A VIOLET MURDER

I let out a "boof" of surprise and slammed against the car, but I knew I didn't have the luxury of collapsing on the ground or even trying to catch my breath. Not if I was going to defend myself. I clenched my hands into fists, whirled—

And stopped cold.

I'd expected to find an assailant behind me, but instead I was greeted by the most astounding animal I'd ever seen.

No, not a bison, thank goodness.

This was a dog. A large dog of questionable parentage. She was tall and long-legged, like an Irish wolfhound. She had the pointy ears of a shepherd and a long curled tail, like a Samoyed. Her luxurious shaggy fur reminded me of a sheepdog. It hung in bangs over her dark eyes and it fringed her ears, and when a breeze kicked up, all that fur rippled this way and that. She was snow-white, and she had a nose that was more pink than it was black.

Now that she was done jumping on me, the dog barked a greeting.

"Hey, there." Though I do not own a dog, I'd always been fond of them, and I knew the best thing to do was to let her sniff my hand. She did, and I got the seal of approval. She gave my fingers a lick.

"Who are you, huh?" She was big enough that I didn't have to bend down to rub a hand over the dog's head, and when I did, I came away with fingers coated in white fur. The dog was wearing a purple collar and there was a tag hanging from it, so shedding or no shedding, I gave her another pat and took a closer look. "Violet. Are you Violet?"

She woofed her answer.

"Well, Violet . . ." I started toward the house, and she trotted along at my side. "I came to see Brody. Is he around?"

Violet put on the brakes, looked back at the barn, and barked.

"Is that where he is?" I asked her.

I turned around and hiked along a stone path bordered with zinnias in every color of the rainbow, past that beautiful covered outdoor entertainment area, around to the far side of the house, and across what felt like a couple of football fields of lawn all the way to the barn.

There was a Dutch door facing me, and I was tempted to yank it open and go inside. But bison, remember? And I wasn't sure how the barn was laid out or how much freedom the animals had inside.

Instead, I inched open the door and called, "Brody? It's Lizzie. From Love Under the Covers. I've got your credit card."

Violet poked her nose between the door and the jamb and popped the door open.

And that's when I saw him.

"Brody?" The name croaked out of me, and my voice was caught behind the ball of panic and fear that wedged in my throat, blocking my breathing.

Brody Pierce was laid out on the floor, his cowboy hat on the ground beside him. Those blue eyes of his were wide open, staring at nothing, and his skin was tinged Grinch green. His left arm was thrown out at his side. His right hand was next to the jagged wound that tore into his denim shirt and ripped his flesh. His fingers were coated with blood dried to the rich brown of a bison's fur.

Violet raced to her master's side. She plunked down next to him, and she howled.

Death
of a
Red-Hot
Rancher

MIMI GRANGER

BERKLEY PRIME CRIME
New York

BERKLEY PRIME CRIME
Published by Berkley
An imprint of Penguin Random House LLC
penguinrandomhouse.com

Copyright © 2021 by Connie Laux
Penguin Random House supports copyright. Copyright fuels creativity, encourages
diverse voices, promotes free speech, and creates a vibrant culture. Thank you for buying
an authorized edition of this book and for complying with copyright laws by not
reproducing, scanning, or distributing any part of it in any form without permission.
You are supporting writers and allowing Penguin Random House to continue to
publish books for every reader.

BERKLEY and the BERKLEY & B colophon are registered trademarks and
BERKLEY PRIME CRIME is a trademark of Penguin Random House LLC.

ISBN: 9780593201565

First Edition: September 2021

Printed in the United States of America
1   3   5   7   9   10   8   6   4   2

Book design by George Towne

When it comes to romance,
this one has to be for
David

Chapter 1

When Brody Pierce walked into a room, folks sat up and took notice.

Eyes got wide.

Blood quickened.

Hearts beat faster.

Men's, because they automatically compared themselves to Brody's six-foot-four-inch muscular frame, strong jaw, straight nose, eagle-eyed stare.

Compared themselves, and found themselves lacking.

Women? They had a whole different kind of reaction.

But then, Brody was that kind of man.

As if I needed proof, my left arm prickled and my cheeks caught fire. Automatically, I gave my arm a thorough scratching and, just as quickly, told myself to get a grip.

It was no use.

Like every other female in Tinker's Creek, Ohio, I couldn't help but fall under Brody's spell.

It must have been those broad shoulders of his. Or that raven-dark hair, shot through at the temples with the slightest hint of silver.

Or maybe it was his voice, a deep, rich baritone with just a tad of a drawl that was as heady as a shot of bourbon.

"Good morning, darlin'."

That voice—and the man standing just a couple of feet from me on the other side of the front counter of Love Under the Covers—shook me out of my daydreams. Was the smile that automatically wreathed my face too dopey? Too encouraging? Did my dark curly hair look as completely unruly as it usually did, and would Brody think the green streak I'd added to it the night before was sexy? Or just alien-weird?

Get a grip, Lizzie Hale!

I did my best to do just that, giving my arm another scratch while I pulled in a long, deep breath. I centered myself on the soles of the pink canvas sneakers that made it possible for me to negotiate way more than my minimum number of fitness steps in the bookstore each day.

Brody was a customer, not a knight in shining armor who'd come to whisk me away.

And I was the owner of the most successful romance bookstore in the Midwest.

I'd better start acting like it.

"Mood gorning." I gave myself a mental slap and coughed away the faux pas. Yeah, like that would somehow prove to Brody I wasn't a total goof.

"Good morning, Brody." I congratulated myself when the words came out right this time, and yes, I managed to keep a sigh from the end of my greeting. Eyes as blue as

Caribbean waters will have that effect on a girl if she's not careful.

"How are . . ." No way I'd be able to finish the sentence. Not while I was looking at the man. I asked the question of the pile of brochures on the counter in front of me advertising the next Love Under the Covers speed-dating night. "How are you this morning?"

When the words came out right, I made the mistake of thinking I was home free and looked from brochures to man just in time to see him smile. It was an injustice to say the spark in his eyes that went along with his "Just fine, ma'am" was infectious. There was more to it than that. Cheerfulness, sure. Friendliness, absolutely.

Heat.

The realization tingled through me head to toe, and I scratched a little more. Yeah, sure, all this talk of Brody's alpha-male superpower sounds crazy, but I knew for a fact I wasn't the only one who felt it.

Callie Porter, who'd stepped into the shop just after Brody, pretended to be looking at the display of newly published books over on my right, but she wasn't fooling anyone. I saw her take a good, long look at Brody's butt-hugging jeans and wave a hand in front of her flaming cheeks.

Tasha Grimes, who'd arrived just a few minutes earlier and should have been comparing my calendar to the scheduling program she had open on her phone so we could come up with a date for the next meeting of the local chapter of Writers of Romance, pressed her lips together and gave Brody the once-over.

Even my aunt Charmaine, who was almost older enough than Brody to be considered a cougar, picked that particular moment—coincidence? I think not—to prance out of the historical romance room. She sashayed into what used to be the wide front entryway of the nineteenth-century home that was now Love Under the Covers, the area where we took care of purchases and featured displays of little extras like herbal soaps and scented oils. Charmaine being Charmaine, she wasn't about to let Brody miss her grand entrance, not even when he was examining a spinning rack of handmade greeting cards.

With her way-too-golden hair scooped loosely at the back of her head in what was more messy than bun and her long green skirt rippling around her ankles like a gentle wave, Charmaine looked more like a ship's figurehead than a bookshop employee. Fists on her ample hips, she stopped three feet from Brody and looked him up and down. "Well don't you look as handsome as that Prince What's-His-Name this morning."

"Maybe as handsome, but nowhere near as rich!"

It was the same playful back-and-forth they always used to greet each other, and just like he always did, Brody laughed. No surprise, there aren't many people who aren't captivated by my aunt's bubbling personality and her wide smile.

It was, after all, why I'd hired her to work at Love Under the Covers. Charmaine Randall was as invaluable an asset to the shop as the books—all those wonderful books—that filled every nook and cranny.

"Is Lizzie helping you with what you need?" my aunt asked Brody, and yes, she fluttered her eyelashes. Charmaine has that kind of chutzpah. "I mean, with *everything* you need?"

This time, the sound I stifled was a groan. Somewhere in her overactive and somewhat warped imagination, Charmaine had decided she wasn't above a little matchmaking when it came to me and every available man in our little town. Honestly, she should have known better. Though I may know everything there is to know about fiction—romance heroes, plots, tropes, and authors—when it comes to real-life romance, I am unfortunately and ashamedly pretty much a dud.

Thanks to my uncanny ability to turn into a puddle of mush with a mouth full of marbles every time an attractive man is near me, my relationships tend to flare like bottle rockets and fizzle just as quickly.

I didn't need to add Brody Pierce to the sad-but-true list.

My smile firmly in place, I assured my aunt, "Whatever Brody needs, I can take care of it," before I turned my attention to my customer and asked, "What I can . . . can I help you with?"

"Oh, just thought I'd look around a bit." Brody inched back the cowboy hat on his head to reveal a strip of scraped skin, new and nasty-looking, on his forehead. "I'll give you a holler if I need you."

Before I could ask what had happened and if he was okay, he strode away from the checkout counter, tipping his hat to Charmaine, Callie, and Tasha before he went into the contemporary romance room.

"Give you a holler."

When Brody said the words, they sounded as sensual as a love poem. Not so much when they were parroted by Ned Baker.

My head snapped up and my gaze shifted from Brody's retreating and delicious form to Ned, who had just walked up to the counter with the newest Nora Roberts paperback in one hand. The thunderous look on his face matched the growl that added a note of acid to his words. He tossed a look over his shoulder toward the contemporary romance room. "Man acts like he just stepped in off the back forty."

"Which he probably did," Charmaine pointed out. I had a feeling she might have said something more, too, something in the way of *how dare you criticize Brody when you're not half the man he is*, if I hadn't shot her a look. She didn't like it, but she got the message. She tossed her head and continued on toward the back of the shop.

I watched her go, then did my best to dissolve the sharp sting of Ned's words with a smile.

"Brody does own a ranch," I reminded him.

The sound that escaped Ned was somewhere between a harrumph and a snort of disgust. "Grown man, playing cowboy, raising those . . ." Ned's shoulders trembled. "Those animals."

The animals in question were bison, and ever since Brody had bought one hundred acres outside of town and established the Pierce Double B Bar Ranch there, he'd gone on to make a name for himself. Not only was he a responsible farmer and landowner, but restaurateurs from places like Cleveland and Akron and Cincinnati flocked to his ranch for what they claimed was the finest, the sweetest, and the healthiest meat around. Of course, Ned knew that. Ned was a successful financial advisor, a middle-aged guy with a doughy nose, a receding hairline, and just-starting-to-sag jowls, who officially lived in Cleveland but spent most of the summer at what I'd heard was an impressive country home on twelve acres that abutted Brody's ranch.

"Not a bison fan?" I asked.

It was an innocent-enough question. I did not deserve the curled lip I got from Ned.

"You haven't heard?" That lip curled even more, enough to reveal Ned's clenched teeth. "I guess that aunt of yours hasn't, either, or the story would be all over town by now. That man . . ." He didn't need to glare toward the contemporary romance room. I knew who he was talking about. "That man . . . last night . . ." As if praying for strength, Ned closed his eyes and clutched the paperback tighter. He tapped the spine of the book on the counter, the sound of his aggravation a sharp tattoo of Morse code. "I had some of my business associates down for a cookout." He shot me a look. "Important people."

Something told me Ned wouldn't have invited them if they weren't, but I didn't point this out. It didn't matter, and he didn't give me time anyway.

"There we were having cocktails on the patio when one of those beasts came over the fence and crashed through my yard."

I'd driven past the ranch. I'd seen the bison. They were big, and I'd heard they could be fierce.

"You must have been terrified!"

One corner of Ned's thin lips twisted. "You think? You ever see one of those things in action? Big as trucks, fast as you wouldn't believe. And ornery." He whistled low under his breath. "I swear that animal came at us shooting death-ray-dagger looks."

"What did you do?"

"Do? I called the police, of course. Right before I called Pierce. Raised a stink, too, I can tell you that much."

"And Brody?"

He hated to admit it. Ned crossed his arms over his chest. "Came as fast as he could, I suppose."

I imagined the scene, and it wasn't pretty. "How did he . . . ? How could he manage . . . ? He got the bison out of your yard?"

I hadn't even realized she'd been right there and listening, but Callie plunked a reissue of a Debbie Macomber classic on the front counter. "Bison don't intimidate Brody," she said. "Maybe he's simply more of a man than you are, Ned. That's why all you did was make a phone call. Brody was the one who had to spring into action."

"Shouldn't have had to do either—call the police or have Brody come over acting like some superhero savior." Ned dug a ten-dollar bill out of his pocket and plunked it on the counter. "That animal never should have gotten over that fence. Besides, I didn't say I was intimidated, I said bison are nasty animals." When I gave him his change, Ned refused a bag. "Mark my words . . ." He pointed at both Callie and me with his book. "No good comes from having animals around that are that wild. Pierce will see. Oh, one of these days, he'll see, all right. My insurance company is giving him a call today. So is my attorney. He's lucky no one was hurt. Or worse."

And with that, he took himself, and his new book, out of the store.

"How awful."

I made the comment to no one in particular, but that didn't stop Tasha from sidling up to the counter just as Callie backed away. "You believe that story?"

I glanced her way. "You don't?"

"Oh, I believe it happened. But my guess is it wasn't nearly as dramatic as Ned makes it out to be. He knows Brody's insurance company will cover any damage, so what's the big deal? No, bison aren't what's bugging Ned. Haven't you heard?" She bent her head closer. "Ned saw his wife, Joy, talking to Brody the other day outside that new bakery shop over on Main Street."

I do not have my aunt Charmaine's imagination. "So? They were talking. That doesn't mean anything."

Tasha rolled her eyes. "Talking. Real close. Standing. Right together. With Brody, that can only mean one thing."

"Ridiculous." Callie pushed in front of Tasha to plunk a copy of *Romantic Gazette* magazine on the counter. "Joy Baker is not Brody's type."

I begged to differ. From what I'd seen, every woman was Brody's type. Not that I was going to step into the middle of these two customers and point that out.

Tasha snickered. "And I suppose, Callie, you know what type that is?"

"I should." Callie was a short, round woman who favored skirts that were too short, tops that were cut low, and plenty of blue eye shadow. Her chin came up and her shoulders inched back. "Brody and I have been out a time or two. We were in the same graduating class," she added as an aside to me. "In high school."

Tasha frowned. "And I was a few years behind you, remember." She didn't have to say this obviously meant she was younger than Callie. "And by the way, I've been out to dinner with Brody, too."

Callie sneered and ignored the comment completely, directing her remarks at me. As a longtime resident of Tinker's Creek, Callie knew what everyone else in town knew—I'd lived there for just two years. In a small town, that meant I was a newcomer. And always would be. "Brody left here and made something of himself. How lucky we are . . ." She glanced toward the contemporary romance room. "A genuine Hollywood star. Right here."

"Commercials are not exactly Hollywood," Tasha pointed out. "Though I will admit, when one of those truck commercials he's in comes on TV, I do tend to watch them. Real close."

"Those incredible stunts he does," Callie purred.

"The aura of manliness," Tasha crooned. "That man could sell me a truck. Any old time."

I put Callie's purchases in a bag, she grabbed it, headed out of the store.

She didn't go far, though.

We have a patio outside the front of the shop, a spot where customers can meet and chat and read that's enclosed by a brick wall and filled with tables and chairs. Callie got as far as one of those tables, plunked down, grabbed her magazine, and flipped it open.

Tasha didn't give her another look. "Jealous," she said. "She hates that Brody's been out with me."

I am the proprietor of the bookstore. I knew better than to offer my two cents.

Instead, Tasha and I came up with a suitable date for the local Writers of Romance meeting, and I promised I'd gather all the latest releases so the members of the group could look them over. While I was at it, I told her I'd see which ARCs I had around. ARCs, or advanced reader copies, are books that are distributed to stores and reviewers before the actual books are published. That way, store owners like me can know what's coming out and we can order the books we know our customers will love. I would never in a thousand years sell an ARC—that's strictly illegal, not to mention unethical—but it was always fun to flash them at readers and see the way their eyes sparkled when they realized I had the inside scoop on what was soon to hit the shelves and what wonderful new books they had to look forward to.

Our business done, Tasha headed for the door just as Brody came back to the counter. She stepped around him and stopped to take a phone call.

"Find what you need?" I asked Brody.

"Not exactly sure." He shifted from foot to foot and picked a long white strand of fur from the sleeve of his denim shirt, looking suddenly as uncomfortable as he always looked self-assured. He reached for the rack of handmade cards and gave it a spin. "I was wondering. About these."

"A card?" To better assist him, I stepped around the counter and did my best to ignore the scent of his aftershave. Tobacco. Musk. Pure seduction.

Cards, I told myself.

Concentrate on the cards.

"What's the occasion?" I asked Brody.

"Um." He stopped to think about it. "No occasion, I guess. I mean, not a birthday or an anniversary or anything."

Brynn Chisolm was the artist who made the cards, and since Brynn is my best friend, I am terribly biased, but I had to admit that each was a little gem. I picked up one with a front that was an intricate combination of hand-cut paper lace, dried flower petals, and tiny buttons in shimmering shades of pearl and cream. "This one says 'Thinking of You' inside," I told Brody.

"How about one that doesn't have anything inside?"

There were other cards nearby that fit the bill. I chose one stamped and embossed with a couple of small hearts, a showy bouquet of flowers, and a tiny little cupid with a bow and arrows in his hands and a mischievous smile on his face.

When I handed it to Brody, he smiled.

"Perfect!" He passed the card back to me so I could ring it up, and I concentrated on that rather than on Tasha, who'd stopped near the door to carefully watch what Brody was up to, and Callie, who was still out on the patio but now had her nose pressed to the front window, the better to keep an eye on the transaction.

When I was done, I found Brody patting his pockets.

"Darn." He shook his head with disgust. "I left my cash at home. I hate to have you go through all the trouble of a credit card just for—"

"No problem at all." When he handed me the card, I took care of the sale. "You want a bag?"

He did.

"Can't thank you enough," Brody said, and he tipped his hat and left.

And yes, I swear once he was outside and the door closed behind him, I heard a dozen sighs escape from women all around the store.

But like I said, Brody was that kind of man.

Thinking about it, I scratched my arm. That's when I realized he'd left his credit card behind when he walked out of the store.

"Brody!" It didn't do much good to call after him. He was already out of the shop, so I raced out to the patio. There was no sign of Brody or of Callie, either.

"I'll just give it to him next time I see him," I told myself, and went inside to tuck the credit card in a safe place.

If only I knew.

The next time I had the opportunity to return the credit card, that would be the last thing on mine—or Brody's—mind.

Chapter 2

"Oh, come on. There's no way it was that bad."

I listened to the calm, even tones of Brynn's voice from the other end of my phone and reminded myself my best friend was levelheaded and very smart. She wouldn't say anything that wasn't true just to keep me from exaggerating the details of what was sure to go down in the annals of history as the Worst Date Ever.

The thought was almost enough to calm my dashed hopes.

My mortification.

My total and complete humiliation.

Almost.

I grabbed the phone from where it had been on speaker on the seat next to me and dragged myself out of my car.

"No, Brynn." To emphasize my point, I slammed shut my car door before I turned off the speaker function and put the phone to my ear. "It really was that bad."

"But he was cute!"

Brynn knew this for a fact. After all, she was the one who'd arranged this blind date with Ben, an attorney she'd met when she'd catered his sister's wedding, a guy she was certain was absolutely right for me. "Cute and smart and funny and—"

"Exactly." I shouldn't have had to remind her. Brynn knows the sad history of my dating life. But Brynn—as all best friends should be—is the eternal optimist. "He was expecting this put-together business owner, and what he got was . . ." I rounded the car and headed across the garden that separated my house from Charmaine's.

We shared the property, me and my aunt. She, in the historic saltbox home with its two stories that faced the town's main street and the roof that sloped down to one story at the back, and me in the Victorian carriage house all the way on the other side of the eighth-of-an-acre garden that at this time of the year was bursting with roses and daisies and Charmaine's treasured herbs.

Just like my aunt, her house was big and artsy and impossible to ignore. Metal sculptures out front and here in the garden danced with the wind. There was a weather vane (a witch riding a broomstick) up on the roof. And did I mention the color? Something told me the early settlers from New England who'd built the house had never anticipated it would be done up in mustard yellow with purple trim. Then again, I doubt any of them ever dreamed there could be a woman as one of a kind as Charmaine, either.

To try to keep some semblance of cohesiveness, I'd used the same mustard yellow on the exterior of my clapboard house with its A-frame roof, but had toned things down with ivory trim.

I had a small stone patio outside my front door, and right

there, right then, I decided that once I kicked off my shoes I was going to pour a glass of wine and sit outside, where I could stare into the half darkness and give myself a figurative kick in the pants.

"You know how it goes every time," I said to Brynn. "I couldn't think of anything to say to Ben. I mean, come on, how lame is it to talk about the weather? He doesn't like sports, so it was no use bringing up baseball. He works so hard, he hasn't been to a museum in years, so I couldn't exactly impress him with talk of that Monet exhibit I went to Cleveland to see. I admit it . . ." My sigh spoke my frustration. "I had to pull out the big guns."

It was Brynn's turn to groan. "You didn't."

"What choice did I have? I didn't want to sit there and look like a total dork. I talked about the only thing I can discuss intelligently. Romance novels. And as soon as I did that—"

If I could have seen through the phone, I know Brynn would have been shaking her head. "Guys don't get it. As soon as they hear 'romance' they think—"

"Love and marriage. Yeah. Like I was trying to trap him into making a lifetime commitment right there in Panera Bread with a woman he barely knew. I could see the fear in his eyes. I could see—"

What I could see—or at least what I thought I saw—was a shadow next to the fountain in the center of the garden. A shadow that definitely did not belong there.

"What?" Brynn is not the most patient of souls. Not when it comes to the details of my (pathetic) love life. "What's going on? Why did you stop talking?"

"I thought I saw . . ." I squinched my eyes and let my squinty gaze roam over the yard, and I had to admit, as reluctant as I was about all that yellow paint on my aunt's house and on mine, at this time of year, with the last of the evening light still glowing in the air, the color made our houses look ethereal, like they belonged in the fairy garden near my aunt's back door.

The color also provided a perfect backdrop for seeing things that I might otherwise miss at night—the deer that came through, the occasional fox, the kids who sometimes used our property for a cut-through from the baseball fields down the street.

This wasn't any of those.

This was a low shadow, like someone crouching to keep out of sight, and I stepped in the direction where it slid between a head-high row of hollyhocks and Charmaine's garden shed, hoping for a better look.

I wasn't fast enough. Just like that, the shadow was gone.

"Hold on," I told Brynn, though it was obviously exactly what she was doing. "I thought I saw something odd. I'm just going to go around to the front of the house and—"

"What?"

Brynn's question knocked me out of the surprise that paralyzed me the moment I rounded the front of the house.

"What is it? What did you see?"

Not the shadow, that was for sure. Whoever—whatever—that was, there was no sign of it out there on the slate sidewalk. No, what I was looking at was—

"Brody's truck," I said.

"So?" Brynn held the phone far enough away to remind her six-year-old, Micah, that it was almost time for bed before she got back to the matter at hand. "So Brody's souped-up, high-end, all-the-bells, all-the-whistles, nobody-could-ever-afford-it-but-the-guy-who-did-the-commercials-for-it truck drove by and—"

"Not drove by." I looked from the truck to Charmaine's

front door. "It's parked. In Charmaine's driveway." Why I whispered this last bit of information is anybody's guess. Maybe it's the same reason I looked all around, just to make sure no one was listening. At that time of night, all the action in town was farther down the hill at the couple of restaurants that brought in locals as well as folks from the city and visitors to the nearby national park. I was all alone, but still, I spoke softly. "Brody is at Charmaine's!"

Like I said, Brynn is smart. She knew exactly where this was going. "They're seeing each other?" She squealed like a teenager reading the latest celebrity love story news.

And I couldn't blame her one bit.

Charmaine?

And Brody?

"No, no, no." I said this as much to myself as I did to Brynn. "It's not possible."

"Then what's he doing there in the middle of the night?"

"It's not exactly the middle of the night."

"You know what I mean!"

I did. "What's he doing here? That's easy. He's . . ." He's what, I didn't know. But as much as I'm a private person myself, as much as I believe in giving people their space and letting them make their own decisions and build their own relationships . . . well, I sure intended to find out.

I didn't actually need to creep. Like I said, there was no one else around. Still, I walked closer to the house on tiptoe and peeked in the window of Charmaine's dining room. The lights were on, and there were two empty plates on the table, two used wineglasses, two candles that had been snuffed out.

"No one in there," I told Brynn, and then because I knew she had no idea what I was talking about, I gave her the play-by-play. "Walking along the front of the house. Pass-

ing the front door. There's a light on in that little room up
front that Charmaine calls her den. That's got to be where
they are. And—" I bent my head, listening to the sound that
tinkled through the night air, as light and as melodic as
wind chimes.

"Brynn, they're giggling."

"You mean like they might actually be—"

"No, they couldn't be. I mean after all, the room is right
at the front of the house and I know there are no curtains in
there and the lights are on and Charmaine wouldn't be doing anything she shouldn't be doing right there where anyone could see. Would she?"

Neither one of us needed an answer to that question.

Worried now and creeping faster, I closed in on the window in question and since I'm only five feet two, I was
fortunate that Charmaine had found an old hitching post at
the antiques mall run by her friend Glory Rhinehold. The
post itself was iron, and just as in the old days, Charmaine
had put down a big rectangular rock next to it. Perfect for
ladies stepping down from their carriages.

Or short, nosy nieces dying to see what was happening
inside the house.

Careful to keep to the side so I couldn't be seen, I
stepped up onto the rock and looked in the window.

In typical Charmaine fashion, the room was a riot of
color and a jumble of objects, from a Thai marionette wearing a sequined shirt and bright red boots hanging from the
ceiling in one corner to a wall of shelves that included
books, antique vases, potted orchids, and a couple of bottles of scotch.

"She's sitting at the desk," I whispered to Brynn. "Brody's standing behind her."

"What's she doing?" Brynn wanted to know.

From this angle, it was hard to tell. "Reading something. Or maybe writing something. He's got his hand on her shoulder!"

"She's too old for him," Brynn decided.

I couldn't help but think of the romance novel trope, older heroine, younger hero. "Brody's what, maybe forty-five?"

"Forty-six." I could just about hear the embarrassment blossom in Brynn's voice. "All right, I admit it. I looked him up online. I mean, when he first came to town. He is gorgeous, after all. And famous. I was curious and—"

I cut her off before I had to admit that when he showed up in Tinker's Creek with all his charm and all his money and more good looks than should belong to any one man, I'd checked Brody out online, too. "Charmaine is my dad's youngest sister," I reminded her. "She doesn't talk about her age and Dad can never keep things straight, but I bet she's not far past fifty. She's not that much older than him."

Brynn digested this news. "Still—"

I didn't wait to hear what else she might have to say on the subject. I had news to report and I did it, my voice tight with excitement. "He's leaning closer. He's looking over her shoulder. He's—" I was so engrossed in spying on my aunt I didn't realize I'd leaned closer to the window and, in doing so, stepped off the rock. I slipped and luckily landed on my feet, but not before I let out a shriek.

I clapped my hand over my mouth—yeah, like that might actually help call back the banshee sound—just as Brody walked over to the window.

"You hear that?" The mellow tones of his bourbon voice oozed through the night from the window right above where I stood with my back plastered against the front of the house.

"Just kids." Charmaine sounded like she hadn't moved from the desk. "Get back here, you handsome devil, and let's finish what we started."

This, I decided, was not something I had any business waiting around to see.

Instead, back to mustard yellow paint, I crab-stepped along the front of the house and toward the far corner of the property, and it wasn't until I was safely in the shadows of Mrs. Castille's mammoth rose of Sharon bushes next door that I dared to take a breath.

"What are you doing?" Brynn hissed.

"Nothing." Not true, of course; the den had a window that faced this side of the house, too, and from where I stood, I could see Charmaine, still at the desk. She looked over her shoulder, said something to Brody. He chuckled, bent nearer, whispered in her ear.

"I never would have guessed it," I admitted. "She plays it so cool when he's around. She never said a word."

"Has to be the hottest secret in town."

"I'll say." I remembered Tasha and Callie, who'd been at the shop that day. I thought about the way heads turned when Brody walked down the street, the way hopes rose. Yeah, sure, Brody was as red-hot as they came. But that didn't keep a thread of worry from worming its way through me. "He's a serial dater. She's going to get her heart broken. You'd think Charmaine would have more sense than to get involved."

"Charmaine? Have sense?"

"Point taken. I guess she isn't any different from any other woman around here, and every other woman is just itching for a chance to be alone with Brody. But she can't possibly think there's a future with a man like that."

"Maybe she's not looking for a future, just a little fun."

Of course Brynn was right.

Who was I to deny my aunt that?

In a feeble attempt to give the happy couple a semblance of privacy, I turned my back on the house. A rose of Sharon flower tickled my nose at the same time my cheeks shot through with fire.

It's one thing reading romance, preaching romance, selling romance, I decided.

It's another thing when the romance in question involves your aunt and the hottest rancher this side of the Mississippi.

"I'm getting out of here right now," I told Brynn, and I scrambled between Mrs. Castille's plants and the lilac bushes Charmaine so loved. They'd been glorious in the spring, but now the branches were bare of flowers and—

"Ouch!"

"What?" Brynn's concern simmered on the other end of the phone.

"Nothing. I'm fine. I just . . ." I wiped a finger over the side of my neck and the wet streak there. "Scratched myself on a lilac bush, that's all. That'll teach me not to go sneaking around where I don't belong. I should just mind my own business."

"You are minding your business. She's your aunt."

"And a grown woman. And what she does and who she does it with . . . well, I'll leave that up to her."

My mind made up, I'd just taken another step toward the backyard when I heard the front door pop open.

Whatever Charmaine and Brody had been up to, they'd finished plenty fast.

From my spot in the lilacs, I caught the purr of Brody's voice, the higher pitch of Charmaine's. But I couldn't make out what they said.

I did hear the front door close, though, and the truck

engine roar to life, and that's pretty much when I panicked. When Brody backed out of the drive, his truck lights would rake this side of the property and in just another second, he'd see me standing there like the proverbial deer in headlights.

Or a shameless Peeping Tom, caught in the act of snooping.

I had to make myself scarce. Fast.

I dove behind the nearest lilac bush, and I'm not sure how I thought it was going to help, but I held my breath, too.

I'd be home free once Brody cruised past the house and headed down Main Street.

Only he didn't.

Instead of the smooth sound of tires against the pavement, I heard the truck stop and jerk forward again. It didn't drive past my hiding place for a full minute, and when it did, it was stop-and-go, with Brody driving at a snail's pace, his brake lights winking off and on through the dark.

"What? What's going on?" Brynn asked.

I stepped out from behind the bush. "I hope he hasn't been drinking and now he's driving," I told her. "Brody's driving funny and—"

"Brody! Brody!"

My report to Brynn was interrupted when Charmaine raced out of the house. She stood on the sidewalk, jumping up and down, waving for all she was worth and calling out.

Brody kept up his herky-jerky drive.

Charmaine grumbled. She mumbled. But she didn't hesitate, at least not for long. She jumped in her car and took off down Main Street after Brody.

"Lovers' quarrel?" Brynn asked.

"They seemed to be getting along so well. But maybe you're right. Maybe they argued. Maybe that's why he left so quickly. But the way he's driving . . ." I leaned forward and craned my neck to see down the street, but by then both Brody's truck and Charmaine's vintage Volkswagen beetle were nowhere in sight.

"There's nothing more I can do," I told Brynn. I pushed my way through the greenery and on toward my house and promised I'd call her later if there were any updates.

In the meantime, I'd ask myself a whole bunch of philosophical questions about love and life, life and love.

An aunt with man problems.

A niece who couldn't get her act together when there was an attractive man around.

And—

The thought flew out of my head when I saw a shadow—that same shadow I'd seen earlier—creep around a metal sculpture just on the other side of the path.

I took off running, but I didn't get far. There was something on the path, something I didn't see until it was too late. I tripped, stumbled. My feet went out from under me. I yelped, flew into the air, and landed on my butt in a patch of chamomile.

It took me a second to catch my breath, and another few seconds to get rid of the shakiness that made my heart pound and my knees weak.

By that time, the shadow—whoever it was—was gone.

I looked around and saw what I'd tripped on was a rake. One that had been set directly across the path.

I knew Charmaine would never be so careless. She cherished her garden and she was always careful about her tools. And I certainly hadn't left the rake there.

There was only one explanation. That shadow, whoever it was and whatever that person was up to, wanted to make sure I didn't follow.

Chapter 3

Love Under the Covers is officially open every day except Sundays and Mondays, and the hand-lettered sign in the front window that features hearts, cupids, and a couple in a torrid embrace gets flipped from **CLOSED** to **OPEN** at ten. But of course I'm at the shop earlier than that. For one thing, I have to put on a pot of coffee and another of tea for customers who often browse and linger. For another, I need to make sure everything is shipshape—that the shelves are clean and orderly; that the lights are shining in the exact right direction to highlight the displays; that the latest stock and the hottest books are front and center, right where they belong.

But truth be told, the real reason I arrive when it's quiet and I have a chance to be alone?

It's the books, of course!

The realization bubbling through me like a sip of champagne, I stopped just inside the front door of the shop, smiled, and pulled in a long breath. Don't get me wrong. I'm a realist. I know there are people who don't love books as much as I do, and standing there and reveling in the wonderful aroma of paper and ink, I couldn't help but wonder how they make it day to day. What about those folks? Don't they sense a change in the air when there are books in a room, that little frisson that tells readers that fictional worlds and the people who inhabit them are nearby? Don't they hear the call of the stories that beckon and tempt book lovers? Don't they know the absolute joy that comes along with wallowing in the marvelous, endless possibilities of fiction?

Honestly, anybody who doesn't get it, I feel sorry for them.

Convinced and ready for the day, I limped toward the back of the shop—rake in garden pathway, remember?—and in spite of the bag of frozen peas I'd put on it the night before, my left knee still ached. Not that I was about to tell anyone about the incident, especially Charmaine. I didn't want her fussing. Or worrying. Not when I didn't know what was going on or who might have been lurking in the lavender.

I stowed my purse and the lunch I brought with me in my office, then convinced myself a little exercise would be good for both my knee and helping to dispel the heebie-jeebies that prickled through me when I thought about that shadow—that person. Why our garden? Why last night?

I had no answers, and that only made me more restless, so I went around from room to room, straightening, organizing, basking in the books and in my good fortune to be able to spend my days with them.

The contemporary romance room was once the dining room of the old house, and while I'd kept the crown molding, the leaded glass windows, and the oak floor that gave

the room a timeless feel, I'd also decided from day one that
the room needed all the snap and pizzazz of a modern-day
romance novel. The walls were painted a gleaming stain-
less steel. The accents in the room (pillows and curtains)
were black. The one wall that wasn't floor-to-ceiling book-
cases featured a metal sculpture of a stylized couple with a
gleaming red heart between them.

Satisfied all was shipshape there, I headed to the room
dedicated to historical romance.

This room had a fireplace, and when the weather permit-
ted, we kept a fire going in it. There was an Oriental rug on
the floor, the shades of deep green and cinnamon in it com-
plemented by walls a color the paint company called In-
verness and I always thought of as atmospheric smoky
gray-green. There were two wing chairs near the fireplace,
and no matter the weather, they were usually occupied by
customers sharing book recommendations, comparing
notes. It was a quiet room, a comfortable room, and the best
compliment I'd ever heard about it was from a woman who
claimed she expected Mr. Darcy to walk in any minute.

If only!

Smiling at the image that flashed into my head, I continued on to the erotica room. It was, of course, in a bedroom
of the house, and I'd opted for lush and opulent in there. In
spite of Brynn's suggestion that I paint the walls in fifty
shades of gray (Brynn could be hilarious), I'd gone for a
carpet in a swirling pattern of plum and lilac, soft ivory
walls, and touches of gold.

There were other rooms in the house, too, and I went
through them one by one—the vintage romance room,
where I proudly displayed a selection of romances from the
twentieth century; a young adult romance alcove; a room
devoted solely to romantic suspense. Inspirationals were

kept in the kitchen, and nearby was the pantry, where I housed the gothics I loved so much.

If asked, I freely admitted that every room and every book in every room was my favorite, but I had a special place in my heart for the solarium, which ran along the back of the building. Once upon a time it had housed some dignified lady's African violets, her orchids, and the geranium cuttings she took in the fall and nursed until the next spring. These days, the greenhouse windows looked out at a small walled garden Charmaine tended, and in addition to lots of bookshelves, we'd filled the room with an array of bromeliads and other assorted odd plants, Charmaine's collection of vintage Halloween decorations, and a fountain she insisted on adding purple food coloring to every day. Add the glass witch balls hung from the ceiling, the dark blue carpet with silver stars, and voila—the paranormal romance room!

I picked a wilted leaf from a plant with dusty purple leaves and tiny purple flowers, then carefully hitch-stepped my way back to the office. By the time I got there, my knee was a little less achy, just as I'd hoped it would be. It had better be, as I had some special orders to pack and send out and lots of paperwork to catch up on. That day like every day, I needed to be at the top of my game. I'd just started into the work when I heard the front door snap open.

"Good morning," I called out, and I had to congratulate myself. I sounded just like I did every day. My smile was the same, too, when Charmaine sauntered in, a stack of books in the crook of her arm and a travel coffee mug in her other hand.

Oh yes, I was the picture of innocence, all right.

Even when I asked, "What did you do last night?"

She set down the books and took a glug of her coffee. Once she was at the shop, Charmaine was more than willing to drink the coffee I brewed, but her favorite was the sludge she made at home. Black, and strong enough to curl hair, toes, and everything in between.

"Do? Nothing, of course."

My head came up, and I guess there was something about the look I gave her that made her feel defensive because she added, "Nothing at all."

Brody and Charmaine in the den.

His hand on her shoulder.

His voice in her ear.

Call me crazy, but that didn't sound like nothing to me!

Still, I managed to play it cool. "You didn't go anywhere?" I asked, remembering how he left her house and how Charmaine raced after him.

"On a Wednesday night?" She waved a hand in a way that told me I was crazy.

"You didn't leave the house at all? Say, around ten o'clock?"

"You were back from your date by then?" I couldn't tell if she was trying to change the subject or she was disappointed that my date with Ben had fizzled so quickly and I hadn't stayed out until the wee hours of the morning.

"We weren't talking about my date," I reminded her. "I asked if you went out."

"Well, I didn't." She lifted her chin. "I had a quiet night at home."

"Alone?"

She whirled and stepped toward the front of the shop. "Of course I was alone. Honestly, Lizzie, I don't know what gets into your head sometimes."

Well, I sure did. And right about then and there, what was in my head was the idea that my aunt had been with Brody Pierce, and that she didn't want me to know about it.

The question, of course, was why.

The answer was what I was dying to find out.

Unfortunately, I didn't have the chance. Not right then, anyway. No sooner did ten o'clock roll around than the Classic Romance Book Club showed up, copies of Mary Stewart's *Nine Coaches Waiting* clutched in their hands. I showed them upstairs to our conference room and left them to it, and for the next hour and a half I heard their chatter rippling down the stairway.

Book talk is like music for my soul, and to its tempo I helped customers, talked to a representative from a publishing house about scheduling an author's signing, and unpacked a carton of hot-off-the-presses books.

And big points for me, I didn't limp or rub my knee.

At least not when anyone was looking.

I had just finished setting out a display of the newest historicals on the round table inside the front door when Glory Rhinehold walked in.

Glory and Charmaine are best friends, but honestly, there couldn't be two people who seem less alike.

Glory is short and so tiny, she reminds me of the statues of fairies in Charmaine's little mystical garden. She favors what I always think of as fairy colors, too. Pastels and creams. Lace at her throat. That day's outfit was perfect proof. Glory looked as delicate as a flower in a pink pantsuit and a white blouse ruffled down the front. She was older than Charmaine by at least ten years, but there wasn't a wrinkle on her face, and her chin-length bob . . . well, even when I visited Tinker's Creek as a child, Glory's hair had already been a glorious silver that made every senior citizen in town green with envy.

She walked up to the counter where I'd just finished packing up three new romantic suspense titles for an eager customer and smiled.

Glory has a great smile.

Achy knee, worries about shadows, questions about Charmaine, it didn't matter. I couldn't help but smile back.

"On your way to Junk and Disorderly?" I asked her. "You look too neat and pink to be messing with dusty antiques all day."

Glory grinned, and when Charmaine joined us at the front counter, the two friends exchanged smiles. "Wash and wear," Glory said. "Everything I own. Believe me, you learn that early on in the antiques business."

"And what can we do for you today?" I asked her.

"Can't linger." She said this more to Charmaine than to me, but my guess was Charmaine already knew that. Glory and Charmaine's time for talk (aka town gossip) was and always had been two o'clock in the afternoon. Glory set down a folder she'd been carrying. "Just wanted to drop this off. I talked to Brynn and she said she'd dress it up and frame it for me. But I know she's busy with that catering business of hers. She's doing some fancy luncheon today. She said she'd get this from you next time she sees you."

"And it is . . ." Curious, both Charmaine and I leaned forward.

"That letter. From Ted." Glory said this to Charmaine because of course, as Glory's BFF, Charmaine knew all about it. I didn't, other than the fact that Ted was Glory's late husband, the local doc who everyone in town had adored. "He wrote it just for me," Glory filled me in. "Right before he died. And I've cherished it since. I'll tell you what, Lizzie, men are full of surprises. Ted and I were married for forty-five years and I never suspected he could write anything so moving, so personal. That man had a little bit of poet in him, and even after all this time, just thinking about it warms my heart. Oh, how I cried when he gave that letter to me. Tears of joy, of course." Even now, her voice clogged. She coughed away her emotion. "I've been thinking I shouldn't keep anything so wonderful locked away. I should put it somewhere where I can see it, where I don't have to worry about it getting dirty or wrinkled."

"So framing it is a great idea," I told her. I reached for the folder. "Do you mind . . . ?"

"Of course not. Nothing private about it. The minister read it at Ted's funeral."

I hadn't lived in Tinker's Creek then, so this was my first look at the letter.

"'My dearest Glory,'" I starting reading the letter out loud, but truth be told, I couldn't keep it up. The words were so tender, so sweet, Ted's love for his wife just about jumped off the page. I got as far as, "'You know there isn't a second of my day when I'm not thinking about you,'" and I was a goner. I had a lump in my throat and tears in my eyes.

Quietly, I finished reading and reverently set the letter back in the folder. "It's beautiful."

"It is." Glory's smile was bittersweet. "You remember, don't you, Char, that day he gave it to me and—" When Glory looked for her friend, it was the first either of us realized Charmaine hadn't stuck around. She was nowhere to be seen.

"Must have gone off to take care of a customer," Glory decided. "I'll leave this with you." She slid the folder toward me. "Tell that aunt of yours I'll see her later."

I assured her I would and tucked the letter in a safe place under the front counter. Before Glory walked away, I glanced around to make sure we were alone.

"Glory . . ." I guess the way I lowered my voice told her this was a private conversation. Glory stepped closer. "Has Charmaine said anything to you about seeing . . ." Charmaine's relationship with Brody might have been a secret even to Glory, and I didn't want to take the chance of giving anything away. "Anyone?" I ended lamely.

She wrinkled her nose. "Seeing? You mean as in dating?" She wiggled closer. "Spill the beans, kid. What do you know?"

"Nothing," I assured her, lying with a straight face. "It's just that I thought I saw a car parked in front of her house last night and—"

"Last night?" Glory eyed me as if I were a dodgy antique. "What happened to your date?"

My shoulders slumped. "Does everyone in Tinker's Creek know about my dating life?"

"They might. If you had much of one." Glory's silvery brows dipped over her eyes. "You need to get out more."

"I know that, Glory, but what I'm asking about is—"

"This one was an attorney, wasn't he? Good catch."

"I'm sure, but—"

"You didn't try talking romance, did you?"

"Romance is something I can discuss intelligently."

"Take it from me, kid"—Glory gave me a wink—"romance isn't what guys are looking for. Not on a first date. At that point, they just want to get a sense of who you are."

"I'm the owner of a romance bookstore."

"Exactly. Businesswoman. Smart. Independent. On the ball." Smiling, she backed away from the counter. "Don't sell yourself short. You've got too much to offer. And if you get a line on what Char is up to, let me know."

"But—" There was no use trying to dig for any more information. Glory breezed out of the shop.

After that, the rest of the morning flew by. All those wonderful Classic Romance Book Club members finished their discussion and trooped down the stairs, eager to buy copies of *Pride and Prejudice*, the next book on their reading list. Other customers, too, came and went, and in between recommending books and listening to their opinions about everything from same-sex couples in romance novels to the artwork on covers, I had just enough time to scarf down the salad I'd brought for lunch. I was back behind the front counter when I looked out the window and noticed someone had left a coffee cup on one of the patio tables, so I called to Charmaine to let her know I'd be outside and pushed through the door.

It was a hot afternoon, but the architect who'd helped me transform house into bookshop had been wise. When we added the stone patio surrounded by a wall that separated it from the sidewalk and the hubbub of Tinker's Creek pedestrian traffic, she'd suggested we plant red sunset maples all around. It was genius. A little less than two years old, the trees already provided decent shade, giving customers who wanted to sit and talk or read out there on the patio a great spot to hide from the sun.

While I was out there, I figured I might as well give the patio a once-over, so I wiped off the tables and straightened the chairs. We'd planted ivy all along the wall and a few of the leaves were droopy so I plucked them off, then grabbed that forgotten coffee cup. I was on my way back inside when I saw Brody walk by.

Only it wasn't Brody.

I did a double take, then realized my mistake and called out a greeting. "Hello, Ernest!"

Ernest Hoyt was, in fact, Brody Pierce's cousin, and by now I should have known better than to mistake one man for the other. Then again, with the sun glaring and the mix of light and shade that dappled the patio and played tricks with my eyes, I could be forgiven.

Ernest was tall. Just like Brody.

Ernest was dark-haired. So was Brody.

Ernest was lean, and though his shoulders weren't as broad at his cousin's, they were wide enough. Then again, Ernest was an instructor at the local community college and an avid and skilled archaeologist whose specialty was the nearby canal and the towns—like Tinker's Creek—that had sprung up to provide the men who built it the supplies they needed. He could often be found poking through the dirt along the canal, searching for bottles and tools and the other treasures the early settlers had left behind. All that digging was bound to build muscles.

Ernest juggled an armful of books, and honestly, I think he was grateful for my greeting. It gave him the opportunity to step out of the sun and onto the patio. He set his books on the wall.

Well, at least that's what he tried to do.

The pile was large and the books were thick and heavy. They tipped, scattered, and splatted to the pavement.

"Doesn't it figure? That's just the kind of day it's been." He grumbled and bent to retrieve the books at his feet while I stepped to the side and took care of the ones that had slid out of his reach. "First Meghan wasn't at the library and now this. I hope I haven't damaged any of the books. They're special orders from other library systems. They look all right, don't they?"

I brushed my hand over the spines of the books I'd plucked off the ground. They were all history books, no surprise there, and though I expected titles like *Nineteenth Century Farm Machinery*, the couple of books about Vikings were unexpected. Luckily, all the books seemed to be in good shape. I handed them to Ernest, who thanked me with a smile that wasn't nearly as dazzling as his cousin's.

He, too, brushed off the books and, not willing to take another chance with his precious charges, piled them on the nearest table. "I guess it's just as well I didn't get all the books I ordered or I never would have been able to carry them all." He shot a look down the street in the direction of the tiny library that served our town. "They told me my entire ordered hadn't come in, but I'm not sure I believe it. A couple of those clerks are not as careful as they should be. No one at that library is as efficient as Meghan."

Meghan Watkins is the manager of the library, a woman who had nothing good to say about romance novels and was never shy about preaching that "nothing good" anytime we happened to run into each other.

It was no wonder my mood soured and I frowned. "I know," Ernest said, mistaking my grumpiness for concern. "I'm worried about her, too. She called in sick, and Meghan is never sick. I hope it's nothing serious. The place would positively fall apart if Meghan wasn't there." His lips puckered. While Brody's face was all planes and angles, from the chipped-from-granite chin to the perfect nose and sweeping forehead, Ernest's was less so. In fact, standing there with him, it occurred to me that Ernest was Brody's shadow. Like him, but not exactly. Close, but not quite.

Something else struck me, too—that credit card Brody had left behind at the shop.

"I don't suppose you're going to see Brody anytime soon, are you?" I asked Ernest.

One corner of his mouth twitched. "I hadn't planned on it."

"I just thought if you were maybe going to stop out at the ranch—"

"No. Sorry." He gathered his books and stepped toward the sidewalk. "Brody and I don't socialize. In fact, I've never been to the ranch."

This struck me as odd, and I couldn't help myself, the comment just fell out of my mouth. "But you're cousins."

"We are." He back-stepped farther from me and the conversation. "But Brody's a busy man what with all those bison to take care of, and I've got my teaching schedule and my own responsibilities." As if thinking about it, he pursed his lips. "No, I have no plans to go out to the ranch."

"It's just that Brody left his credit card here. I thought you could take it back to him, and—"

"Then for sure my answer is no. I don't want to be responsible for a credit card I won't return anytime soon. You understand, don't you?"

Of course I did, and I told Ernest as much.

I also knew Ernest was right. It wasn't fair to hold on to a credit card Brody might need, one he might assume had been lost or stolen.

It was time for me to drive out to the Pierce Double B Bar Ranch myself.

Chapter 4

Like Ernest, I'd never been to Brody's ranch, but since his one-hundred-acre property was on the road that led out of Tinker's Creek and toward Cleveland, I'd driven past it many times. From the street there wasn't a whole lot to see. A fence that went on and on. Two stone columns that flanked the curving driveway. An iron archway over the drive that announced visitors were entering the domain of the Pierce Double B Bar Ranch and featured Brody's unique brand, two sturdy, macho letter *B*s, back to back.

Once or twice when I'd cruised by I'd caught a glimpse of bison in the distance, and that Thursday evening I kept an eye out for them as I swung my car into the drive. The way I remembered it, those critters looked plenty big, even from out on the road, and I didn't want to take the chance of one of them hopping the fence as it had that night of Ned's cocktail party and darting in front of me.

I shouldn't have worried.

A couple of hundred feet down the drive flanked by towering oaks, I realized that the fence along the front and on either side of the drive was just for show. The bison themselves were enclosed by another, higher fence that circled acres of land where the grass was green and lush.

Maybe bison are intelligent creatures.

Maybe they're just nosy.

Just as I cruised by, a bison with a massive dark head and a lighter brown body looked up from where it was munching its dinner. He had horns and dark eyes that watched me roll by, and I had no doubt he wanted to know who I was and what I was doing on his turf.

"Trying to find the house," I grumbled, more to myself (obviously) than to the bison. Up ahead, I saw a structure and thought I'd been successful, but when I rounded a corner and saw that the fence keeping in the bison ran straight up to the building, I knew it wasn't the house but the barn.

And what a barn it was!

I'd seen houses in fancy-schmancy magazines that weren't nearly as jazzy.

The cedar-sided barn glowed in the evening light, its warm brown color reminiscent of the fur on the bison that grazed nearby. The barn had wide front doors that were thrown open, windows that winked a greeting. There was even a cupola on the roof. Oh yes, these lucky bison lived in the lap of luxury.

As it turned out, so did their owner.

Another twist in the driveway, another turn around a stand of oaks, and I found myself in front of the house. I'll confess this: I have never been fond of things Western. Not movies. Not clothing. And certainly not houses that looked like they belonged on the range. This was nothing like those weather-beaten cowboy bunkhouses. This was a ranch on steroids. And so beautiful, it took my breath away.

The house had a main, two-story structure at the center that branched out left and right to a one-story living space. On one side of the house between the two-story part and the one was a covered stone patio where there was a table, chairs with red all-weather cushions, a barbecue grill and smoker, and an outdoor bar stocked to the gills. Just like the barn, the house had cedar siding and a rustic metal roof, and there was a wide courtyard out front and a pond where a couple of ducks and one glorious white swan paddled in contentment.

It was impressive, all right, and when I parked and took another look around, I thought of two things:

Number one, guys who were the face of rough, tough trucks in commercials made a whole lot more money than I ever imagined.

And number two, as much as I told myself it really was none of my business, I wondered how many times Charmaine had been there, lounging on that patio, sipping a margarita or two.

Just thinking about my aunt made me grumble. No wonder, as I'd tried and failed to get her to fess up to her relationship with Brody just as we were locking up back at Love Under the Covers an hour earlier.

"I've got to get Brody's credit card back to him," I'd told her.

"Uh-huh." Charmaine was engrossed in reading reviews of the newest romances in *Publishers Weekly* and barely looked up.

"I've got a whole bunch of paperwork to catch up on," I lied with a straight face and added a sigh, too, in an effort to make her feel sorry for me. "Maybe you'd like to get out tonight. You know, go out to Brody's for me."

Her head snapped up. "Out? To Brody's? Tonight?"

"I just thought—"

"No, no. No can do." Charmaine pushed through the front door ahead of me, and after I flipped our OPEN sign to CLOSED, I followed her and locked up. "Sorry," she said. "Tonight I've got a date with a frozen pot pie and a couple of episodes of *The Crown*."

"No worries." I hoped the smile I gave her hid my devious intentions. "I just thought if you wanted to see Brody again . . ."

"See Brody? Again? I haven't seen Brody since last time he was here at the shop. Why would I want to see him again?"

I managed to make my shrug look casual. "Oh, I dunno. I just thought maybe if you wanted to, I don't know, have a talk with him, or have a nightcap with him, or—"

"Oh, Lizzie!" When she turned and sailed off the patio, Charmaine's laughter trailed behind her. "You're pulling my leg."

Sitting out there in front of Brody's magnificent home and thinking about it, my shoulders drooped and my spirits flagged. Charmaine was being cagey about her relationship with Brody, all right. And it was driving me crazy. Then again, that didn't mean . . .

I pictured Brody surveying his domain from out there on the front porch, wearing cowboy boots, a big ol' hat, and those butt-hugging jeans, and I realized there was more than one way to uncover the truth. I was there to return Brody's credit card, sure, but that didn't mean I couldn't use this one-on-one time with the red-hot rancher to try to find out a little more about what he and my aunt were up to.

Reminding myself to play it cool and keep my questions for him low-key, I rolled down the car windows to let in the cool evening air. I got out of the car and had just turned to close the door when I was hit from behind and nearly knocked off my feet.

I let out a "boof" of surprise and slammed against the car, but I knew I didn't have the luxury of collapsing on the ground or even trying to catch my breath. Not if I was going to defend myself. I clenched my hands into fists, whirled—

And stopped cold.

I'd expected to find an assailant behind me, but instead I was greeted by the most astounding animal I'd ever seen.

No, not a bison, thank goodness.

This was a dog. A large dog of questionable parentage. She was tall and long-legged, like an Irish wolfhound. She had the pointy ears of a shepherd and a long curled tail, like a Samoyed. Her luxurious shaggy fur reminded me of a sheepdog. It hung in bangs over her dark eyes and it fringed her ears, and when a breeze kicked up, all that fur rippled this way and that. She was snow-white, and she had a nose that was more pink than it was black.

Now that she was done jumping on me, the dog barked a greeting.

"Hey, there." Though I do not own a dog, I'd always been fond of them, and I knew the best thing to do was to let her sniff my hand. She did, and I got the seal of approval. She gave my fingers a lick.

"Who are you, huh?" She was big enough that I didn't have to bend down to rub a hand over the dog's head, and when I did, I came away with fingers coated in white fur. The dog was wearing a purple collar and there was a tag hanging from it, so shedding or no shedding, I gave her another pat and took a closer look. "Violet. Are you Violet?"

She woofed her answer.

"Well, Violet . . ." I started toward the house, and she trotted along at my side. "I came to see Brody. Is he around?"

Violet put on the brakes, looked back at the barn, and barked.

"Is that where he is?" I asked her. I judged the distance between where I'd parked my car and the barn, then explained to Violet, "I worked all day, and I'm tired. It's a lot closer for me to check the house first."

Violet didn't argue. At my side, she stepped up on the front porch and over to the door. She sat down when I lifted my hand to ring the bell.

No answer.

"What do you think?" I looked at the dog. "I'm thinking I should give it one more try." I raised my voice and called out, "Brody, are you home?"

Violet barked and looked at the barn.

This time, like it or not, I got the message. I turned around and hiked along a stone path bordered with zinnias in every color of the rainbow, past that beautiful covered outdoor entertainment area, around to the far side of the house, and across what felt like a couple of football fields of lawn all the way to the barn.

There was a Dutch door facing me, and I was tempted to yank it open and go inside. But bison, remember? And I wasn't sure how the barn was laid out or how much freedom the animals had inside.

Instead, I inched open the door and called, "Brody? It's Lizzie. From Love Under the Covers. I've got your credit card."

Violet would have none of this pussyfooting around.

She poked her nose between the door and the jamb and popped the door open.

And that's when I saw him.

"Brody?" The name croaked out of me, and my voice was caught behind the ball of panic and fear that wedged in my throat, blocking my breathing.

Brody Pierce was laid out on the floor, his cowboy hat on the ground beside him. Those blue eyes of his were wide open, staring at nothing, and his skin was tinged Grinch green. His left arm was thrown out at his side. His right hand was next to the jagged wound that tore into his denim shirt and ripped his flesh. His fingers were coated with blood dried to the rich brown of a bison's fur.

Violet raced to her master's side. She plunked down next to him, and she howled.

Josh Randall was not only one of Tinker's Creek's finest, he was my cousin, Charmaine's son from her first (or was it her second?) marriage. He looked toward the barn where a team of techs from the Ohio Bureau of Criminal Investigation had set up lights and was taking photos and measurements.

"Man, the chief is going to lose it when he hears he's missing out on something this big," he said. "He's got a broken leg, you know. Chief Goodrich. Fell off a ladder painting his kitchen. It's going to make him crazy to have to sit this one out. We've never had a murder in Tinker's Creek. We're not exactly a big, dangerous city. Not like Chicago."

I was not in the mood to discuss the benefits or disadvantages of my hometown. There were more important things to worry about.

"What do you suppose happened?" I asked Josh.

We were sitting side by side in the back of an ambulance, the big back doors open, our legs swinging over the side. The paramedics who'd arrived not long after Josh screeched down the drive insisted on checking me out. Yeah, my blood pressure was high. No surprise there. And my heartbeat was doing a cha-cha inside my chest. That wasn't a shock, either. Convinced I was as well as a woman who'd just found a body could be, they'd sat me down, given me a bottle of water, and thrown a blanket over my shoulders before they told me to wait a little while, then they'd check my vitals again.

Josh put an arm around that blanket and my shoulders long enough for a quick squeeze.

"Can't say what went down. Not yet." He had a notebook in his hands, and he looked over the notes he'd scribbled there. "Want to go over it again?"

When he'd arrived, lights flashing and siren screaming, I'd told him what I knew. But I understood he had a job to do. Even if I didn't like the idea of reliving the nightmare of what I'd found in the barn.

"Brody . . ." The name stuck in my throat. "He left his credit card when he came into the shop to buy one of those cute handmade cards. I came here to give it back to him."

"And you found him. Dead."

I nodded. There really was nothing else to say.

"Did you see anyone else around?"

Josh's question snapped me out of the misery that had settled on my shoulders and made me feel as if I'd been loaded down with leaden weights. A rush of fear will do that to a girl.

"You mean . . ." There were three cop cars there now, all of them with their light bars going. The crime scene truck was parked nearby, too, as well as the ambulance where we sat and a truck from the coroner's office. I was surrounded by the good guys, and perfectly safe. Still, I couldn't help but peer through the shadows that winked in and out between the crazy patterns the red and blue flashing lights made against the barn. I swallowed hard. "You mean like the murderer?"

Josh scratched a hand along his chin. He was short and stocky, with sandy hair, a square jaw, and eyes the color of the night sky. "My guess is Brody's been dead awhile," he said. "So I don't know." As if he were trying to align his thoughts, he shook his head. "If you killed someone, would you stick around the scene of the crime for twenty-four hours?"

Twenty-four hours.

I digested the information.

Or at least I would have tried if it didn't make my stomach flip.

It was Thursday, and just about twenty-four hours earlier, I'd played the spy, watching Brody in that crazy mishmash of a den with Josh's mom. I'd heard him leave. Saw his car lurch away. Watched Charmaine hurry out of the house and race after him.

Twenty-four hours.

Which meant that just a little while after I'd seen him, Brody had come home. And that's when he was killed.

Had Charmaine been here with him?

As if he might actually be able to read my mind, I batted the thought away before Josh could somehow sense it, and did my best to wash away the sour taste in my mouth with a drink of water.

"Where were you yesterday evening?" Josh asked.

I didn't hold the question against him. He was getting his ducks in a row. "I had a date," I said, "and—"

"You had a date?" He grinned and bumped me on the shoulder in a way-to-go gesture that wasn't nearly as encouraging as I imagined he intended it to be. "How'd it go, cuz?"

I shot him a sour look. "What difference does it make? And who are you to preach about dating to begin with? You're not exactly out there being Casanova. If you'd loosen up a bit and pay a little more attention, you'd realize that Brynn—"

"What time did you get back from your date?"

When he cut me off, I grumbled a curse. Brynn was crazy about Josh, and Josh was crazy to pretend he didn't notice. This time at least he had a good excuse for interrupting me when I attempted to point that out. I mean, what with the murder and everything. But he did the same thing every time I brought up Brynn's name. And it pretty much drove me up a wall.

I set aside the idea of Josh's love life, my dating, and Brynn always hoping Josh would wake up and notice her.

We had more important things to think about, and the realization chilled me to the bone.

I pulled the blanket closer around me. "It was after dark," I told him.

"And . . . ?"

"And nothing. What else is there to say? I got home from my date and I stayed home. Back in town. I can't tell you anything about what happened out here." Aside from the fact that my stomach rebelled just thinking about it, my brain wouldn't leave it alone. "How was he killed?"

"Stabbed." Someone in the barn called to Josh, and he slid out of the ambulance. Fists on hips, nose wrinkled the way it always was when he was deep in thought, he stopped long enough to say, "Weird wound. Probably a knife, but . . ."

He shrugged the thought away. "You going to be okay here by yourself for a while?"

"I'm fine," I assured him, even though it was far from true.

He patted my shoulder. Josh is a few years older than my twenty-eight, and he's always considered himself the big brother I never had. "I'll tell you what. Until I get back, see if you can come up with a list of people you think I need to talk to. You know, anyone Brody might have had a relationship with."

This I did not agree to do, but honestly, I don't think Josh noticed. He hurried off to the barn, and I kept my thoughts to myself.

People Brody had relationships with?

Did he mean, like, women?

Brody was a serial dater, and Josh was going to have his work cut out for him, that was for sure.

And if one of those women was Josh's mother?

I told myself I wasn't going to say anything about that. Not until I knew more about what had been going on between Brody and Charmaine.

Reminding myself not to forget it, I settled into the soft folds of the blanket and did my best to ignore the hubbub all around me. I closed my eyes, concentrated on my breathing, did my best to chase away the prickles of horror that shot through my bloodstream when I thought about finding Brody on the barn floor.

It was no use. My nerves were strained. My head pounded. My imagination spun with all the terrible possibilities. What had happened? Why? And, most important, who could have possibly hated our red-hot rancher enough to stab him and leave him there, his life's blood flowing out on the barn floor?

Too antsy to keep still, I slid out of the ambulance. All the action was in the barn, and I turned my back on it, hoping to find at least a few moments of peace in the darkness that settled over the ranch. Crickets sang in the distance. Tree frogs babbled. I pulled in a breath, concentrated on the night and on the soft shadows thrown by the trees at the far end of the property beyond the house.

And that's when I saw it.

A beam of light, raking the woods.

"Josh!" Keeping my eye on what must have been the light of a flashlight, I called out to my cousin, but of course, he was in the barn and he didn't hear. As I watched, the light skimmed the edge of the woods. It came closer, then faded back into the cover of the trees.

"Josh!" I called again, and when there was still no response from him, I turned. It was the exact moment Josh stepped out of the barn, and I caught his eye, spun, and pointed.

At nothing.

The light was gone.

When he walked over, I explained what had happened, and Josh didn't have the heart to tell me I was imagining things. Instead, he said I must be exhausted, and that I should get home and try to get some sleep. He called the paramedics over to check me out again, and when they told me I was good to go, I gave them back their blanket and began the long trudge back to my car.

"I will need to talk to you about this again." Josh walked along at my side, his flashlight lighting the stone path that led back to the house. "This is going to be the talk of the town," he said. "I'd appreciate it if you didn't mention it to anyone tonight. I mean . . ." He gave me a sidelong glance.

"Especially my mom. There will be no peace in Tinker's Creek once she gets hold of this news."

"And you don't want the killer to know, do you? That we found the body? That you're on the case?"

This time the look Josh gave me was more penetrating. "You're thinking like a cop! How'd you know?"

"I read a whole lot of romantic suspense," I told him when I dug my car keys out of my pocket. "But if I keep that secret for you tonight, can you do me a favor tomorrow?"

"Anything. You know that."

I fumbled with my keys. "I'd rather not let anyone know I'm the one who found Brody. Not yet, anyway. If word gets out—"

"I get it!" He chuckled. "They'd be lined up around the block to get into your shop, and it wouldn't be to buy books. This town loves its gossip. No worries. I'll keep that bit of info under wraps as long as I can."

"Thanks, Josh." I gave him a quick hug and opened my car door.

"Call me when you get home," he said.

I promised I would and slid into the car, and I guess considering everything that had happened, I can be excused for being muddled because it wasn't until I started the car and pushed the gearshift into drive and checked my rearview mirror that I realized I should have known better than to leave my windows open.

I wasn't alone.

Two big brown eyes looked back at me.

A pink nose sniffed my ear.

Violet leaned over the seat and gave me a sloppy kiss.

Chapter 5

What one does with a wildly shedding, albeit friendly, dog is up for discussion.

For my part, I did the only thing I could think to do. When we got home from the ranch, I poured myself a glass of wine, drank it while I shared half a box of Ritz Crackers with Violet, and made a bed of blankets for her in my kitchen. She spent the night there, quiet and well behaved, and for that, I was grateful. The next morning, since I didn't have kibble in the cupboard, I treated her to a breakfast of scrambled eggs, then walked her to the center of town and back, a long silk scarf tied to her collar since I didn't have a leash.

She did not complain about any of this.

In fact, when I left for work and promised I'd check in at lunchtime, she was snuggled in the blankets, and maybe I was imagining it, but I thought there was sadness in her eyes, and I knew what that was all about. New person looking after her. New place to sleep. And a beloved master, suddenly gone. I know I didn't imagine her heavy sigh when I closed the door behind me.

What would happen after that day—to Violet, to this new living arrangement—was anybody's guess, but my plan was to call Josh when I got to the shop and ask him who, ultimately, was responsible for the animal.

As it turned out, I didn't have the time. I'd already stowed my purse and was headed to unlock the door when I realized there was a customer out on the front patio, her nose pressed to the glass.

I plucked a long strand of white fur from my alligator-green shirt and reminded myself that sleepless night or not, disturbing memories or not, it was time to open for business.

At least until I saw who was waiting there.

That's when I froze with astonishment.

The last person I ever expected to see that day or any other day at Love Under the Covers was Meghan Watkins.

See, Meghan, as the manager of the local library, is one of those types who thinks Shakespeare and Dickinson and Atwood are Literature (and yes, the way she says it, the word does need to be capitalized). Everything else, anything that's genre fiction—especially romance—she considers trash.

Cheap.

Tawdry.

Vulgar.

Insipid.

Just some of the words I'd heard Meghan use when she talked about romance.

And those were some of the nicer ones!

Wondering what was up, I shook away my surprise and unlocked the door. And I mean, really, since the last time I'd run into Meghan and she'd greeted me with, "Well if it isn't the smut peddler," I can be excused for passing right by "Good morning" and "What can I do for you?" and going straight to "Are you sure you're in the right place?"

She stepped into the store so quickly, I had no choice but to hop back or get bowled over.

"I need to talk to you," Meghan said.

She was closing in on forty, a woman who wasn't as thin as she was simply flat, like a cardboard cutout of a real person. She was average height, had unremarkable features and nondescript hair of a color writers of Regency romances are given to call mouse-brown.

The only thing good or bad—in fact, the only thing at all—anyone ever said about Meghan was that she was Prepared. (Yes, another capitalization and, like the last one, totally apropos.)

Summer or winter, Meghan always had a navy blue cardigan draped over one arm—so she'd never catch a chill in whatever place she happened to be.

Breezy or tranquil, she always had a headscarf in her pocket, like those filmy ones that look so charming on the Queen of England and make the rest of us look like peasants—so her hair never got mussed.

Sunny skies or gray, she always kept an umbrella tucked in her purse—just in case.

Yup, there she was, sweater over her arm in spite of the day's sweltering temperatures, scarf peeking from the pocket of her black pants, umbrella within easy reach.

In fact, the only thing different about Meghan that morning was that she was wearing enormous sunglasses with tortoiseshell rims. No doubt she'd seen some new scientific study about just how damaging UV rays could be to her eyes. Or maybe she was keeping pollen at bay.

"Talk? Sure." I waved an arm in an indeterminate direction, behind me and toward the front register. "You can wait right there while I finish turning on the lights and—"

"Now. I need to talk to you now."

I am not usually swayed by pushy. Yet there was something about the tremor in Meghan's voice, a something that made me realize something was up. I walked toward the historical romance room and motioned her to join me.

"We can talk in here," I said, and I staked my claim to the wing chair nearest the window, brushing a piece of Violet from the leg of my army-green pants when I settled myself.

"How can you just sit there?" Meghan paced a pattern on the Oriental rug in front of me. Her voice trembled. Her hands fluttered from her crisp white blouse to her black pants and back again. "How can you act like nothing is wrong?" she said, planting her feet directly in front of me. "After what you've seen."

Uh-oh.

I did not need Meghan to tell me the proverbial cat was out of the felonious bag.

In an effort to chase away the memories of dried blood and knife wounds, I crossed my legs and swung one pink-sneaker-shod foot. "You've heard about Brody."

"Heard?" She hiccuped. "Everyone's talking about it. Everyone knows you . . ." Honestly, I thought she was going to fall to her knees and grab my hands, and rather than take the chance, I popped out of my seat and moved a safe distance away. "Oh, Lizzie! How your heart must ache. You're the one who found him!"

"Who spilled the beans?"

"Does it matter? At a time like this? No, it does not!" She lifted a chin that could best be described as weak. "What matters is the darkest depths of the horrible truth.

The terrible, mind-numbing reality of a world turned upside down. The inescapable facts, so dreadful in their certainty that they chill the soul and turn day into night."

This from a woman who thought romance authors were hacks.

"Brody is dead!" she wailed.

"Yes, he is, and why don't you . . ." I dared to latch on to her arm and swung her toward the chair. I don't think she actually sat down as much as her knees just gave out. She plunked onto the cushion. "Is that why you're here, Meghan?" I asked her. "Because of what happened to Brody?"

"Well, yes. I thought I could . . . that is, I hoped you would . . ." Her words were drowned by her burbling. She dug a tissue out of her purse and whisked off her sunglasses to dab her eyes.

That's when I saw what those sunglasses were all about.

Meghan's eyes were red and swollen. Her cheeks were blotchy. Her nose was raw.

As the finder of said dead body, I pretty much figured I was the one entitled to that sort of reaction.

And the reason Meghan had beat me to the punch in the grief/shock/heartache department? Thinking about that made a couple dozen questions pop into my mind.

"What did you come here hoping I would do?" was just one of them, and the first one I had a chance to voice.

She gulped a sob and settled her sunglasses back in place, but not before she aimed one desperate, pleading look in my direction. "I thought you could tell me about it."

"You're kidding me, right?"

Not the answer Meghan was hoping for, but I'm not sure she was thinking straight.

"I'm not being morbid or anything," she said, and before

I could beg to differ, she added, "I just want to be able to share in Brody's last moments."

"Except I don't know anything about his last moments." As long as we were in the historical room and I was getting increasingly uncomfortable with the conversation, I went through my usual morning routine, righting a couple of books that had tumbled from the display table in the center of the room, moving a Georgette Heyer back to the H's from the M's where some careless customer had left it, turning on the overhead spotlights. Since word of Brody's death was already all over town, I didn't think I was breaking any confidences by adding, "He was already dead when I found him. It looks like he was killed Wednesday night."

"Wednesday." The way Meghan wailed the word made it sound like a hoodoo curse. She clutched her hands at her waist. "I don't suppose . . . the police, do they have any clues?"

I wasn't sure if she could see me shrug, what with the weeping and the gnashing of teeth. "Clues aren't something that are any of my business. Or anybody else's," I added and hoped she got the message. "The cops are on top of things."

"But what if they found something?" As if she'd just run a mile, Meghan's breaths were fast and shallow. "What if the killer left behind something suspicious like . . . oh, I don't know . . . like a glove or a hat or something? That's what always happens in those awful paperback mysteries everybody and his brother take out from the library. If the police found some sort of clue last night . . . well, you were there. You would have heard them say something about it, right? You would know."

A nicer version of Lizzie Hale would have been reluctant to destroy her hopes. But this was Meghan, remember? Hater of romance. Disparager of all popular fiction. I wasn't looking for revenge, and I sure didn't want to be petty. But I needed her to face facts.

"I don't know anything," I admitted.

"But you must." She popped out of her seat. "You were there."

"I was there. And yes, I found Brody. Then I called the police and hightailed it back to town," I told her. Since I'm a big believer in show rather than tell, I brushed my hands together in the hopes of getting my message across. "My part in the whole business is done. Finished. I'm as much in the dark as everyone else is about what happened to Brody."

"Everyone else but maybe . . ." She swallowed hard. "The police. Which is why I asked about clues. If they found some evidence, it might lead them to a suspect." She swallowed hard. "Right?"

It was a no-brainer, and I might have pointed that out politely if Meghan hadn't blurted out, "You could ask that cousin of yours."

"No." I didn't know how to be any clearer. "No, no, and no. You want to follow the details of a case, Meghan, I can sell you some terrific romantic suspense. There's Nora Roberts and Sandra Brown and Jayne Ann—"

"Read? That stuff?" As if she were a vampire and I'd just showered her with holy water, Meghan reared back, turned on her heel, and hightailed it out of the shop.

"She's an odd duck, that's for sure."

I'd been so engrossed in talking to Meghan, I didn't realize we had an audience. Penny Markham toed the line between the hallway and the historical romance room.

"With everything that's going on, she's just upset."

"Yeah." From where she stood, I was pretty sure Penny

couldn't see Meghan, but she looked toward the front door anyway. "Except the way I heard it . . ." Penny turned my way. "Meghan was already plenty upset when she showed up at work for a meeting early this morning. And that's before word ever got out about what happened yesterday."

I didn't ask Penny how she knew this. In a town as small as Tinker's Creek, folks always knew everyone else's business and weren't above minding it. Penny was a real estate agent, a woman who was whip smart, savvy, and had a reputation as a ruthless negotiator. She'd done a good job for me when I bought the building I'd converted into the shop, and she'd also handled the deal soon after I arrived in town, when I purchased both my home and Charmaine's. She was president of the local Chamber of Commerce, had once served on the town council, and was the niece of Cal Patrick, our longtime mayor. If anyone had a direct connection to the local grapevine, it was Penny.

"What was Meghan upset about?" I wondered.

She barely controlled a smile I can only describe as predatory. "Her poor sense of fashion? Her failure to ever find a stylist who can do anything with that awful hair? Hard to say. But there's no question now, she's upset about Brody. Really upset."

Didn't I just tell Meghan my small part in the whole thing ended when I discovered the body? I'd meant it, too, but that didn't stop me from asking Penny, "Why?"

Penny strolled toward the front counter, and I walked along behind her. She was a woman in her late thirties, tall and lithe, with a mane of Titian hair that was braided that morning and swung over the back of her black power-suit jacket. "Women like Meghan," she told me, "are too easily controlled by their emotions. She heard about the murder and, as you saw, she got carried away by her reaction."

"Were they friends? Her and Brody?"

"In Meghan's dreams!"

"Well . . ." I stepped around Penny so I could check the cash register and make sure we had enough change to take care of the day's transactions. "I wish word hadn't gotten out so quickly. I don't want to spend my day repeating the details."

Penny waved a manicured hand. "Too late! Everyone's heard he's dead, and they know you're the unlucky one who found him. Ken's Diner is packed this morning with people chewing over the news along with their bacon, and I saw Ryan Guttreig, that kid who reports for the *Tinker's Creek Times*, running down Main Street just as I was coming in. I bet he's hot on the trail of the story. Doesn't it just figure?" When she shook her head, a shaft of sunlight flowing in the window behind the counter glimmered against her coppery hair. "Brody was an arrogant blowhard in life, and now just look at what's happening. Even after he's dead, he's making sure people are going to keep talking about him."

I knew my share of gossip, too. After all, Charmaine was my aunt. "That's a pretty cynical attitude considering you dated him."

Penny swung her Coach bag onto the front counter. "Just about every woman in this town dated Brody."

"But if you thought he was arrogant—"

Her laugh cut me off. "I know that now. I didn't. I mean, not when I first agreed to have dinner with the man. My goodness, that one night should have taught me a lesson. Brody Pierce could talk about one thing and one thing only: Brody Pierce."

"But you went out with him more than once."

Penny's smile told me she appreciated my honesty. "You do have your ear to the ground, don't you?" Somehow, a

filament of Violet fur had escaped my notice and hitched a
ride on Penny's jacket sleeve. She brushed it away. "Three
times total," she said. "I went out with him three times. The
first time, well, I figured Brody was just nervous. You
know, the way some men get around a woman who isn't as
impressed as they think she should be by all their macho
chest pounding. I thought that's why he couldn't think of
anything to talk about but himself. Then the second
time . . . well, when it happened again, it was a little harder
to excuse."

"And the third time?"

She laughed. "Guess I'm a glutton for punishment. I
learned my lesson after that. Every time he asked, I just
happened to be busy that night. Don't get me wrong, I'm
sorry the guy's dead. But the good news is I won't have to
listen to him talk about what a big star he was. Big star!"
She rolled her eyes. "Man was in truck commercials."

"Lots of truck commercials."

"And he acted like he was a household name."

"Maybe they wouldn't know his name, but I bet plenty
of people recognize his face when they see it."

"Whatever." It was clear Penny was bored with the subject. She glanced around the shop. "Is Charmaine here?"

Now that she mentioned it, I realized Charmaine wasn't.
A prickle of worry touched the back of my neck. If news of
Brody's death was all around town, then Charmaine had
certainly heard it. Was she upset? Despondent? Had she
gone out to the ranch on some sort of pilgrimage to see the
spot where Brody had met his end? Or was she home, hiding under the blankets of her bed with one of those little
airplane bottles of vodka like she'd done the night Matthew
Crawley bit the big one on *Downton Abbey*?

I refused to let myself get sucked into the worries.

At least until I knew what was going on.

"You can wait for her," I told Penny. "Or maybe there's something I can do for you?"

Thinking this through, Penny tapped the toe of one black pump against the floor. "She said I should stop by today. That she'd have it ready."

"It . . . ?"

"Oh, my horoscope!" Penny laughed in a way designed to tell me it was a silly thing to have to admit, though if she thought it was all that silly, I wondered why she'd asked for Charmaine's astrological expertise. "We were talking a few weeks ago," Penny informed me. "About this and that. And Charmaine, she told me she dabbles in astrology. Said if I gave her my birthday and where I was born and what time, she'd work up my horoscope and I thought, why not? Not that I believe in it or anything," she was quick to add. "But I thought it might be worth a laugh."

As much as I tried to keep my worries about Charmaine from upending me, I couldn't make them go away. I needed to reassure myself, and there was nothing like killing (the word made me cringe, I mean, considering) two birds with one stone.

"I'll tell you what," I said to Penny. "If you can wait here for about five minutes and take care of any customers who might come in, I'll pop over to Charmaine's and see if she's got your horoscope."

"Deal." Always ready to take charge, Penny stepped behind the cash register. "I've got everything under control."

"And I'll be right back," I assured her.

I went out the door that led into the garden because from there I could cut across the back patio of the restaurant next door, snake around the old lovely church that had been a mainstay of the town for as long as anyone could remember, and zip past the square with its gazebo and its bubbling fountain. Our houses, mine and Charmaine's, were only a little way beyond.

"Charmaine!" She never locked her side door, so I knew I could easily get in that way. When I did and didn't see her either in the kitchen to my left or in the dining room to my right, I called again, "Charmaine, are you here? Penny's looking for her horoscope."

No answer, and it was so reminiscent of what had happened to me out at the ranch the night before that I couldn't control the bubble of panic that made my heart squeeze. I took the steps two at a time up to Charmaine's room.

The curtains were open and sunshine poured into the room, and I could easily see she wasn't there. Her bed had been slept in, the yellow-and-orange blanket thrown back. But there was no sign of her there or in the attached bathroom.

I muttered my displeasure. "Well, if you can't find Charmaine, maybe you can at least find Penny's horoscope," I told myself, and to that end, I hightailed it over to the French provincial desk near the windows.

I knew my aunt better than to think there would be a place for everything on her desk, or that everything would be in its place. No sign of Penny's horoscope. Charmaine's latest water bill was thrown on top of a catalogue for garden tools and that was tossed next to her grocery list and that was lying right next to—

I looked at the card on the desktop and my heart banged against my ribs.

Stamped and embossed.

Small hearts, bouquet of flowers.

Tiny cupid with a bow and arrows in his hands and a mischievous smile on his face.

The card Brody had bought at Love Under the Covers the day he died.

Sure, I felt like a busybody. I mean, that's why I looked over my shoulder to make sure Charmaine was nowhere near, right? But I just couldn't help myself. I was dying to know more about what had been going on between my aunt and Brody. Maybe the card . . .

I picked it up, and like the paper itself was as hot as the man who'd sent it, I juggled it in suddenly trembling hands. I reminded myself to get a grip, both on my overactive imagination and on the card, flipped it open, and read the words written inside in thick, manly letters above Brody's signature.

I wanted to know more?

A perfectly good example of be careful what you wish for.

Because now I knew more, and what I knew was that Brody Pierce, he of the too-hot-to-handle body and the bigger-than-life personality, a man who'd made a name for himself selling macho trucks and who'd set every woman's heart afire, had sent my aunt Charmaine a love poem.

Chapter 6

Don't ever forget . . .

> *Love isn't Love*
> *'less the person you Love*
> *Loves Love like you Love Love*
> *And Loves you like you Love*
> *Like the person you Love*
> *Loves Love*

Keeping you in my thoughts. Thank you for the warm memories, bright laughter, and your dear, generous heart.

Brody

All right, so it was lousy poetry.
   But poetry, it was.
And there was no doubt what it was all about. I mean,

really, how many mentions of *Love* does it take to get a message across?

I stared at the words above the flourishing signature *Brody* and a million thoughts whirled through my head. I'd suspected something was up between him and my aunt, but honestly, I thought it was no different from the kind of flirting he did with every other woman in town. A quick kiss, maybe a couple of candlelight dinners. A loaf of bread and a jug of wine and blah, blah, blah.

I hadn't expected the L-word to enter the picture.

And certainly not so many of them.

I can be excused for standing there like a statue, staring and wondering. Speculating. Theorizing. Pondering.

At least until I came to my senses.

"No way!" I told myself to get a grip, shook the thoughts out of my head, and set the card back where I'd found it. "You've got to stop believing everything you read between the covers of a romance novel," I mumbled to myself. "Women like Charmaine and men like Brody don't—"

My advice to myself petered out when I glanced over at the bed and saw something familiar glimmering in the morning light. Sure my eyes were playing tricks on me, I hurried over for a closer look.

Violet fur!

On Charmaine's bed!

Since I'd yet to see my aunt that morning and she had yet to encounter the dog at my house, there was only one way the strands of fur could have gotten there. They rode in on Brody.

And that meant Brody and Charmaine . . .

Fire raced through my cheeks, and as if I'd been discovered to be the trespasser I was, I took a guilty look all around, hoping against hope Charmaine wasn't lurking somewhere in the room, watching as I invaded her privacy and destroyed all trust between us.

I should have known better. No way Charmaine could stay quiet as long as I'd been in the bedroom.

And no way did I want her to find out what I'd been up to.

I darted toward the doorway, then had a thought and turned right around and raced back to the desk. Before I skedaddled out of the room, I took pictures of both the outside and the inside—that telling inside—of the card and that love letter from the red-hot rancher.

So that's what I'm thinking. I mean, there's really no other way to look at the whole thing, is there? Brody and Charmaine . . ." It was Friday evening and the shop was closed. I was home, sitting in a pool of sunshine that splashed over my patio and turned the roses near my door to neon colors. Electric red. Crisp mango. Cinderella pink. There wasn't another person around, but I lowered my voice anyway.

"They were in love! I know, it's totally crazy, but there you have it. Living out there at the ranch, you must have known all about it."

Violet sat at my side, and since I'd zipped to the pet store on my way home and bought real dog food and some treats I'd let her sample, she looked a little happier than she'd been since we discovered Brody's body together. Still, she listened, but she didn't say a word.

"She was upset when she finally showed up at the shop," I told the dog. "I mean, everybody who walked into Love

Under the Covers today, that's all they could talk about—
Brody's murder. He was something of a hero, local boy
makes good and all that, and people are visibly shaken. But
you know that. And I wouldn't have thought a thing of
Charmaine's sniffling and sobbing like everyone else if I
hadn't seen that card. That puts a whole new spin on things,
doesn't it? Even then, I couldn't get Charmaine to open up
and talk about Brody. 'He was such a nice man.' Can you
believe it? That's actually what she said. And when I asked
why she was late for work? She had the nerve to tell me
she'd been at the hair salon. I bet not. I think she was somewhere all by herself, grieving the love of her life. It's so sad! I
just wish I could be there for her. If she'd admit to the relationship, I could help." The futility of my words crashed
down on me. "Somehow." It was my turn to sniffle. "Somehow, maybe I could help."

Though I usually avoided caffeine this late in the evening, it was hot out and I'd treated myself to an iced tea. I
watched condensation form on my glass and saw it trickle
down the side, like tear drops.

"I feel bad for you, too, of course," I made sure to tell the
dog. "Brody was your master. I bet you miss him and your
life on the ranch. If Josh ever calls back . . ." I knew he
hadn't, but I checked my phone for voice mails anyway. "I
get it. He's busy." I plunked the phone on the table. "A murder in Tinker's Creek! I bet it means reams of paperwork
for him, and tons of interviewing people. But I told him you
were with me and asked him what he wanted me to do with
you, and . . ."

Violet settled herself on the sun-warmed stones of the
patio and sighed and I sat back, my gaze automatically
drifting across the garden to Charmaine's house. She'd shot

off for home practically before I had the door of Love Under the Covers locked that evening, and I hadn't seen hide nor hair of her since. What with the heat, her dahlias were drooping, and Charmaine loved her dahlias.

I dragged myself out of my chair and got up to retrieve the watering can nearby, filled it, and crossed the garden to give her flowers a drink. Pouring water over the dahlias and watching them perk up lifted my spirits. At least for a moment. Unfortunately, by the time I was done and returned to my patio, the familiar worries were marching through my head again.

My aunt was generous and free-spirited. Sure, she was a little out there, but she was also lovable, sweet, and kind to children and animals.

Still . . .

I flumped down in my chair. "It's not possible," I told myself and Violet, who was so comfortable, she'd never moved a muscle while I tended the dahlias. "They were in love. There's no way Char would hurt Brody."

On the way home, I'd also picked up a take-away salad for myself, and my romaine was quickly wilting in the heat. I stabbed a piece of it along with a slice of radish and a cherry tomato and popped it all into my mouth. Chewing got me thinking, and all that thinking made me remember all the books I'd read where passion disintegrated into jealousy and jealousy led right on down the road to perdition. Straight to murder.

I hated to even consider it, but I had no choice. "You don't suppose . . ." I looked Violet's way and took out my frustration on an artichoke heart, cutting it in half, poking it, munching it.

"Charmaine must have known about the other women

Brody was dating," I said, and yes, I was talking with my mouth full, but I'd seen the way Violet wolfed down her dinner. She was hardly one to criticize. "Everyone in town knew everything about Brody's love life."

Except they didn't, did they?

The thought hit, and I sat up like a shot.

If Charmaine and Brody's relationship was common knowledge, it never could have been kept under wraps. Which meant maybe there was someone else Brody was leading on, too, some woman no one knew about, some relationship Charmaine discovered and felt threatened by.

If she'd fallen for all that schmaltzy talk, then found out there was another woman, poor Charmaine would have been knocked for a loop.

What if she believed Brody was her soul mate?

How would she feel if she found out he thought of her as nothing more than another one of his conquests?

What would she do?

A sour taste filled my mouth and even another sip of iced tea didn't wash it away.

I screeched my frustration, and that brought Violet to her feet. "If the cops get wind of what was going on between Charmaine and Brody, she's going to be suspect numero uno. Especially if they find out he was here the night he was killed, and that she followed him home. Oh, Violet!" The dog put her head in my lap and I raked my fingers through her fur. "We can't let Charmaine get accused of a crime this horrible. It would break her heart. You know what that means, don't you?"

Violet's eyes sparkled.

"That's right." I rubbed her head and came away with a hand covered with white fur.

"Before the police get any crazy ideas into their heads

about Charmaine, we're just going to have to find the killer ourselves."

Violet barked her agreement.

In my book (not a romance for once), the best place to start a murder investigation is with the most obvious suspects. To that end, though Saturdays are always busy at the shop, I told Charmaine I had to go out and promised I'd be back in just a couple of hours. If she couldn't handle the press of customers herself, I reminded her, I was sure any number of our regulars would be only too happy to step in to help.

That taken care of, I hopped in my car and drove out of town, exactly the way I'd gone that fateful Thursday evening. Except this time, I cruised right by the ranch and turned into the property next door.

Let it be known here and now that I have never been impressed by McMansions. I'd bet anything that wasn't the reaction Ned Baker wanted visitors to have to his home. Then again, when you build a gigantic multistoried Mediterranean estate in Tinker's Creek, Ohio, my guess is you don't care if people like it or hate it. You're going for unforgettable.

Ned certainly accomplished that.

Try as I might, I was pretty sure I would never be able to erase the image of the house, with its lemon-yellow stucco, terra-cotta-tiled roof, iron railings around porches on every level, terraces, statues, and fountains, that was now burned into my brain.

Oh my!

It took me a moment to catch my breath just to settle my stomach.

Grateful I wasn't planning to stick around long, I parked outside a four-car garage and headed to the double doors right below a gigantic window that spotlighted the chandelier that hung above a two-story entryway. I rang the bell and a minute later, Ned opened the door a crack and peeked outside.

"Go away," he said.

"I'm sorry to bother you. I just wanted to stop and talk and . . ." The way he was standing, it was impossible to see Ned clearly. I moved a little to my left.

He stepped to his right.

I took another step, but Ned was too quick for me. He darted to the side to be sure I couldn't see him.

I wondered if he walked around the house nude.

And decided I wasn't going to take the chance of glancing down to find out.

Instead, I kept my eyes on the bit of his face I could see. Which wasn't much. "I just stopped by to see if you're all right. After all, your neighbor was murdered."

Ned huffed out a breath. "What about him?"

"Well, I just thought . . ." It felt weird talking to the sliver of the man on the other side of the door. "I was worried you'd be upset. I wondered how you felt about the whole thing."

"You mean how do I feel not to have that arrogant so-and-so living so close by? How do you think I feel?" As if he'd just had a new thought, he cocked his head and I caught just a glimpse of his face. I couldn't be sure, but—

"What's going to happen to those bison of his?"

Ned's question interrupted me processing the quick peek I'd gotten of him. "I have no idea," I had to admit. "But you know, I'm the one who found Brody. And that got me to thinking about what might have happened to him, and I just thought I'd ask . . . you know . . ." Maybe it was a good thing I couldn't see much of Ned. If I focused on the double doors with their panels inlaid with scroll carving, it meant I didn't have to look him in the eyes when I asked, "Where were you Wednesday night, Ned?"

He reared back and farther into the interior shadows. "Where were *you* Wednesday night?"

"Home," I answered automatically, even though it was not technically true because I was really out with that cute lawyer where I made a total fool of myself, then lurking in Charmaine's yard where I discovered things about my aunt I wasn't sure I wanted to know, then following that shadow in the garden where I lost my footing and . . .

I rubbed my still achy knee.

"It doesn't matter where I was," I told Ned. "I'm not the one who was mad about Brody's bison jumping over the fence and ruining my cocktail party."

"You're also not the one who has any business asking me any of this." Just to prove his point, Ned slammed the door in my face.

But here's the thing. In order for that slamming to be as dramatic as a slamming should be, Ned had to inch open the door just a little more. For full slamming effect. And when he did, I got confirmation of what I thought I'd seen earlier.

As I headed back to my car, I realized I'd learned something in spite of Ned's less-than-cordial reception.

Ned Baker, never reluctant to let anyone and everyone know how much he disliked Brody, had two black eyes and a scraped cheekbone. His eyelids were purple. His nose was swollen.

Yeah, like he'd been in a fight.

Did it mean what I thought it meant? Did Ned have

something to do with Brody's death? Had I just been face-to-face (well, sort of) with the murderer?

I couldn't say, but it was certainly a possibility, and honestly, I liked the idea that Brody hadn't gone down without a fight.

I was still smiling about it as I neared the ranch. On Thursday night, after everything I'd seen, I'd sworn I'd never want to set foot on the property again, but that day, with puffy clouds in the blue sky above me and birds chirping from the oak trees, I turned in, drove up to the barn, and stopped my car.

As if life went on at the Pierce Double B Bar Ranch with or without Brody, the bison were out in the meadow. The sun caressed the wood barn. All those zinnias between here and the house looked bright and cheery.

In fact, if it wasn't for the yellow crime scene tape draped over the barn door, a visitor would think nothing horrific had happened there just a few days earlier.

I knew better.

I suppose that's why I'd stopped in the first place. I'd wanted to see proof that there was still hope, even after a tragedy as awful as Brody's death. I wanted the reassurance that his beautiful ranch wasn't an illusion, that he'd left something solid and tangible behind.

Eager to squeeze every bit of contentment out of the moment, I slipped out of the car and leaned against it, my head tipped back. A breeze kissed my cheek. Quiet wrapped around me and—

At the sound of metal on metal, I flinched and stood up. There was no one out in the meadow with the bison, and the sound wasn't loud enough to have come from the barn.

I heard it again, far away, carried on the wind.

Curious, I rounded the back of the barn and looked all around.

Had the sound come from the house?

I'd already started that way when I heard the sharp ping again.

No, not from the house, from the woods on the other side of the bison enclosure.

Too intrigued not to check it out, I started the trek toward the trees and discovered soon enough that over open meadow, distances can be deceiving. I walked for fifteen minutes, the fence that kept the bison where they belonged was over to my right and the animals themselves were scattered on the other side of it, some lounging, others grazing. I stopped once to catch my breath and fan my face and wish I'd brought along a water bottle, and while I did all that, I leaned against a fence post.

What had Ned Baker told me about the bison that invaded his party? That the animals can move fast?

I'll say.

Before I saw him coming, one of the males roared up to within ten feet of the fence. He was bigger than I had even imagined, and he dropped his head and gave me a look that said he was clearly in charge. And I was an intruder.

"Okay. I get it." I raised both my hands and backed away slowly. I can't say I understand wild animal behavior, but I knew better than to stare him down. The fence was at least six feet tall, but if he jumped it as he had the night of Ned's party, I was a goner.

"Leaving." I don't think the critter cared that I smiled at him. I backed up another dozen steps. "Going. Won't be back. Promise!"

It was the distance I put between us, I think, that finally

made him happy. He backed off a couple steps and stomped the ground in a way that said *Good riddance*, and even when I was far enough away that I felt safe to turn my back on him, I knew he was still watching me. I could feel his gaze drill between my shoulder blades.

It wasn't until I made it all the way to the shade of the trees along the far property line that I dared to let go a shaky breath and glance back at the enclosure. The big male was gone and I was limp with relief. I dropped onto a tree stump and took a few minutes to gather my composure. The metallic ping rang out again, closer now, it's high-pitched echo vibrating through the morning air.

"Hello?" I stood and called out.

No answer.

I made my way through a tangle of fallen branches and knee-high weeds, zigzagging in the direction where I thought the sound originated.

And I found absolutely nothing.

One more look around, and I gave up the hunt. Whoever was out there, whatever had made the noise, it was none of my business anyway.

Keeping my eyes on the strip of sunshine that showed where the trees ended and the meadow began, I made my way back. I didn't need to remind myself to give the bison enclosure a wide berth, so I swung around to my right and followed a meandering path that led out of the trees. I was almost back to the meadow when something in the bushes caught my eye.

Binoculars.

I picked them up and looked them over and I looked all around, too, but there wasn't anyone anywhere. At least not that I could see. What I could see in the distance, though, was the barn, the enclosure, just a hint of the house even farther off. It was the perfect vantage point to keep an eye on the Pierce Double B Bar Ranch.

A memory flashed through my mind.

That shadow in the garden the night Brody visited Charmaine.

Another thought followed on its heels.

That gleam of a flashlight I'd seen in the woods the night I found Brody's body.

Considering it all, I set the binoculars down exactly where I found them and made my way back to the car. I'd call Josh and let him know about the binoculars, and I'd let him know something else, too.

I think someone was keeping an eye on Brody.

Chapter 7

I was back at Love Under the Covers, where I belonged, before noon. I found the shop hopping (a very good thing). Tasha was there with a few other romance-writer-wannabe buddies, and they bought armfuls of the latest books.

It was enough to make a bookshop owner's heart sing!

I finished bagging their purchases and took advantage of a brief lull to seek out my aunt. I found her with the gothic romances. The left side of her hair looked as if a family of mice had been in there building a new home. The right side hung around her shoulders. All she needed was a castle behind her and a bolt of lightning slicing through the air to be the twin of the heroine on one of the nearby covers.

"You want to talk about it?" I asked her.

"How did you know?" she asked me.

Relieved she'd finally decided to open up about Brody, I felt the curl of worry inside me untwist. "It's not common knowledge, if that's what you're afraid of."

"Thank goodness." She swiped a hand across her eyes. "I'd hate to look like a horse's behind in front of everyone in town."

I put a gentle hand on her arm. "Not at all! That's not what anyone would think. It's not your fault you believe the best in people. When someone tells you something—"

"Exactly." Charmaine nodded. "And oh, yes, I did believe. And now this! I don't know what I'm going to do, Lizzie."

"Of course you're upset." I gave her arm a pat. "How can you not be? When the love of your life—"

"Huh?" Charmaine towers over me, but when she threw back her shoulders and gave me a penetrating look, I felt smaller than ever. "What on earth are you talking about, girl?"

There were no customers in the vicinity, but I made sure to keep my voice down. I didn't dare violate the secrecy of Charmaine and Brody's relationship. And not just because I was trying to nip the Tinker's Creek grapevine in the bud. Cops, remember? Cops who might look at Charmaine as a suspect.

I moved a step closer to my aunt. "I'm talking about Brody, of course."

Her brows dropped low over her eyes. That is, right before they shot up her forehead and Charmaine let out a whoop of laughter. "You're talking about . . . !" She laughed some more, so hard she had to brace herself against the kitchen doorway to keep from toppling over. "Oh, honey! I'm talking about the ham salad over at the Sparkle Market. They told me it was homemade, and I believed them. Even tasted it there at the deli counter and told everybody within earshot that it was their best ever. Then Marva Stickler stopped in here at the shop. You know, that woman who's always winning top prize at Bring Your Best Casserole Night at the town hall. Marva, she told me she was at the market and saw the commercial containers the salad was delivered in. Oh!" Charmaine groaned. "If she finds out I thought it was homemade, I'll never hear the end of it. She's just that petty."

I chewed this over in much the same way I imagined Charmaine had sampled the offending food. "You're this upset? Over ham salad?"

"Well, I wouldn't be. If not for Josh. He's coming for cocktails tonight. And bringing a friend. I wanted to make a good impression. You know, salsa and chips, deviled eggs, ham salad piled on those cheesy crackers shaped like stars. And now this." She threw her hands in the air and let them fall back to her sides.

"Then you're not upset about Brody?"

One corner of her mouth pulled tight. "Of course I am! Everyone is. Poor, dear man. It's so wrong. And so horrible. But I'll tell you what, at times like this, it's more important than ever to realize just how short life is, to get enjoyment out of small things. That's why I talked Josh into stopping over."

"And he's bringing a friend." I did not like the sound of this. If Brynn found out Josh had a girlfriend, she'd be heartbroken.

"You're going to be there, too, right?" Someone called from the front of the shop, and Charmaine headed that way before I could tell her I'd let her know. "Seven o'clock sharp. In the garden. I'm making margaritas. I've even got some of those darling little paper umbrellas to stick in them!"

Just like that, she was gone, and I was left questioning

my skills—apparently abysmal—at counseling the grief-stricken.

Before I had a chance to give myself a figurative swift kick in the pants, though, Becky Nilender, a longtime customer, came around the corner.

"Found this." She poked a thick hardcover book at me. "Out on the patio. Looks like it slipped under the ivy and got lost. I bet someone's looking for it."

I bet so, too, and I bet I knew exactly who it was. Ernest and I must have missed the book when we gathered the ones he'd dropped the day I chatted with him. It was a history book, *At Sea with the Vikings*, and it had a sticker on the back that showed it belonged to the Tinker's Creek library.

"No worries," I told Becky, and tucked the book under my arm. "I was going to go out and pick up a sandwich for lunch. I'll stop by the library on my way."

Tinker's Creek is far from a sprawling metropolis. In fact, we have one main street with a half-dozen side streets branching off it. There are three restaurants that cater to the needs of visitors to the nearby national park, a bike store, and a few gift shops, their windows filled with beautiful art that beckoned me when I walked to the library. It was only in the last few years that developers had been buying up the land around the town for upscale houses and the kind of country estates Ned Baker owned. What was once a sleepy village pulsed with activity, especially on weekends. Crossing Main Street, I dodged a van with a satellite dish on its roof, darted through a line of traffic waiting to turn into the parking lot of Ken's Diner, and waved a hello to Mayor Cal Patrick, who was on his cell, busy as usual and unable to chat.

The library itself had been built back before the influx of new growth. It was a single-story brick building on the corner of the side street just east of the bridge over the canal. Its windows faced the street and I knew there was a wide foyer just inside the automatic doors.

I did not expect said foyer to be chockablock with cartons and ladders.

Meghan Watkins, her navy cardigan perched on her shoulders, was ensconced in the center of it all.

"What's up?" I asked her.

"Oh, this and that and the other thing!" In her own buttoned-down, uptight way, Meghan looked as tousled as my aunt. A yellow sticky note clung to her sweater, and her left cheek was streaked with dust. "I'm trying to get the memorial display done today. You know, for Brody."

I looked where she was looking, at the wall of the foyer where the doors were thrown open on two floor-to-ceiling cabinets with glass fronts. Her display had already begun to take shape. At the center of the cabinet on my right was a nine-by-twelve glossy of Brody, his eyes narrowed just the slightest bit, as if he were checking the horizon for any signs of danger and preparing himself to face it.

"That's an especially nice picture, don't you think?" Meghan looked at the photo, too, and a bittersweet smile played its way around her lips. "He autographed it. See?" She approached the cabinet as reverently as if she were a commoner getting ready to bow to royalty. "'To Meghan.' See, it says that right there." She pointed. "'Keeper of the books, a pillar of Tinker's Creek.' He called me a pillar." She twittered and her cheeks flushed. "Brody, he had a way with words."

"And you've got quite a collection of his things." I glanced over a model of the truck that Brody flogged in all those commercials, a drone view of his ranch, a picture of him performing the stunt he was most famous for, the one where he hang glided over a moving truck and landed in the open bed. "Where'd you get all this stuff?"

Meghan shrugged. "Oh, you know. When a local boy makes good, people accumulate memorabilia. Take a look at this!" She dug through the nearest box and pulled out a copy of a high school yearbook and skimmed a gentle hand over the cover. "Brody's senior year. I don't have the heart to cut the book apart for pictures for the display, but I'll scan them and use them. Imagine this!" As if she were doing just that, she backed away and looked from one cabinet to the other. "Brody's early years in Tinker's Creek in that cabinet, and in this . . ." She swung her gaze toward the cabinet that featured that glossy photo of Brody. "His later years here, you know, after he was famous and came back to town. It's the least we can do"—she held the yearbook to her chest—"for a real hometown hero."

"He certainly would love it."

Meghan beamed with pride. "Yes." A long sigh escaped her, the sound nearly lost in a rush of humid air when the doors behind us swished open and a young man with a mop of wild hair even curlier than mine walked into the library.

"Cool!" The second he saw the display, he whipped out his phone and snapped a few pictures. "It's great to see this kind of tribute to a giant in the industry."

"Was he?" Funny, I'd never thought of Brody that way. "A giant, I mean?"

The young man laughed and introduced himself as Kevin Markowitz. "Today's News Network. I'm in town to cover the story."

"That explains the van with the satellite dish on top." I looked out the window to the parking lot and saw the van there. "Is there really that much interest in Brody?" I wondered.

"Are you kidding?" Meghan and Kevin answered at the same time and laughed when their words overlapped. She let Kevin explain.

"Back when Brody was discovered, using a nobody in commercials was unheard of. He blazed a trail."

Meghan nodded. "A producer just happened to have a flat tire on the road outside the ranch where Brody was working at the time. Naturally, Brody came to his rescue and that producer, he knew right away he'd found the face of his new commercial campaign. And what a face it was!"

"He was photogenic, all right." As if to prove it, Kevin took a few more snaps of the Brody picture. "But everyone knows that part of the story. I'm looking to dig deeper. Brody was born here in Tinker's Creek, wasn't he?"

"That's right." Meghan flipped the yearbook around so Kevin could see the cover. "Graduated from high school here. Of course, that was before he left to go out west and find his fortune."

"Find his fortune . . ." Mumbling the words, Kevin grabbed a small spiral notebook from the pocket of his golf shirt and scribbled down what Meghan had said. "That's a great way of putting it. He really did find his fortune, didn't he? That guy was the epitome of the western hero. You'll let me look through the yearbook?" he asked Meghan.

She agreed with a giggle and handed the book over. As long as her hands were free, I gave her the book that had been left on our patio. She took one look at the cover and frowned. "Ernest is going to be very disappointed this one got away from him," she said. "I'll give him a call and let him know it's here. He's been reading a lot about Vikings lately. Probably preparing a new class. And you . . ." She looked over to where Kevin was studying a page of the yearbook that showed Brody in his senior year and the Drama

Club production of *Hamlet*. It looked like Ernest was Claudius to Brody's Prince of Denmark. "You might want to come back when the display is finished. Then you'll get a better sense of just what kind of man Brody was."

"Sure, sure. I've got to get over to the police station in just a couple of minutes anyway. Want to find out if they have any leads on the case." Kevin handed the yearbook back to her. "And maybe when I come back, we can sit down and chat. You don't mind if I video you, do you?"

Meghan plumped like a peacock.

Kevin stepped toward the door. "You seemed to know Brody pretty well. Maybe you can explain something to me. He was so successful out west. He went from working on a ranch to owning his own spread, and I was just wondering, you know, what brought him back to Tinker's Creek."

"What?" Meghan jiggled her shoulders. "Or who?"

"Ah!" Kevin pointed to her with his pen and backed out the door. "This is an interview I'm definitely looking forward to. See you later!"

"Who?" My question made Meghan snap her gaze from Kevin to me. "What are you talking about, Meghan? The story I heard was that Brody came back here when his folks were getting older and he wanted to be close to them. I actually once heard him say what a bonus it was because buying property for his ranch here was cheaper than buying something of the same size out west. Do you know something no one else does?"

"Maybe," she admitted with a coy lift of one shoulder.

"You want to tell me about it?"

"Oh, I don't think so." She tucked the yearbook back in the box it came out of. "I'll save that for the reporter. I'd hate for word to get around too soon and for the other women of Tinker's Creek to get too jealous of me."

"You?" All right, so blurting out the question probably didn't win me any points. Still, no one could blame me. Sure, Brody dated a whole lot of women. And yes, he may have been in love with Charmaine. That is, if he wasn't playing her for the fool. But Meghan? Navy cardigan Meghan?

"Are you telling me you and Brody—"

"Oh, Lizzie!" She tossed her head and let out a trill of laughter before she sailed into the library. "I'm not going to tell. Not yet. Some secrets are worth savoring."

Secrets, huh?

I watched her slip behind the library reference desk, the word playing through my mind.

It seemed the more questions I asked, the more I found out people in Tinker's Creek had plenty of secrets.

There was Charmaine, using classic displacement to convince herself worrying about ham salad was better than facing Brody's death.

And Ned, who didn't want me to know he'd been whooped in a fight.

Now I had Meghan to add to the list. If she was involved with Brody, the revelation would shake Tinker's Creek to its foundations.

I considered all the angles when I went to pick up lunch and naturally, one question led to another. The most important of those seemed the most obvious, too.

Which of those secrets could have led to Brody's murder?

I guess it's a good thing I didn't have much of a chance the rest of that afternoon to wonder about Brody's death and people's secrets and their motives. My questions were getting me nowhere, and besides, not having time to worry about the murder meant I was too busy talking about and selling books.

And that, I reminded myself, was the best thing possible!

I thought nothing of it when Charmaine asked if she could leave a little early that evening. By then, the crowds were gone and the store was quiet. I always enjoyed closing, wrapping things up for the day, making sure the cash register balanced and everything was in order. There was comfort in knowing I was leaving the shop and the books in it in good order. On my walk home, I made plans for my long weekend. The store was closed on Sundays and Mondays, and I had a to-be-read, or TBR, pile a mile high. The very thought of diving in made me tingle with pleasure.

I got home, took Violet for a walk, and fed her. I was all set to head out to the patio with a tall glass of sparkling water and the half of my sandwich I'd never had a chance to finish when I heard Charmaine's trill waft across the garden.

"Lizzie! Josh just parked up front."

Josh.

And ham salad on cheesy crackers.

I'd completely forgotten.

I set the sandwich aside and took Violet to Charmaine's patio with me. Lucky for me, she was a homebody and not interested in exploring any farther than the hollyhocks that bobbed on one side of the garden and the tomato plants on the other. The dog was my own version of displacement, I admitted to myself. If Josh was going to show up with a new girlfriend, I was going to be annoyed on Brynn's behalf, and I'd tell them Violet needed dinner. Or she went to bed early. The dog would give me the perfect opportunity to make my excuses and ditch this little soiree.

"What a cutie!" Charmaine wasn't talking about me. She ruffled a hand through Violet's fur and handed me a margarita. "Josh told me she was staying with you."

"She's a good dog." As if to prove it, Violet sat at my side, tail thumping.

She didn't stay still for long. A minute later Josh rounded the corner of the house. Violet, though, was not nearly as interested in my cousin as she was in the man who strode into the garden behind him.

Good news for Brynn. Josh didn't have a girlfriend.

Bad news for Lizzie.

One look at the guy with the dark hair and the coal eyes and my left arm started itching like all get-out.

He was tall, with long legs and a slim torso. His nose was a little crooked. His ears were a tad big. Two little minuses that made zero difference when it came to the overall looks department. Yeah, this guy, I'd say he landed somewhere right between intriguing and irresistible. He was dressed in faded jeans and a dark, short-sleeved shirt that enhanced shoulders that didn't quit.

I scratched my arm and watched Violet zip over to him, and our guest squatted like a catcher behind the plate and got to know Violet face-to-face. He crooned a greeting to her and laughed when she licked his cheek.

"Good girl!" He gave her head a final pat, and it took him longer to get to his feet than it had to hunker down. "Sorry, ma'am." The smile he aimed at Charmaine crackled with a thousand watts of power, and I knew she felt it, too. Like it would help her cool off, she gulped half her margarita. He stuck out a hand to her, his voice all charm and Texas. "Max Alverez."

It hit me then. Just like that. The way he'd squatted to greet Violet. How he'd done his best to hop to his feet, like he was all set to throw out the runner headed from first to second.

"Max Alverez, the catcher?" I was so amazed, I forgot to scratch when he turned to me and beamed a smile.

There were lines at the corners of his eyes that bunched when he studied me. "Looks like you know your baseball."

"My cousin is a whiz when it comes to b-ball." Josh wrapped an arm around my waist. "Ask her anything. Go ahead. This girl knows her stuff."

"No. Really." My cheeks caught fire. I stepped out of Josh's grasp and away from the magnetic pull of Max's smile. "Why don't I just help Charmaine . . ."

Help her do what, I didn't know and I didn't care. I darted into the house. It was cooler inside. That's why I was able to catch my breath, right? After all, the funny little patter inside my ribs couldn't have anything to do with the six-foot-three of gorgeousness out on the patio. If it did, I was doomed—and about to prove to my aunt, my cousin, and most of all, to Max, that when it came to romance I was lame, a nonstarter who couldn't string two sentences together.

Sticking my head in the fridge cooled me off a little more and had the added bonus of putting me up close and personal with a dish of deviled eggs. I took them outside and found Josh, Max, and my aunt already seated at the round table. The fountain was to Max's back and Violet sat at his side, his hand playing through her fur. With any luck, I wasn't drooling the way she was when she looked at him.

"Eggs." I made an attempt to set down the serving plate with a flourish, and the eggs on it shimmied and slid. Two of them landed on the table. One of them plopped onto Max's lap. He laughed, asked no one in particular if it was all right to give the treat to Violet, and earned another whopping dose of her undying love when he held it out to her.

"I'll get the rest of the stuff." Josh beat me to the punch. He went into the house and because I had no choice, I sat in the chair to Max's right.

"So, is he right?" Max finished off a deviled egg in two quick bites. "You a fan?"

Of baseball? Or of you?

Another woman would have dared the words along with a flutter of eyelashes, a flirty smile.

I tried for a sip of margarita to deal with the sand that suddenly filled my mouth and got poked by the orange umbrella in my glass. *Think baseball,* I told myself. *Concentrate on statistics. Not on the electric smile just a couple of feet away.*

I plucked the umbrella out of my glass, took a drink, and gave Max a careful look that didn't waver. At least not too much. "First-round draft pick, St. Louis Cardinals. You played forty-three games in your first season, threw out nearly seventy percent of the runners who tried to steal on you, batted .303."

"Actually, it was .304." The gleam in his eyes told me he didn't hold the mistake against me.

"Don't let any of this give you a swollen head, Max." Josh was back, and he brought the ham salad with him. He put it on the table along with a stack of mismatched china sandwich plates and purple linen napkins. "Lizzie's not some kind of crazed stalker. She knows that kind of stuff about every player."

"I like it." I wasn't sure if Max was talking about the sip of margarita he'd taken or my ability to call up baseball statistics at will.

When Charmaine dealt out the plates like cards, I grabbed

one along with a cheesy star-shaped cracker and thought over this curious turn of events. The ham salad was decent. It was not homemade good. Rather than point this out to my aunt, I chewed and thought and glanced Max's way.

"So what are you doing—?" Dang, I wished I had another cracker I could stuff in my mouth to smother my own colossal faux pas. Max Alverez, Major League game number forty-four. The Cardinals played the Cubs, and I was watching on TV. Who could forget that collision at home plate, the sound of bones cracking that could clearly be heard above the voice of the startled commentator? A career-ending injury.

Since my hands were shaking, I didn't dare reach for my drink. "I'm sorry," I said.

"Hey, don't be." Max sat back in his chair. "It was quite a ride while it lasted and, hey, if I was still playing ball, I couldn't be doing this, and I really love doing this."

I looked from him to my cousin. "This?"

"Oh, I didn't explain." Josh swallowed down a cracker. "Max is a ranger at the national park. Until they find a permanent position for him at one of the other parks, he's here on temporary assignment. We met a couple of weeks ago when we did a joint training. You know, local police departments and the rangers in charge of law enforcement in the park. Promised him I'd show him around if we both ever had the same evening off and hey, it doesn't get any better than this, does it?" He raised his glass in his mother's direction. "Max wants to learn about Tinker's Creek, and this is the place to start."

"Well, we'll need all the law enforcement we can get. You know. Now." Charmaine covered her son's hand with her own. "Not that I'm criticizing our wonderful police department, but you know, a murder . . ." She washed away the thought with more lime-and-tequila goodness. "No doubt there's a lot of extra work to do."

"I'll say." The chips and salsa were already out on the table, and Josh loaded up his plate. "One of the things I've been doing is compiling a list of anyone who might be able to tell me anything about Brody. Chief Goodrich, he suggested I start by interviewing the women Brody dated."

"Oh my." Maybe Charmaine got a hot pepper in the bite of salsa she swallowed. She fanned her face. "That's going to keep you very busy."

Max must have heard about Brody. His murder was the talk of the town. That didn't stop him from asking, "This Brody, he was quite the ladies' man, huh?"

"I'll say." Josh shook his head, and I couldn't tell if it was in disbelief or admiration. "Brody dated just about every woman in Tinker's Creek."

"Did he date you?"

It took me a second to realize Max was looking at me when he asked the question. "Me?" I pointed a finger at myself. "Brody was one of my customers and—"

"Yoohoo!"

I was saved from saying anything dumb when Glory called out a second before she sailed into the garden. "Hoped you'd be home, Char. But I'm sorry. I didn't know you had company."

"Always room for one more." Charmaine told Josh to get a chair, poured another margarita from the pitcher she had close by, and handled the introductions. "Max is new in town. He's a ranger."

"Well, then maybe you two Sherlocks"—Glory looked from Josh to Max—"can help me solve a little mystery. It's what I came over to run by you, Char, but now that we've got the brain trust here, we might as well see what they have to say. It's about this." She smoothed a fifty-dollar bill out on the table. "I was away from Junk and Disorderly most of the day on Tuesday, and when I came back, there it was, on top of a Depression glass cake dish."

"Somebody bought something." It was the most logical explanation, so I didn't feel goofy suggesting it.

"Maybe." Glory sipped her drink. "But if they did, I can't imagine what it was. Then again, I've got a lot of new merchandise in. You know." She glanced at Charmaine. "From the Tussock homestead. Old farmer," she added for Max's sake. "Been dead a few years now, but his family is finally cleaning out all the stuff they had in storage. Owned the land Brody turned into his ranch. Though why anyone would pay fifty dollars for any of that stuff . . ." Glory jiggled her shoulders. "Don't get me wrong, young man," she told Max. "I'm a sucker for old stuff, and I love most of it. But I only agreed to take Tussock's possessions because I've known the family forever. Most of it . . ." As if she were sharing a secret, she leaned over the table. "Junk. Pure and simple."

"Then be glad someone was willing to pay for it," Charmaine told her.

"And I know exactly what I'm going to do with this." Glory scooped up the money and tucked it in her pocket. "Going to save it. To help pay for that letter Brynn is framing for me. Now . . ." She finished her drink and stood, and when she did, Max got out of his chair. "I've got to run." She gave each of us a peck on the cheek, even Max. "My grandsons are coming for dinner tomorrow and I've got to get the ribs in the marinade."

We watched her leave, and Max was the first who spoke up. "Did Brody date her, too?"

"Nah!" Josh laughed. He leaned over and gave his mom

a pat on the shoulder. "These old chicks were immune to Brody's charm."

It wasn't a topic I'd hoped would come up, and I did my best to divert it. "More ham salad?" I passed the plate around, then to be sure we would avoid talk of Brody's love life, I said to Josh, "I hope you're considering that there are other possibilities when it comes to Brody's murderer. Everybody knows Ned Baker and Brody didn't get along."

"Understatement." Josh grabbed another cracker. "As a matter of fact, I gave Ned a call earlier today. He told me he was in Cleveland the night Brody was killed."

I grumbled my disagreement. "Maybe that's what he said, but have you seen the man?"

"Have you?" Max wanted to know.

"Um." I unfolded my purple napkin. Folded it again. If Max found out I'd been playing Stephanie Plum, he'd think I was a bigger dork than ever. "Do you need anything from the kitchen?" I asked my aunt.

She didn't.

Fortunately, the mosquitoes were biting that evening and they descended right on time. After what Charmaine called "just one more little margarita" and another pass of the deviled eggs, we called it a night.

For this I was grateful.

With Violet at my side, Charmaine and I walked Josh and Max around to the front of the house.

"Oh, nearly forgot!" About to climb into the passenger seat of a very muddy Jeep, Josh reached into his back pocket and brought out a red bandanna. "Picked this up at Brody's. Inside the house," he added for Max's benefit. "It's not evidence. Thought maybe this young lady"—he waved the bandanna at Violet—"might be missing her master. What do you say, huh?"

Violet sniffed the air and closed in on Josh. She buried her nose in the fabric, lifted her head, let out a whimper that broke my heart.

"Oh, isn't that sweet?" Charmaine clapped a hand to her heart, and we all watched Violet gently take the bandanna out of Josh's hands. Her prize secure and me brushing away a tear in my eye, I watched her head back to the garden while my cousin and Max got in the Jeep.

Finally I was able to breathe a little easier. With any luck, this was the last I'd see of Max. No more handsome hunk meant no more scratching and no more tripping over my own tongue.

"I appreciate your hospitality," Max told my aunt before he slid behind the wheel. "And, Lizzie—" When he turned my way, I automatically gulped in a breath and bit my tongue. "I hope I'll see you around again soon."

"Around? Here?" Okay, it teetered on silly, but I somehow managed to make the questions sound more like small talk than *OMG, what are you talking about?* "I'm sure you're much too busy at the park to come into town often."

"Well, maybe not." Josh gave his mom and me a smile. "Didn't I tell you? What with Chief Goodrich being laid up with his broken leg and not able to help with the investigation, he talked the folks at the park into lending us Max for a little while."

"Which means I will be around," Max told me, his smile gleaming in the last of the evening light. "A whole lot."

Chapter 8

Max was just what I didn't need.

For one thing he was way too hot for stumbling, bumbling Lizzie Hale to handle.

For another, he was smart.

I knew this because he was, after all, a catcher, and a baseball catcher is basically the general of the team. He not only catches the ball, he calls the pitches and is the leader on the field. When people talk about what it takes to be good at the position, they always say a catcher never lets anything get by him. By that, of course, they mean he never lets a ball get by him, he never lets a runner get by him and cross home plate to score.

But I knew in my heart of hearts that Max Alverez would never let a nugget of information get by him, either.

And I couldn't let him find out about the Charmaine-Brody connection.

Oh yeah, I'd have to avoid Max, all right, and I decided to start the morning after Charmaine's get-together. It was Sunday and the shop was closed, but there was always plenty to do and I didn't mind spending a few hours doing it. Locking myself in the shop meant I could eliminate any chance of running into Max in town.

I took Violet (and that red bandanna of Brody's that she now carried with her everywhere) with me to Love Under the Covers and instantly regretted it. Violet meant Violet fur. And it was everywhere.

I vacuumed, then as long as I was at it, I dusted. With Violet finally napping under the front counter, that bandanna under her chin, I settled down to take care of Internet orders.

I'd already finished two when I heard tapping on the front window.

Violet's head came up. She stretched, got to her feet, and went to the door to see what was up.

Even above the sounds of her excited barking, the tapping continued.

I squinted at the computer screen to double-check the order. Julia Quinn? Or Tessa Dare? A bookseller couldn't be too careful and every order had to be just right. I also muttered to myself and to the unseen tapper. "Closed on Sundays. Read the sign!"

More tapping.

Rather than be driven crazy by both the dog's barking and the person who ignored the sign in the window, I went to the front of the shop and stopped cold. Max was out on the patio, tapping at my window. I shook away the unwelcome surprise and gave my arm a scratch before I pointed to the CLOSED sign.

"Not open today!" I said it nice and loud so he'd be sure to hear me through the window. "You can see the shop another day."

"I didn't come to see the shop. I came to see you."

"Great." Violet missed the sarcasm and took me at my word. She danced around me, eager for the door to open so she could get up close and personal.

It was two against one, and I knew a losing cause when I saw one.

I opened the door.

"You don't look like a romance reader." I stepped back and Max walked in, all loose limbs and masculine energy. He didn't look around until after he greeted Violet, and then that dark gaze of his took in everything, from the table of new releases right in front of us to the display just beyond, where I featured scented candles, essential oils, and bubble bath. Over on the right was a poster advertising a book talk and signing by Madeline Gaffney-Brown, an up-and-coming historical romance writer whose books displayed all the talent I knew would propel her to the top. In her publicity photo, Madeline was wearing a low-cut black sweater and pearls, smiling at her readers as if she knew all the secrets of romance and if only they read her books, they'd learn them, too. I swear, the moment Max walked in, Madeline's smile inched up a notch.

That morning, Max was dressed in jeans and a Rock & Roll Hall of Fame T-shirt. He had a blue plastic grocery bag hung over one wrist, and when he propped his fists on his hips, it swung back and forth. "Don't have to be a romance reader to be a romance lover," he announced.

I instantly fell down the rabbit hole, struggling between finding something to say and saying something totally stupid. I was saved by none other than Violet, who trotted toward the back of the shop, turned, and gave me a bark that reminded me I'd put on a pot of coffee when I arrived.

"Coffee?" I blurted out.

Max followed me to the alcove where we kept a pot on for customers. Lined up nearby was an assortment of the mugs we also sold up front. I poured his coffee in one that said *Keep Calm and Read Romance* and took *Do Not Disturb, I'm with My Book Boyfriend* for myself.

"So . . ." I was afraid to ask, and afraid if I didn't, it would only make me look as if I had something to hide. "What can do I—" I coughed politely. "What can I do for you?"

"Just looking to talk."

About what, he didn't say, and it was that more than anything that made me nervous. Okay, all right, not that more than anything. Max made me nervous. And itchy. Max made me instantly tongue-tied and left me feeling totally and completely off-center.

Eager to keep my reaction to him under control, I grabbed my coffee and strolled to the computer where I'd been working when he showed up, peering at the screen again to confirm the order.

"Tessa Dare." I knew the titles and loved every one of the books, but I wrote out a list anyway to give my shaky hands something to do, then made a beeline for the historical romance room.

I can't say I was surprised when Max followed.

"Hey, nice!" He looked around the room and nodded his approval, then plopped into the wing chair nearest the window and sipped his coffee. "Fires in the winter?"

I wondered if it was against some ordinance, then decided if it was, Josh would have already warned me.

"Yes." I went to where the D books were lined up and

plucked the ones I wanted from the shelf. "I know you do the same thing at the park in those—" I made the mistake of glancing at him over my shoulder and blanked. "I mean, you know, those places where they do the nature education programs and—"

"The park visitors' centers." He crossed his long legs. "Truth be told, they don't let me anywhere near the nature programs. Don't tell anyone, but I wouldn't know a possum from a porcupine! I'm a protection ranger."

I'd lived in Tinker's Creek going on two years and the park surrounded our little town. Still, I'd never heard the term.

Max read the confusion in my expression. "We're peace officers. Just like that cousin of yours. Those other rangers, interpretive rangers is what they're called, they take care of things like wildlife programs. The rest of us, we enforce federal and state laws inside the park."

"Which is why Josh asked you—"

"To help with the Brody Pierce murder investigation. Yes, ma'am. And speaking of that—"

That was exactly what I didn't want to talk about.

I swept out of the historical romance room and blindly took refuge in the room next to it, and it wasn't until I realized I was in the erotica room—and that Max had followed me there—that my cheeks caught fire.

"My car's been making the most terrible noise." Yes, I know. No segue. And considering we'd been talking law enforcement, the words that tumbled out of me made absolutely no sense. But desperate times, desperate measures, and all that. At times as desperate as these, words just fall out of my mouth. This time, they sounded something like, "Phtt, phtt, phtt." At least I managed not to spit on Max when I made the raspberry noise. "I don't usually worry about car troubles. I mean, my car isn't that old and I'm pretty much a homebody who doesn't do much driving, but Charmaine, she had a problem with her brake lines recently. They split. Or broke. Or leaked. Or something. Whatever it is brake lines do when they're not doing what they're supposed to do. And so naturally when I heard my car making that crazy sound—"

"Phtt, phtt, phtt." How Max managed to echo the noise without grinning is anybody's guess, because his eyes sparked with amusement. His expression, though, was solemn. "Definitely not your brake lines," he said.

"Good. That's good." I hadn't even realized I set the Tessa Dare books down, but now I scooped them up again and held them close to my chest, and oh, how I scrambled for something to say. I glommed on to the only thing I could remember that we'd talked about. "That whole ranger thing, that explains why you're helping Josh. Because you're a law enforcement ranger."

He nodded. "Have been. Ever since I left the big leagues."

Baseball. Ah. We were finally on firmer ground. Some of the tension inside me uncurled. "A player with your experience could coach. Or be a scout. Or a commentator. Lots of retired players become commentators."

"Not this one." He finished off his coffee and hung on to the mug. "Majored in criminal justice in college. Always loved the great outdoors. Didn't think I'd ever find a way to combine the two, but when I found myself at loose ends—"

The memory of his injury crashed into me much like that runner had plowed into Max at home plate. I winced. "You must have done an awful lot of rehab. The way I remember it, your left leg . . ." I dared to check out said appendage and my train of thought derailed. Just like that, I was out of things to say, and for a few awkward moments, Max and I didn't say anything at all. We stood there, surrounded by covers that screamed sex and titles designed to titillate.

He looked me up and down, and I knew better than to try to do the same. I looked up at the ceiling. I looked down at the floor. I looked anywhere but at Max.

Finally, he reached into that grocery bag he'd brought with him and pulled out another clear plastic bag, one with something soft and fuzzy inside.

"I know you're busy working, and I don't mean to take up a lot of your time. I was just wondering," he said, "if maybe this belonged to you?"

I honestly couldn't say. At least not until I leaned forward for a better look.

Just as quickly, I jumped back. "Is that a tail? The tail of a fox? That is so gross. Why would you think that I—"

The laugh that cut me off was deep and throaty. "It's a fox tail, all right. But not a real one." He opened the plastic bag and pulled out the tail. It was maybe twenty inches long, and it had an elastic strap on one end designed to hook around the wearer's waist. Like the real foxes I'd occasionally seen around town, the tip of the tail was white, but the rest of it was luxurious russet, the color distinctive against the cream and purple of the room.

"Not mine," I said.

"You're sure?" He closed the distance between us in three steps and held out the tail to me. "Maybe you could just try it on!"

At that moment, I was sure my cheeks flushed the same color as that tail. I didn't care if it looked like an all-out escape or not. I pushed past Max, out the door, and took refuge behind the front counter.

It didn't take him long to catch up to me. His legs were long, even if his stride was slow and there was just the slightest bit of a hitch in his left leg. "I'm sorry." He set the tail and the bag on the front counter. "I didn't mean to embarrass you. Really."

"You didn't. It's just that . . ." His smile was so genuine, I couldn't help but smile back. "All right, you did! It's not every day a man attempts to try a fox tail on me."

He pursed his lips. "Wouldn't dare. At least not until I was invited."

Rather than let them slip from my trembling hands, I set the books down on the front counter. The top one in the pile had an especially beautiful cover and I concentrated on it, on the woman in the gorgeous pink dress and the shirtless hunk who had his arm around her waist. I loved every moment of romance in books. Reading, I never felt like my throat was closing and my breathing was about to stop. So what was it about even a hint of romance in real life that made me quiver like a bowl of Jell-O?

I stared at the book. "Why did you show me that tail?"

"Because it was found near the barn. At Brody's."

My head came up and my gaze snapped to Max's. "The night of the murder?"

"Well, not that night. By the time you called in the incident and Josh and the forensics team got there, it was already dark and hard to see much of anything. At least that's what they all told me. Honestly, I think they were a little afraid to look too hard until they had some light and could see the lay of the land. You know, so they knew exactly what those bison were up to."

I couldn't say I blamed them.

"Your cousin found the tail the next morning. I thought maybe if you'd seen it lying there on the ground—"

"Definitely not. And that elastic band . . ." I took a closer look. "It's snapped. That means someone was probably wearing it, the band broke, the tail fell off. And you say it was near the barn?" There was only one conclusion to be drawn from that fact. "Someone wearing the tail was there. The murderer?"

It was a deadly serious situation and a deadly serious question, but as soon as the words were past my lips, I couldn't keep a smile from erupting. "Sorry." I did my best to fan away the smile, but that only made me smile more, and in another couple of seconds, my smile dissolved into laughter.

I clapped my hand over my mouth.

"What?" Max should have known better than to try to get a woman who was laughing uncontrollably to talk.

I laughed some more. Swallowed the sound. Tried to drown my giggles by grabbing the mug I'd set down before I went to retrieve the books. The coffee in it had already gone cold.

"It's just that . . ." I still quivered with laugher and, rather than take the chance of spilling, I put down the mug. "I just can't picture . . . I mean, a murderer wearing a fox tail?"

A smile played around his mouth, but he wasn't much better at controlling it than I was at stopping mine from blossoming again. "Funky, I will admit that much."

"And plenty strange. Do you suppose the murderer used the tail as some sort of bait? Maybe he thought the bison would smell the fur and think there was a predator around? That he'd be safe from running across them?"

"Nah. This thing is as phony as phony can be. Even I can tell that. And bison are way smarter than I am. Nobody sprayed it with scent, either." To prove it, Max held the tail up to his nose, then held it out for me to sniff. "Besides, I've seen bison. Something tells me a little thing like a fox wouldn't scare them off."

"You got that right," I concurred. "But if that's the case, why would anybody—"

"Wish I knew," Max admitted. "Wish I knew a whole lot about what happened out there that night. That's what got me to thinking about you this morning."

Another gulp of cold coffee. Hardly enough to distract him. "Me?" I wasn't laughing now. "What do I have to do with any of this?"

"Well, you are the one who found Mr. Pierce. I know you told Josh you didn't see anything that night, but it's not unusual for witnesses to remember details days after an incident. Think about it. You're sure you didn't see anything out of place at the ranch? See anyone?"

I shook my head. "Just Violet. Except—" The memory poked its way to consciousness. "I saw a light. Out in the woods on the far side of the property. I told Josh about it but by the time he had a chance to look, the light was gone. It looked like the beam of a flashlight."

"Like somebody keeping an eye on what was happening?"

I nodded. "And yesterday I heard someone in the woods. Beyond the barn. I took a look, and I found a pair of binoculars. I left them right where I found them," I was sure to add. "And I meant to tell Josh about it but I haven't had a chance. I think someone was keeping an eye on Brody."

"And I think someone's been poking around our investigation."

I gave myself a figurative slap on the forehead for running off at the mouth. "It wasn't that I was poking, I was just—"

"I thought so." He saved me from tripping over my own explanation. "Yesterday when we were talking about the murder at your aunt's, I had a feeling you knew more than you were willing to say."

I'm not sure how I thought it would prove my innocence, but I clasped my hands behind my back. "I really don't. Nothing more than I just told you. Sorry to disappoint you."

"You don't know anything? About anyone here in Tinker's Creek we might not have considered as a potential suspect?"

Three cheers for me, I played it cool. "I know the killer could have been keeping an eye on Brody. What with the light in the woods and the binoculars, and—"

"And?" He leaned over the front counter.

I weighed the wisdom of telling him about the shadow person in my garden and decided against it. I didn't want Max to know Brody had been at Charmaine's that night.

"And nothing. Flashlight. Binoculars. That's it. And both of those things make sense, don't they?" I warmed to the theory. "If someone was planning on killing Brody, they might have wanted to keep an eye on him. To follow his movements and know his schedule. They would definitely want to make sure he was alone. That person may have discovered that late at night, Brody went out to the barn to check on the bison and figured it was a good place to attack him."

"Did he? Go to the barn at that time every night?"

I had to admit I didn't know. "It makes sense, since that's where I found his body. And you know, where I saw the light of the flashlight, that was over on the far side of the ranch where Brody's property abuts Ned Baker's place. And when I saw Ned yesterday—"

"Where?"

There. I stepped in it again. Max had already accused me of poking my nose where it didn't belong. I didn't need to give him any more ammunition.

"I saw Ned . . . around," I told him.

"I haven't seen him around."

My smile came and went. "You're not around as much as I'm around."

"I'm going to be around more as long as I'm involved in this investigation and until I get my new assignment. That's another thing I thought I'd run by you when I was here this morning. As long as I'm here, I was wondering if you'd like to go to a baseball game sometime."

Baseball game? In a car? With Max?

I fell back on my best defense—busy businesswoman. "Sounds great, but Cleveland is a long way off and going up there for a game—"

"I was thinking of the Tinker's Creek Diggers. At the field right down the street from your house. There's nothing as much fun as high school baseball. Thought we could eat popcorn and talk about the game, maybe see if you're as good at calling up facts and figures as your cousin says you are."

I inched back my shoulders. "Oh, I'm good at it, all right."

He knew a challenge when he heard one, and just as I expected, Max rose to it. "Yogi Berra batting average?"

"If you're talking lifetime, .285. Post season, .274."

"Then how about Johnny Bench. Home runs?"

"Three hundred eighty-nine," I said.

"So that proves it." Max slapped a hand against the front counter and started for the door.

"Proves?" I scurried after him. "Proves what?"

"That you are one smart cookie." His hand already on

the door, Max turned to face me. "And that when you're talking about things you know and care about, you're not so self-conscious. Baseball. Murder. And romance. I'll tell you what, in my book, those might be the three most important things the two of us ever need to talk about."

Too bad I was tongue-tied until after he left. Then Max might have heard me when I called out, "No, not romance. Romance novels!"

Chapter 9

Lucky for Meghan Watkins, Monday dawned bright and beautiful. Plenty of sunshine and a breeze from the north. Temperatures weren't nearly as high as they had been the week before, and the humidity was down.

Otherwise, Meghan's black weeping veil would surely have drooped.

"You've got to be kidding." Brynn stopped midway between where her van was parked and the table where she'd be depositing the tray of cupcakes she was carrying and looked where I was looking—at Meghan bustling around the gazebo in the center of the town square, dressed in a black suit, wearing black stockings and shoes. And that hat!

I whistled low under my breath, amazed at the size of the thing and wondering where on earth she'd found a black hat with a gigantic brim and a crown wreathed in black roses. The black filmy veil fluttered just under her chin.

"Widow's weeds," I said to Brynn, and then because I

knew she was going to ask, I explained. "Traditional mourning clothing in Victorian times. A woman wore black after the death of her husband, usually for a year. They called it widow's weeds. Black this, black that, black everything. See, you do learn a thing or two reading historicals."

Brynn's taste in romance did not range as far as mine. She was strictly a fan of contemporary romantic suspense. Even though Meghan was fifty feet from us, Brynn leaned in that direction, as if a closer look might help her make sense of what she saw. "Okay, I get it when it comes to widows. But why's Meghan dressed like that?"

"I guess because . . ." I shrugged. "Maybe because she's in charge of this memorial service?"

Brynn was taller than my five-two, but not by much. Her blond hair was short and cute and spiky, and she had apple cheeks, nicely curved hips, and the best laugh, one that usually erupted at the most inappropriate times. She wasn't laughing now.

"I heard Meghan pretty much pushed her way into taking charge of the whole shebang," she confided. "In fact, she's the one who convinced Cal that the town should have a memorial for Brody in the first place. Cal, he said he'd put his staff right on it, but Meghan insisted she knew more about Brody than anyone else in Tinker's Creek, so it was not only her job, it was her duty."

"Well, she certainly took it to heart."

I glanced around and wondered at the organizational skills of our local librarian, who had somehow managed to transform our sleepy town square overnight. The gazebo stood at the center of the square, a round structure with three steps leading up to a platform and a roof overhead. This time of year, red, white, and blue bunting decorated the railing all around the gazebo, interspersed here and there with planters overflowing with red geraniums, white petunias, and yellow marigolds.

Four pathways led to the gazebo, one from each corner of the square, and between each was a wide swath of grass where on weekends, people set up chairs and laid out blankets and listened to local bands or a high school choir performance. I remembered once seeing a ranger at the gazebo, kids gathered all around, giving a program about raptors.

Not Max, I was sure.

I had it on good authority he wouldn't know a possum from a porcupine.

Most Monday mornings, I liked to take a nice long walk, stop for coffee, and bring it to the square along with a book. Nothing beat sitting outside in a pool of sunshine and listening to the nearby fountain trickle while I was reading with not another soul around.

Not so much that Monday morning.

A sound system had been set up in the gazebo, and Cal was standing in front of it doing a one-two-three test and generating enough feedback to make the speakers squeal and my teeth hurt. The high school band, all twenty-eight of them, was gathered at the farthest corner of the park, tuning up and donning the blue-and-silver jackets and tall silver hats they usually reserved for football games. Rows of folding chairs had been set up all around the gazebo, and they were filling quickly.

Penny Markham was already there. In the front row, in fact. It should be noted that in spite of the fact that she'd dated Brody, she was not in widow's weeds. Penny looked as cheery as the sunshine in a yellow top and orange capris.

Love Under the Covers customers—and rivals when it came to who went out with Brody how many times—Callie Porter and Tasha Grimes were seated just rows apart, look-

ing appropriately somber. Seeing them reminded me to
mention both women to Josh. He might not know about
their connection to Brody and, hey, as far as I was concerned, anything that made Josh look at anyone as a
suspect—anyone other than his mother—was good news.

Refreshment tables had been set up near the sidewalk,
and I walked over to them along with Brynn. While she
arranged cupcakes, I sidled up to her six-year-old, Micah,
who, his tongue caught between his teeth, was carefully
setting out napkins, paper plates, and cups for the lemonade
and iced tea we'd be serving. Micah had his mother's straw-
colored hair and his father's big brown eyes. I knew better
than to mention this particular portion of Micah's heritage
within his mother's earshot. Micah's dad was a total loser
who'd never stepped up to the plate when it came to loving
Brynn or taking care of his son. He didn't show up in Tinker's Creek often, and that was just fine with Brynn. In my
book, if he never came back at all, it would be too soon.

Micah, fortunately, took after his mother when it came
to personality. When I offered to help, he grinned, and
while we worked he chattered away about school and T-ball
and the adventure he'd gone on with Brynn to collect fossils
from a local stream. I listened and responded. Of course I
did. But as I worked, I also realized I had the perfect vantage point to keep an eye on everything going on.

Kevin Markowitz's news van with its rooftop satellite
dish was parked nearby. Ryan Guttreig, the one and only
reporter for the local weekly *Times*, walked through the
crowd, a camera flung over one shoulder.

"Somebody sure did a good job getting the word out," I
commented when Brynn came over to see how Micah and
I were doing.

"That was Meghan, too." Brynn ruffled her son's hair.

"She spent all weekend sending emails and making phone calls. I'm grateful she thought of me for the refreshments, but I'll tell you what . . ." She stretched and rubbed her back. "I spent all day yesterday baking. I feel like I got flattened by a dump truck. I'm so glad you offered to help set up."

"Hey." I returned her smile. "What else am I doing?"

"I hear handling that piece of gorgeousness." Brynn gave me a wink and looked toward where Max was walking along the edges of the crowd. That day, he was wearing his formal park ranger uniform—an olive suit, white shirt, dark tie. He saw me watching him and tipped his khaki Smokey Bear hat in a way a Regency heroine would have said was rakish.

I scratched a hand over my arm.

"He's not here to stay," I told Brynn. "And besides, he's not my type."

She squealed a laugh that wasn't exactly appropriate considering what we were there for, and when I ignored her, she poked me in the ribs. "Oh, honey, admit it! That type is every woman's type."

"Good." There was a plate of cookies nearby, Brynn's famous chocolate-cranberry chunk, and I grabbed one and took a bite. "Then you date him."

Brynn pursed her lips. "I don't think so. On the other hand, that cousin of yours . . ." She scanned the square with an eye out for Josh and found him helping elderly Mrs. Mannon roll her walker up the path and negotiate her way to a seat. "He can be so friendly sometimes, and when he is I think maybe this time we'll get somewhere. Then the next time I see him, he acts like he barely knows me."

I gave her a quick, one-armed hug. "I think he's just got a thing about commitment. He's afraid of getting too close."

"Josh and commitment. You and romance heebie-jeebies. Looks like Charmaine is the most normal person in your family!"

This, she knew to be total baloney, so Brynn laughed and wound her arm through mine. "I'll tell you what, I'll make more of an effort with Josh if you promise to do the same. Go for the ranger!"

She should have known better. "It would take him about two and a half seconds to write me off as dull as dishwater."

"Unless you're talking baseball."

I remembered what Max had said the day before.

Baseball.

Romance.

Murder.

As if just thinking about Brody's untimely end conjured them, Ned and Joy Baker walked by at that exact moment. I was grateful for the distraction.

"Suspect numero uno," I told Brynn with a look at Ned that I hoped wasn't too conspicuous. In spite of the pleasant weather, he was wearing a green hoodie, the hood pulled up around his head and sunglasses perched on his nose. "Hiding his face," I whispered. "He's got bruises. Like he was in a fight. You know, there's talk about Joy and Brody, and that would sure explain a slugfest. It would give Ned a motive, too, in addition to how he was angry at Brody about the bison crashing his party."

"Joy and Brody? Not a chance!" With one hand, Brynn waved away the very idea. "Where have you been, girl? You miss all the good gossip. Joy didn't have time for Brody. She's too busy messing around with Cal."

"Mayor Cal?" I nearly choked on my cookie. "How do you—"

Brynn laughed, and when she noticed Micah was having

trouble opening a package of paper plates, she zipped over to help him. "You need to get out of your shop more often."

No sooner had Brynn walked away than Charmaine sashayed up to me, her outfit as appropriate to the occasion as her Technicolor closet allowed. Dark navy skirt that billowed around her ankles. A top the color of the sky above us. A filmy scarf in shades of yellow, red, and blue.

I didn't waste any time. "Why didn't you tell me?" I asked her. "About Joy and Cal?"

"Old news." My aunt dismissed the whole thing with a lift of one shoulder. "Besides, I did tell you. You had your nose in a book and didn't pay the least bit of attention to me. Never mind that. Joy's not nearly as interesting as . . ." Even though Charmaine is tall, the crowd was getting bigger by the minute, and she had to stand on tiptoe and crane her neck. When she plopped back down on the soles of her gold, sparkly sandals, it was apparently because she'd pinpointed whoever she was looking for.

"Did you see Ned?" she asked, and since the last thing Charmaine is worried about is being subtle, she pointed to where Ned and Joy had taken a seat in the back row to the right of the gazebo. "Why is he dressed like that?"

For once I knew something she didn't know. "Bruised," I said, making sure to keep my voice down. "Two black eyes and a swollen cheek. I think he got into a fight."

"Or he had some work done. The last time I did—" Charmaine, ever vain, swallowed the rest of her words. "Never let anyone tell you men aren't every bit as worried about their looks as women." She patted my arm, and when she saw Max across the park, her eyes lit. "Oh, doesn't he look handsome in that uniform! Why don't you go over there and talk to that nice park ranger?"

My smile was tight. "I don't want to go over and talk to that nice park ranger."

"Is that why you're scratching your arm?" she wanted to know.

I hadn't realized I was, and I dropped both my hands to my side at the same time Charmaine grinned.

"Well, if you won't go talk to him, I will!" With that, she was gone.

I got back to helping Brynn. One platter of cookies needed to be filled, and I took care of that, checked to be sure there was enough ice in the cooler nearby, and because Micah couldn't reach, I pulled a serving platter closer to him so he could fill it with tiny cucumber sandwiches. Before we even pushed the platter back in place, Kevin Markowitz swooped in and grabbed one.

"I didn't think anyone would mind," Kevin said with his mouth full. "That is what the food is for, right?"

It was, but most of the people there knew it wasn't going to be served until after the memorial program concluded. Since it didn't seem worth pointing that out to the reporter, I asked him, "How was it?"

"Delicious." He reached for another one, but at the warning look I shot him, he pulled back his hand. "Glad I ran into you," he said. "Didn't have a chance to talk to you at the library the other day."

"There's nothing I can tell you about Brody," I said.

"That's not what I heard. Meghan told me you're the one who found the body."

"I thought you were interested in digging deeper into the story. Not Brody's murder, Brody's life here in Tinker's Creek."

"You got me there!" He slid out a pencil he'd had tucked

behind his ear and pointed at me with the tip of it. "Still, the woman who found the injured hero—"

"He wasn't injured. He was dead."

"Better yet!" His eyes lit.

I glared away his exhilaration.

Kevin bit his lip. "What I meant is that I know we could sell that story. How you drove out to the ranch. How you found Pierce. Your gut-wrenching reaction to everything you saw. You must know details, plenty of details. And if you can't remember them, we'll embellish a little. Go straight for the jugular. Readers eat up that kind of stuff. Oh yeah, there are a few outlets that would pay a pretty penny for a story like that."

"Not interested," I told him in no uncertain terms. "I've got nothing to say."

"You don't even want to talk about your relationship with Pierce?"

"Relationship? What relationship?"

"Well, I just assumed . . ." He shuffled his feet against the grass. "Every other woman I've talked to around here had a relationship with him."

It wasn't easy to keep my gaze from sliding to Charmaine, but I managed and said, "Not me."

His smile was sly. "Maybe you're just being shy. I get it. I really do. After the trauma of finding him, telling the world the details of your relationship with Pierce—"

"The only relationship I had with Brody Pierce was professional. He came into my bookstore once in a while. He was a man I said hello to when I saw him on the street. End of story."

I guess for a short woman with a green streak in her hair, I could be pretty intimidating when I put my mind to it.

When I stepped nearer to Kevin, my fists on my hips and my eyes narrowed, he backed off.

"Duly noted," he said, and then he actually duly noted it in the little notebook he carried.

"Except you were at the ranch."

I closed in another step. "I'm sure you've read the police report. You know all about that."

He swallowed hard. "I do, actually. I just thought if there was anything you wanted to add to what happened that night . . ." When I lifted my chin, he backed up a step. "No, I can see you don't. Then how about you provide some insight into how people here in town reacted when they found out Brody was coming back for good."

"I didn't live here then." A breeze blew up and scattered the napkins Micah had worked so diligently to set out, and I raced over to gather them before they hit the ground.

"Then what about how they felt about all the hoopla?" Kevin was right behind me. "You know, the lawsuit and the scandal."

"Scandal?" I didn't mean to sound so interested, but it was kind of hard not to. Scandal might mean suspects. And I was plenty interested in suspects. I turned to Kevin. "What are you talking about? I never heard any mention of scandal in connection with Brody in all the time he lived in Tinker's Creek."

"Oh, not here. Back in Wyoming. You don't know the story?" Eager to tell it, Kevin dared to shuffle closer. "They were filming that commercial. You know, the one he's most famous for."

"Hang gliding." I didn't need Kevin to nod to tell me I was right. Of all Brody's truck commercials, that was the most iconic. Brody hang gliding along the horizon, drifting over the truck, landing in the bed. "Meghan has a picture of it," I reminded Kevin. "In her display case at the library."

"Yeah, yeah. A publicity picture from the ad agency. But of course the PR agency never mentioned what happened behind the scenes." He whistled low under his breath. "This was years ago, of course. Maybe twelve? Fifteen? But I bet there are people who are still sorry they ever listened to Brody. He's the one who thought up the stunt. They worked on it for hours, filming it again and again. The director was sure they'd finally gotten it right, but Brody insisted on just one more take. He said he wanted to make sure the camera caught his expression just right when he landed. You know, tough and daring. Said folks would pay attention, and he was right, wasn't he?"

"I bet people here right now are talking about that commercial," I commented.

Kevin nodded. "But do they know the rest of the story? There was a cameraman, see, guy by the name of Dean O'Brien, who put up a fuss about the hang-gliding stunt right from the start. Said the whole thing was too dangerous. Said he didn't want Brody to get hurt and, more important, he didn't like it that the only way to film the stunt from a really good angle was for him to be on the top of the truck cab when Brody landed in the bed. Said it wasn't safe, and as it turned out, O'Brien was right."

"Brody got hurt?" It was a wonder I'd never heard about it.

"Brody? Nah!" Kevin chuckled. "Brody was made of iron. No, no. He was fine. It was on the last take, the one Brody absolutely insisted they do. He misjudged the landing and came in on top of the cab."

I could picture it and my stomach jumped. "On top of O'Brien?"

"Oh yeah. Brody somehow managed to keep his footing, but O'Brien's safety gear snapped and he went flying. Broken back, I think. O'Brien never worked again, that's for sure. In fact, he never walked again."

My heart clenched in sympathy. "That's terrible."

"And not something we need to talk about. Not today." I'd been so engrossed in Kevin's story, I never saw Meghan walk up beside me looking like the Ghost of Christmas Future. She might have glared at Kevin. It was a little hard to say, what with the black veil and all. I did hear her click her tongue. "Today is a day of solemn remembrance," she said. "There's no place here for gossip."

"Hey, I'm not gossiping." Kevin defended himself. "And since you wouldn't discuss it with me the other day, Ms. Watkins, it's only natural I should ask other people about the incident. O'Brien sued Pierce, said his career was over and he had a kid to support and he didn't know what he was going to do. Pierce's publicity people stepped in and swept the whole thing under the rug. Settled out of court. The way I heard the story, there were big bucks involved."

Meghan clutched her hands at her waist. It was the first I noticed she was wearing black elbow-length gloves. "Accidents happen."

Kevin nodded. "And when you're dealing with someone with an ego as big as Brody's—"

"Oh, look!" Meghan whirled and walked away. "There's Ernest. He's next of kin. I need to talk to him."

She did, and a minute later, I saw her escort Brody's cousin to one of the seats inside the gazebo. Right after that, the memorial started.

Cal welcomed everyone and reminded us that Tinker's Creek is a family and, as a family, we could all support each other through this terrible tragedy.

Meghan recounted stories about Brody's life. It actually might have been easier to understand her if her black veil didn't keep getting stuck in her teeth.

Ernest was up next, and since I was standing out by the refreshment tables in the sunlight and he was in the gazebo and in the shade, I could be excused for once again nearly mistaking him for his more handsome, richer, more famous cousin.

"Thank you all for being here." The moment Ernest opened his mouth, all comparisons flew out of my head. He wasn't as smooth as Brody. He wasn't as slick. Ernest was a nice enough guy, but he wasn't an icon, that's for sure.

What he was, it turned out, was a bit of a showman.

He talked a little about Brody's parents, told a story about fishing with Brody when they were kids. Then Ernest asked all of us to be very quiet and listen.

We did.

And for a minute or two, the only things we heard were the sounds of the crowd. Wondering what Ernest had in store for us, people shifted in their chairs. A few kids, bored with the ceremony and playing at the far side of the square with their buddies, called to one another. Someone sneezed and my aunt's voice rang across the square, "Gesundheit!"

And then we heard it.

It started small, a far-off buzz that grew louder and closer with every second. It didn't take long for us to realize it was coming from above, and one by one people raised their hands to shade their eyes, the better to see into the morning sky. Cal and Meghan walked to the top of the gazebo steps and bent forward to look up.

The band started up, playing the theme from *The Magnificent Seven* just as an ultralight aircraft came into view.

It veered off and a second later, a hang glider sailed over the gazebo.

The kids in the band stopped playing. After all, they wanted to watch, too.

The audience gasped.

A few people applauded.

Meghan scrambled down the gazebo steps and into the open.

She pointed at the flyer.

She wailed.

And then she fainted dead away.

Chapter 10

It wasn't the fact that Meghan took a header that had people still talking when I opened for business at Love Under the Covers the next day.

Sure, they were sufficiently concerned when the incident happened. But one whiff of the smelling salts Charmaine pulled out of her purse and Meghan was back to her old self in a jiffy, insisting she'd be fine once she had a moment to collect herself.

No, if that's all there was to it—Meghan emotional, Meghan upset—tongues wouldn't have kept wagging nearly as long.

See, when Meghan landed with a flump, her black skirt tangled around her waist, revealing the very un-Meghan-like purple thong she was wearing.

Grief, the people of Tinker's Creek could understand.

Heartbreak, they could handle.

Skimpy underwear on a librarian known for her navy cardigan sweater?

This was the stuff gossip is made of.

And the town was awash with it.

"Never would have thought it of her. Meghan, of all people."

Behind the counter, in front of the cash register, I gladly accepted Callie Porter's credit card and ignored her comment. She didn't get the message.

"It was disrespectful, don't you think? I mean, I'm the one who dated Brody." Reverent hand to heart. "And even I never thought to go to his funeral wearing . . . well, you know."

I put the three books she'd bought into a bag and handed it to her along with a smile. "Have a nice day."

Callie sucked in her bottom lip and walked out the door.

"You handled that well." No sooner had Callie disappeared than Brynn stepped up to the counter.

Callie was gone, but I looked toward the front door anyway. "I don't know what people expect me to say. We all saw the same thing. And coming up with crazy theories to explain it—"

"Like?"

I puffed out a breath of annoyance. "Well, let's see. There's the one I heard when I got stopped by Tasha Grimes on my way in this morning. About how Meghan runs a house of ill repute out of the basement of the library."

Brynn grinned.

"And then there's the one proposed by old Mrs. Rafferty." Cora Rafferty was still in the store somewhere, so I made sure to keep my voice down. "She's convinced that wasn't Meghan at all. Some sort of body double. No sooner had she said that than Beth Parker piped up and said maybe an alien had sucked out Meghan's soul and was using the lifeless husk as a sort of home away from home." I threw my hands in the air. "It's ridiculous. Why can't people just accept that women want to look and feel pretty? If sexy lingerie does that for Meghan, then good for her."

"Amen!" Brynn and I slapped high fives. "How's Meghan taking the whole thing?"

"Haven't seen her," I said. "But I'll tell you what, in my book, the kind of upset that triggers a response like fainting has to be rooted way down deep in a person. What do you think?"

Brynn wrinkled her nose. "You mean, like, do I think Meghan was in love with Brody?"

"I was wondering if it was more like hate."

She sucked in a breath. "You mean, another suspect? In addition to Ned?"

"Maybe." It wasn't the ringing endorsement I would have liked to give the theory, but I didn't know enough yet to be certain about anything. "I'm going to talk to her for sure."

"Good for you. But actually, I didn't come to talk about Meghan. I came to ask you a favor."

"Anything. Whatever you need."

She set a flat package wrapped in brown paper on the counter. "Glory's letter," she said. "You know, the framed poem from her husband. After everything that happened yesterday, you'd think I would have gone home and collapsed, but I was overly tired and that made me too antsy to sit still. I worked on the poem last night. But today, well, there's a reception for the new president over at the community college later this week and I've got to get my act together and start getting ready for it or I'll never get all the cooking and baking done. If I could just leave this here for her?"

"No." I must have sounded pretty convincing because

Brynn's mouth fell open. I laughed. "I'll go over to Junk and Disorderly and deliver it to her."

"Would you? You're a gem!" Brynn smiled. "There's no hurry."

"Sure there is." I tucked the package under my arm. "Glory loves that poem, and I'm sure she's itching to see what you did with it. It will give me the perfect opportunity to get out of here for a while. There aren't many customers around, and the ones that are here mostly just want to talk about Meghan. I've had it with that. I'll leave Charmaine in charge."

I said my goodbyes to Brynn, found my aunt and told her to keep an eye on things, and since the weather was perfect and I wasn't in the mood to hurry back, I took my time and walked, stopping along the way for a to-go cup of coffee.

Junk and Disorderly was Glory's brainchild, and as I stood on the sidewalk in front of the old grocery store that housed it, I had to give her credit for being innovative and a risk-taker. Everyone else in town had seen the vast, empty store as an eyesore. Glory envisioned new life for it as an antiques mall where individual dealers each had their own area to stock and care for. Glory sold antiques there, too, but she also handled overall management of the place, including assigning one dealer each day to handle sales for all the others.

That particular Tuesday, Scott Claresdale was up front behind the cash register. His booth—toys, dolls, trains— was nearby, so it was easy for him to keep an eye on things and handle customers coming and going.

"Glory?" I asked him.

"Not in. Something about a haircut. Said she'd be by

later. You want me to take that?" He looked at the package I was carrying. "Or you could just put it back in her booth. Not busy in here today, no one will bother it."

Since Glory had told me she'd recently bought a stack of vintage Harlequin romances at an estate sale, taking the letter to her booth gave me the perfect excuse I needed to poke around.

Far right corner, all the way in the back, next to the Junk and Disorderly office where Glory spent so much time.

I wound my way in that direction, through uncomfortable-looking furniture and colorful quilts, chiming clocks and battered books, gleaming glassware and ladies' hats that looked like they belonged in some old black-and-white noir movie.

I didn't see the Harlequins in Glory's booth, but I promised myself I'd come back another time, tucked the framed letter from Ted in a safe place, and, done with my mission, took the top off my coffee cup. Even before I had a chance to take a sip, I heard a low rumbling.

Annoyed bear?

Dissatisfied customer?

Whatever it was, it was coming from Glory's office, and I peeked inside.

Park ranger. Sitting in front of a TV and mumbling to himself.

I stepped away from the doorway as quickly as I could, but I wasn't fast enough. Or maybe Max has super spidey-senses. He caught sight of me before I had a chance to retreat. "What are you doing here?"

"Just came to see Glory." I inched away from the door. "She's not here, so I'll just—"

"No, wait! Don't." He hit a couple of buttons on a machine next to the TV and spun Glory's desk chair so he was facing me. But not before he yawned and stretched. "You can help me."

"Me? Help you? Do what?"

"Security tapes." As if it explained it all, he pointed toward the TV. "I've been watching security tapes. Hours and hours of security tapes."

I was interested in spite of myself. "Because . . . ?"

Max kneaded the back of his neck with one hand. "Because of what Glory said about that fifty-dollar bill that was left at her booth the other day."

"Tuesday," I said.

He nodded. "The day before the murder."

Interested morphed into intrigued. I stepped farther into the office. "You think that money has something to do with Brody's murder?"

"Darned if I know." Max unfolded himself from the chair, stood, and stretched. He was young, fit, and athletic. He was dressed in nicely worn jeans and a shirt that hugged abs and pecs and biceps.

When I scratched my arm, I hoped he didn't notice.

"There's a whole lot I still don't know about this town," he told me. "You're the perfect person to help."

Was I? Perfect? Somehow, I thought not, but my curiosity got the better of me. When he motioned me closer, I couldn't have stopped myself if I tried. Max sat down and I stood at his shoulder.

"You're thinking about the timing," I said. "Money one day, murder the next. It doesn't prove anything."

"Actually, what I'm thinking is that if you could just help me understand the lay of the land, I might be able to get a better handle on things. Not like you're investigating or anything. Just like you're . . . consulting?"

"Sure. Sure." I was, in fact, not as enthusiastic about this consulting thing as I was about all-out investigating, but I knew better than to disagree with him. Cops are cops, whether they work for a city or work for the parks. And I knew Max wouldn't appreciate my sticking my nose where it didn't belong. Of course, that didn't mean I couldn't be cagey and float a couple of theories by him.

"But it does seem odd, doesn't it? The bit about how the money was left just a day before the murder?" I asked, as innocent as can be. "And you know what else is weird? I've been thinking about it. That wound on Brody. Not that I've seen any other mortal wounds in my life, thank goodness. But it looked strange and misshapen to me."

Max did some technological mumbo jumbo and made the video on the screen in front of him jump and rewind and honestly, I think he was so busy concentrating on the uber-outdated equipment he forgot I was there. He mumbled to himself, "The folks at the lab say the wound was thin and straight, not pointed like it was made by the blade of a knife. And there was rust under Brody's skin."

"Rust? Like from an old piece of metal?"

When he looked over his shoulder at me, it was as if he just remembered he wasn't alone. And that if he was smart, he'd better keep his mouth shut. "Could be. But that's not what I was asking for your help with."

My smile was sour, but I didn't let that distract me from this new and interesting information. "What you're thinking is that someone bought something from Glory's booth, something old and made of metal. That makes sense. She told me she got a whole load of farm implements from the Tussock place, and my guess is plenty of those were old and metal. There was so much stuff, she can't even say what's missing. If there's something missing."

"And like I said," Max reminded me, his smile tight now, "not what I wanted to talk to you about."

He cleared his throat in a way that made it clear the matter wasn't open for discussion. "I know it's a long shot thinking I might find anything useful on these tapes. But what the heck. I've been here . . ." He glanced at the time on the phone he'd set next to the TV and yawned. "No wonder my eyes are so crossed that everyone and everything on these tapes is starting to look the same to me. This place is open from ten in the morning until nine at night on Tuesdays, and that means eleven hours of tape. I've already fast-forwarded my way through all the tapes once, and I'm getting a little bleary-eyed. A fresh set of eyes would be a real help. You know, just to help me figure out who's who."

"Maybe this will, too." I handed him my cup of coffee.

Hope blossomed in his expression. "Black? Two sugars?"

"Sorry. No sugar. A little bit of cream."

"I'll take my chances." He breathed in deep. "You just saved my life."

"I doubt it." There was another chair nearby and I pulled it over. "But I'll help you if I can."

He gulped down some of the coffee before he pointed to a stack of tapes on the desk. "VHS system. Can you believe it? I guess when they talk antiques, they mean everything about the place."

I glanced at the grainy picture on the screen in front of him. "Looks like it works. Sort of."

"Yeah. Sort of. See, here's what I did . . ." He leaned toward me. I leaned back. "I started at the beginning of the day. You know, that Tuesday Glory came in late and found the money at her booth. I was just curious about who might have been here and, as it turns out, there were plenty of people in and out that day."

"Well, that's good, right? That gives us something to go on."

"It gives *me* something to go on," he corrected. "Except." He hit a button to get the tape playing again. "The system is antiquated. The color is lousy. It was raining that day, and the lighting in here isn't the best to begin with. The camera is up there." He pointed over his shoulder, out toward the sales floor. "In the far left corner of the building all the way in the back, so it takes in the whole space. Kind of."

I looked at the screen and saw what he meant. The security camera showed a panoramic view of Junk and Disorderly, but it was a big space, and between that and the picture quality, it wasn't easy to make out details.

"There's Glory's space." I leaned over, pointed, squinted. "But you can't see the whole area, just one corner of it."

"Yeah." Max propped his elbows on his knees. "That's not helping."

"And the customers?"

"Exactly why I need your expertise."

He rewound the tape, fast-forwarded it to what he was looking for, stopped it.

"First person in all day."

I watched the front door open, watched the person who walked in flop back the hood of her rain slicker.

"That's me." There was no use denying it, and it didn't matter anyway. It wasn't like Max thought I was guilty of anything.

Did he?

Ice water gushed through my veins. "You don't think that means . . . you can't possibly think I had anything to do with—"

"Give me some credit, Lizzie. If I thought you were a cold-blooded killer I'd have you down at the station, not here in the back room of the Land That Time Forgot. All I'm saying is that you were the first person in that day. See, there you are, waving to the guy unpacking those boxes over on the right of the screen and dripping all over the floor."

I was. Big, splotchy puddles.

It wasn't pretty.

"Nasty morning," I said.

"And yet you stopped in."

He was waiting for an explanation I didn't feel I needed to give, but if I didn't, I'd look like I had something to hide.

"Valentines," I said, then in answer to his blank look, added, "Glory bought a batch of vintage valentines at an auction." Just thinking about it made me grin. "You know, those cool old ones that have like an ear of corn on them and say, 'It's *corny* but I'd sure like to *ear* you say you'll be my Valentine.'"

I guess Max didn't share my taste in vintage schmaltz because he gave me a blank look.

"Got a lot of boyfriends you send valentines to?" he wanted to know.

Since I couldn't be sure if he was kidding, I rolled my eyes. "They're for a display. At the shop."

"And that's why you were here? Even though it was a real toad-strangler out there?"

"I wanted to stake my claim to them before anyone else did. Vintage valentines are a hot item."

He scratched a finger behind his ear. "If you say so."

"You can see me . . ." I pointed to the TV screen. "Well, part of me. See, I say hello to Davy Kirk. He was the one taking care of sales that day. Then I disappear for a while. That's because I was back at Glory's booth, looking through the valentines, picking out the ones I wanted."

He slanted me a look. "Which was all of them, right?"

"Hey, you *are* a good detective!" I was already smiling before I realized he was, too. I wiped the expression off my face and clutched my hands on my lap. "Glory told me to take whatever I wanted, and I could pay her later."

"Did you leave the fifty-dollar bill?"

"Definitely not. You can ask Glory. I paid her when she stopped in at the shop later that afternoon for her daily gossip session with Charmaine. It should have been twenty-five dollars for the cards. She charged me twenty. And by the way . . ." Just so he wouldn't miss my exit from Junk and Disorderly, I tapped the TV screen with one finger to point out how I tucked the bag of valentines under my slicker, flipped up my hood, walked out the door. "I didn't pick up a murder weapon while I was there."

"Hey, I have to cover all the bases. If I didn't make note of you being here"—he did just that on a legal pad at his elbow—"somebody might want to know why I was protecting you. You know, like I was playing favorites because you're going to go to that baseball game with me."

I wished I had my coffee back. It would give me something to do with my hands. I unclasped my fingers. Wound them together again. I forced my mind away from thoughts of pleasant summer nights and popcorn in the bleachers with Max by keeping an eye on the screen when he fast-forwarded the tape.

Together, we watched someone walk into Junk and Disorderly and, just inside the door, shake raindrops from a Burberry trench coat. I squinted for a better look and when that didn't work, I rolled back my chair, hoping a little distance would give me better perspective.

"Ned?" I asked.

Max looked where I was looking. "That's what I was hoping you could tell me."

"Or maybe . . ." I rolled up to the desk. "I don't know. It could be the mayor. Or that guy who comes through town once in a while who sells plumbing supplies to the local school districts. He always stops at Ken's Diner for breakfast. Maybe he stopped here, too."

I took another look. "My money's on Ned, and look, he's walking in the direction of Glory's setup." I shot Max a look. "You know they didn't get along?"

"Mr. Baker and Brody?"

"Bison. Crashing cocktail parties."

Max made a pained face. "Heard all about it."

"And, of course, they're neighbors, which would give Ned the opportunity to be in the right place at the right time. He could have been the one keeping an eye on things from the woods."

"If that's Ned Baker." Max made another note on his pad.

By this time, the figure on camera had his back to us and was heading out the front door.

"Who else showed up that day?" I wanted to know.

"Funny you should ask." The machine whirred, stuttered, stopped. "Kind of hard to tell with the way this person walks in with an umbrella still up and is all hunkered down inside a raincoat." He gave the picture on the screen an eagle-eyed look. "I'm pretty sure it's a woman. And I'm thinking it's the librarian."

I held my breath, waiting for him to say something condescending about the purple thong, ready to defend the rights of a woman—any woman—to wear what she wanted, when she wanted. When he didn't, my opinion of Max rose a notch.

My attention, though, was on the TV screen, where I saw a figure gingerly step around the splotches of water left behind by a certain bookseller and carefully lean an umbrella at just the right angle against the wall, right in a corner where it wouldn't be in anyone's way.

"Absolutely," I told Max. "That's got to be Meghan."

"What would she want here?" Max wondered.

"Can't say," I admitted. "But look, there's someone right behind her." No sooner had Meghan drifted out of the picture than the door opened and closed again. Hair swathed in a silk scarf, collar turned up. It was impossible to get a clear look, but still . . .

"It could be Penny Markham," I said. "She's our local real estate guru. She dated Brody."

"Were they serious?"

"She didn't look especially upset at yesterday's service. And she told me . . ." Even to my own ears, I sounded like one of the gossips over at the shop. I reminded myself this wasn't idle talk. This was reporting facts. To a person in authority. "She told me she went out with Brody three times, and that was enough for her because he was a big ol' bore."

To my surprise, Max chuckled. "Is that what you women talk about? How boring men are?"

"Sometimes," I admitted. "When they're boring."

His eyes sparked. "And when they're not?"

There was no use staring deep into those dark eyes of his. Even if I wanted to. It would only make me crazy. And itchy. I forced my gaze back to the TV and to the woman who might be Penny.

"Penny's all into stylish and trendy," I told Max, because it was important for him to know and because I had to say something to keep my mind off the heat of his smile. "I can't believe she'd ever shop in a place like this. It sure looks like her, though. She waves to Davy there at the front counter, just like I did. Then she walks toward the back of the building and now . . ." I hadn't even realized I'd pulled my chair closer to Max's and leaned way over the desk and toward the TV until it was a done deal. "She disappeared from the picture. And Meghan's nowhere to be seen, either. Either one of them could be back at Glory's booth, picking up a murder weapon."

"Just trying to identify the people on the tape. Not trying to put some kind of half-baked backstory together," he grumbled. "I need to stay objective. I can't just come up with theories because they pop into my head." He had the good grace not to point out that this was exactly what I was doing. "Either one of them could be someplace totally different, looking at some other dealer's spot. Don't go jumping to conclusions." He made note of it, then hit the right buttons again. "They both leave." We watched them, first the woman who was most certainly Meghan, and a little while after, the one who was probably Penny. "It's three hours before anything else of interest happens. Three long hours." He covered up a yawn. "And I've watched every minute of it. A couple of people came in and bought some china up front, but they never moved from that dealer's space. No one else goes to the back of the shop. Not until this guy." He started the tape.

Lightning sparked just as the door flew open and a man in a long, loose-fitting duster swept into the building. He wore his Stetson tipped low over his eyes, and he didn't say a word to Davy up front. He strode through Junk and Disorderly like he owned the place. And like he knew exactly where he was going.

I sat up. "Brody?"

"That was my first thought, too. But at yesterday's service, I had a chance to check out that cousin of his. They look a lot alike."

I narrowed my eyes and stared at the screen. "Could be."

"And Ernest, he's the one who arranged for that hang glider to make an appearance at the memorial yesterday, right?"

"That's what I heard."

"And that hang glider, seeing that is what made Ms. Watkins so emotional."

"It was Brody's most famous stunt. And I guess it made Meghan think about him, and that was too much for her."

"And that explains why she reacted that way." Was that amusement in Max's eyes? Or plain ol' curiosity? I chose to believe the latter.

"You've got to wonder why Meghan would have such an over-the-top reaction," I said, then held up a hand to stop what most certainly would have been some kind of warning about my half-baked theories. "I'm not jumping to conclusions. Or coming up with motives. I'm talking human nature, that's all. We were all supposed to think about Brody when we saw the hang glider. That was the whole point. But Meghan's the only one who got that emotional about it."

"And I'm told they never dated." Max tap, tap, tapped the legal pad with the tip of his pen.

"What's Brody . . ." I watched the screen. "Or Ernest. What's he doing? It looks like he's at Glory's space, all right, but now . . ." The man spun from the camera and moved away.

Somehow I'd hoped there would be more revelations contained on the tape. Disappointed, I sat back in my chair. "Is there more?"

"One more." Max ejected the tape from the machine and put another one in.

A thought occurred and I sat up. "That one other person, was it late in the day?"

"How did you know?"

"Well, I didn't. Except that you changed the tape so that must mean a few hours went by. And that got me to thinking. All these people came and went. But you'd think they would have noticed a fifty-dollar bill just sitting at Glory's booth. That they would have taken it up front to Davy to keep safe, or at least mentioned it to him. That tells me the person who left it must have come in late."

"Excellent deduction. So tell me . . ." He ran the new tape. "Here's the last person in. Who is it?"

By late that afternoon, the rain had let up, from a downpour to a drizzle, and a slice of sunlight shone through the glass front doors of Junk and Disorderly. Silhouetted against it was a large figure shaped more like a cone than a person.

It took me a second to see that the shape was caused by the long raincoat the figure was wearing, and only another second after that to catch sight of the color.

Purple.

The figure stepped inside, and the overhead lights gleamed against the glass beads and sequins embroidered on the oversized pockets of the coat.

"Do you know who that is?" Max asked.

I shook my head before I found my voice. "I have no idea."

"You sure?"

To play along, I watched the tape for another few seconds. Her head was bare, and her crazy blond hair flew around her shoulders when she shook off the raindrops and waved to Davy with all the enthusiasm of a cheerleader.

"That's your aunt," Max said.

I pretended to have to take a closer look. "You think so? I'm not sure."

"Oh, come on." He slapped his knee. "I just moved here

and I've seen your aunt parading around in that crazy rain-coat of hers."

My shoulders shot back. "'Parading' is an awfully harsh word." Then before he could tell me it was also a totally appropriate word because parading was exactly what Char-maine liked to do, I stood up so fast, my chair rolled back and away from me. "I think you're wrong."

He stood to face me. "I think I'm going to need to talk to her about it."

My gaze slid back to the TV screen in time to see Char-maine disappear in the direction of Glory's booth. "She'll have a perfectly good explanation."

"I'm sure."

"And you can't possibly think . . ."

I couldn't say it. I couldn't even think it. I mumbled something about needing to get back to the shop and high-tailed it out of there, kicking myself in the pants the whole time.

There was Charmaine. One of the last people in Junk and Disorderly the day before the murder.

And there was me, giving Max some fool explanation about how the last person in must have been the one who left the money and maybe, picked up the murder weapon.

Yeah.

I'd been trying to protect Charmaine this whole time.

And I'd just handed her to Max as a suspect on a silver platter.

Chapter 11

After my trip to Junk and Disorderly, I popped home and picked up Violet, then took her to the shop for a couple of hours. My customers adored her, and because they knew she'd belonged to Brody and saw her carrying around his bandanna and understood how much she must be missing him, they showered her with affection and the occasional treat. She was in doggy heaven, and I was happy to have her good company once I closed and cleaned up.

Note to self: I would not need to vacuum so often if Violet stayed home and didn't shed here, there, and everywhere.

Second note to self: I felt bad about leaving her home alone all day, every day. Violet was used to a home where the buffalo roam, and the poor thing needed to get out and about. She was a sweetie, and like it or not, I was responsible for her. The least I could do was include her in my life as much as possible.

Even though when she was around, my life seemed to consist mostly of vacuuming.

I finished up in the historical romance room and un-plugged the vacuum, and when I wound up the cord, she made growly faces at it.

"What all this means," I told her, continuing the one-sided conversation we'd been having before I started vacu-uming, "is that I have to put on the afterburners and find the killer before a certain someone"—the look I gave her told her exactly who I was talking about—"convinces himself that Charmaine is his best bet for the bad guy. It makes sense, don't you think?"

Violet did not pipe up and offer her opinion.

"I told you about everyone who was over at Junk and Disorderly that day," I reminded her, taking the vacuum into the erotica room. "Of course, it might not mean any-thing. And I should just mind my own business. Maybe Max is right."

At the very mention of the name, Violet sat up and panted.

I wondered if I looked the same when I thought about Max.

"But what if that fifty-dollar bill is connected to the murder?" Together, we finished up in that room, stowed the vacuum, and went to the front counter, where I closed out the register. "The least I can do is talk to everyone, right?"

Violet agreed.

At least I think that's what it meant when she plopped down on her hindquarters, looked up at me, and her tongue lolled out of the right side of her mouth.

In the best of all possible worlds, *everyone* would in-clude Charmaine, but that day had been busy, and every time I went looking for my aunt to have a heart-to-heart with her about what she was doing at the antiques mall the day before the murder, she was deep in doing something else. The Young Adult Book Club. Her sacred afternoon time with Glory. Charming the socks off the UPS driver who not only delivered three cases of books to our front door but, thanks to Charmaine, offered to haul them all the way back to the office so we could unpack them and get them entered into our inventory program.

"It's not like we won't see her later," I told Violet and myself. "For now . . ." I checked the clock above the register. It was a promotional gift from a publisher, a round clock with elaborate numbers and words scrolled around the dial in old-fashioned curlicue script—ADDICTED TO TIME TRAVEL.

It had taken longer to vacuum than I realized and it was nearly eight o'clock.

"What do you say?" I asked Violet. "Let's start by talking to the other people I saw on that tape. Want to go for a walk?"

This, she understood, and she got the red bandanna so she could bring it along and danced around while I hooked on her leash. It was purple to match the collar she'd been wearing when she came home with me, and with it swinging between us, we locked up the shop and headed down Main Street.

Second Tuesday of the month.

Chamber of Commerce meeting.

And since I'd checked the website, I knew this evening's event was scheduled to take place at Ken's Diner.

Yes, I'm a member of the Chamber and yes (again), I do try to attend meetings as often as I'm able, but that's not where we were headed.

Not to the meeting, anyway.

I walked Violet down the street, stopping now and again

when people passing by commented on how pretty she was, how friendly, tears welling in their eyes when they saw the bandanna and knew she missed her master. Violet's fur is so plush it's irresistible, and more than one person wanted to pet her.

Every single one of them ended up brushing their hands against their clothing.

And brushing Violet's fur off their clothing.

And mumbling when it stuck like those promotional decals on race cars.

Even that didn't keep my fellow townsfolk from telling Violet what a good girl she was. She took it to heart and pranced all the way to our destination.

I bet there's a place like Ken's Diner in every small town everywhere, a squat single-story building with windows all around, red vinyl booths just inside with a bird's-eye view of Tinker's Creek life, and stools at the front counter. Ken's has been a fixture in Tinker's Creek for as long as anyone can remember. Great breakfasts. Decent burgers. Stick-to-your-ribs meals that always include something greasy to go along with the mashed potatoes.

Our timing was perfect. The Chamber of Commerce meeting was just breaking up when Violet and I arrived, so we stood out on the sidewalk, watched, and waited.

As mayor, Cal Patrick couldn't play favorites when it came to the businesses in town. Not openly, anyway. But he was there, glad-handing everyone as they left and, I noticed, waving to Joy Baker when she just so happened to be walking by as he stepped outside. For the record, they disappeared together in the same direction. Glory walked out of the diner and we talked about the Chamber's plan for the Fall Festival in October. She also told me what a fabulous job Brynn had done on the poem from Ted and invited me to stop at her house sometime soon to see it. Diane from the pharmacy came out of the diner, and we exchanged small talk.

By that time, there was only one other person left at Ken's other than Mick, the guy who owned the place (Ken was long dead), and Violet and I closed in on the front door, waiting for that person to come outside.

"Hi, Penny!" It was still light out, so it wasn't like we were lurking in the shadows, but it seemed Penny's mind was a million miles away. At the sound of my voice she flinched, looked at me and Violet, and joined us on the sidewalk.

"Out enjoying the weather?"

When she started walking, we trotted beside her. "Actually, I was hoping to see you," I told her. "I felt so bad that I looked for that horoscope Charmaine prepared for you and couldn't find it. I wondered if you ever had a chance to pick it up."

"Oh, that." When we stopped to let a long line of bike riders glide past us on Main Street, Penny laughed, looked both ways, and we crossed once it was safe. "Truth be told, I forgot all about it. Like I said, I thought the whole thing was silly right from the start."

"But Charmaine did take the time to work on the horoscope for you," I said. "Silly or not, she puts her heart and soul into doing them, and it takes hours."

We were on the other side of the street now, near the bridge over the canal, and Penny glanced my way. "You're absolutely right. It would be rude of me not to get it and show her how much I appreciate her work."

Everyone in town knew where my shop was and, of course, they knew where Charmaine and I lived. It was up the street, to the left. Penny looked that way.

"Headed home?" she asked.

"Oh, I thought we'd just walk a little longer." When she turned to the right, Violet and I did, too. "There's something I'd like to discuss with you."

"Not the Brody thing, I hope."

"What makes you think that?"

A soft breeze blew bits of Violet everywhere, and Penny plucked away a strand that landed on her red, red lips and stuck. She looked at the three-inch-long filament, wrinkled her nose, flicked away the fur. "That yummy ranger for one thing," she said. "He stopped by today to ask if I went to Junk and Disorderly the day before the murder."

"Did you?"

"Does it matter? To you?"

We were in front of Penny's real estate office, a trim white building with mullioned windows and a sign that blinked off and on in a shade of blue that was impossible to ignore.

OPEN

"You're still working?" I asked her.

"Just some papers to clean up. I figured it didn't hurt to leave the sign on. You know, just in case someone like you got it into their head to buy up big chunks of Tinker's Creek."

"I didn't exactly—"

She laughed. "Just kidding. Believe me, with as lousy as the economy was a couple of years ago, having you show up and buy the building you turned into the store, then rescue your aunt's just-about-to-be-foreclosed property was a dream come true. Come on, Lizzie, everyone in town knows you've got deep pockets, oodles of money from all that Apple stock your parents bought in your name from the day you were born. How about buying a few more buildings? The old tavern's going to be on the market in a month or so. And Mrs. Portage's house. That's not far from your shop. You could use it as a sort of annex."

She wasn't exactly kidding, but I laughed anyway. "Maybe someday. Right now, I'd rather just concentrate on the shop I have."

She stuck her key in the front door.

"Could I . . ." I looked down at the dog. "Could we come in and chat for a bit?"

I think she would have told me no way if she hadn't just mentioned that I was a dream come true with a bigger-than-most bank account. "Sure." Her smile was tight when she swung open the door and stepped back to let us walk in ahead of her.

The reception area was just inside, neat and trim and organized. Penny's private office was to the right. It was spacious and tastefully decorated in the same sort of boring way real estate agents always recommend to people trying to sell their properties. Not too much color. Not too many personal mementos. Not too much personality.

I guess I'd been around Charmaine long enough to crave at least a splash of pizzazz. The way it was, the office reminded me of vanilla ice cream.

I took a seat in the straight-backed chair with beige upholstery in front of Penny's desk, and Violet sat at my side. When she dropped the red bandanna, I picked it up and tied it around her neck.

Penny sidled behind the desk and into a black leather desk chair with a high back. "Water?"

She offered a bottle from the mini fridge behind her desk, and I accepted and asked for one of the plastic cups stacked nearby so I could pour a little for Violet. She slurped it down with gusto.

Penny's stiff smile told me she wouldn't have ignored the noise—or the dog—if I were anyone else. "Tell me, what did you say I can do for you?" she wanted to know.

"Well, you can tell me what you told Max . . . er, Ranger Alverez. Were you at Junk and Disorderly the day before the murder?"

She picked up a pen and poked it against the desk blotter. "Like I said, I can't imagine why it matters."

"I wouldn't be asking if it didn't."

Penny tossed the pen on the desk. "Why, is someone going around pinching trashy old things? You can't possibly think I would ever—"

"Never crossed my mind," I assured her. "In fact, I think if you wanted something, let's say from Glory's booth, you'd buy it outright. You wouldn't even quibble about the price. And if Glory wasn't there, maybe you'd take what you wanted and leave the money behind. You know, like a fifty-dollar bill."

"What is it with you people?" Penny asked no one in particular. "You and that ranger? Why are you both concerned about a fifty-dollar bill?"

"I'm more concerned about what you bought with it."

"Nothing. Okay?" She twined her fingers together on the desktop in front of her. "I'll tell you exactly what I told Mr. Hot Ranger. I stopped in to Junk and Disorderly that morning, all right. But I didn't go anywhere near Glory's booth. I have a client who's into those hokey old salt and pepper shakers. You know, two cows. Or two apples. Or two little Mason jars, though, gads . . ." She rolled her eyes. "Why anyone would want those on the table is a mystery to me." She got rid of the thought with a shake of her shoulders.

"I wanted to show my appreciation to the customer for letting me handle the recent purchase of his house. So I went to that junky place . . ." She shivered. "And I went to that booth all the way in the back. Not to the right, where Glory's booth is. Over on the left."

I knew the space she was talking about. It belonged to Katrina Ionoca.

"And I looked at salt and pepper shakers. I didn't buy any, by the way. Not that day. I had a hard time wrapping my head around the idea of kitsch. In fact, it took a couple of days. Then I went back and picked up two fat pink pigs. Perfectly horrendous. And my client loves them to pieces. I can prove when I bought them." She slid open her top desk drawer and drew out a piece of paper. "This is exactly what I showed that ranger. The receipt. Dated last Thursday, two days after the visit you're asking about."

It was.

Which proved Penny had made a legitimate purchase just recently.

And didn't prove she hadn't slipped a murder weapon into the pocket of her coat that rainy Tuesday.

"Meghan was at Junk and Disorderly that Tuesday morning, too," I said.

"Was she?"

"At the same time you were."

"I didn't notice her. Of course, until yesterday . . ." Penny didn't hide her sly smile. "Up until she pulled that stunt at the memorial, I don't think anyone ever noticed Meghan. Now, well, I guess she accomplished what she wanted. She's got everyone talking about what she wants them to talk about."

"Her underwear?"

Penny laughed. "Don't be ridiculous. Who cares what

the woman wears under her no-style clothes? I mean everyone's talking about Meghan's reaction to the hang-gliding stunt. They're wondering what it says about her and Brody, if it means the two of them had something going on. I'll tell you what, they should be wondering about her mental state. That woman's got a screw loose."

"Because she was overcome with emotion?"

"Because she wanted to show the world that Brody had a special place in her heart. And you know, I think she's nuts enough to believe she had a place in his."

I stroked a hand over Violet's head. "You don't think it's true?"

"Oh, come on." She tipped back her chair. "Meghan's about the only woman in town Brody never dated. Her." She shot me a look. "And you."

I did not rise to the bait. I didn't know what was lurking on the other end of the hook.

"You dated him but never liked him," I said instead.

"You got that right." She sat up straight. "Which doesn't mean I killed him. I mean, if anyone was inclined to murder . . ." Her brows dropped low over her eyes and for a minute, she was lost in thought.

"What?" I finally asked her. "Or should I say who?"

She shook her shoulders. "Just my crazy imagination. I told you, I'd pretty much had it with Brody from the start, but he was one persistent guy. Since I wasn't as into him as he was into me, I was just going to say that if anyone was going to plan a murder, it would be him."

"Brody? Murder you?" The pitch of my voice reflected my surprise.

"Like I said, my wild imagination. He never threatened me or anything, I was just thinking, that's all. If a person is so crazy about another person, and that other person doesn't pay the least little bit of attention to . . . her." The look she gave me told me exactly who she was talking about.

"You think Meghan's capable?"

"I think jealousy makes people do loony things."

"It makes sense." It did, so it's not like I said that just to cozy up and soften her before I asked my next question. "Where were you? The night Brody was killed?"

Penny sat as still as a statue, the soft light highlighting her coppery hair, her high cheekbones, her small straight nose. Once again I had the impression she would have blown me off if she could risk it. But I was a customer. I might use her services again. And Penny was smart. "As a matter of fact, I was right here," she told me with the sweep of one manicured hand. "All alone. Catching up on paperwork. Not much of an alibi, is it? And believe me, if I killed Brody, I'd come up with a better story than that."

I can't say how a professional like Max or Josh would have handled things from there. I only knew that little ol' amateur me was long on theories and short on questions.

"I've taken enough of your time." I stood and Violet got to her feet, too. "I hope you don't mind me being nosy. It's just that the whole town would like to know what happened to Brody and I thought, oh, I don't know, maybe I could help out a little."

"I would mind"—she came around the desk, laughing—"if you weren't such a good customer! It's always nice to see you, Lizzie, and if you ever want to buy up more of Tinker's Creek . . ."

"You'll be the first to know." Violet and I turned toward the door and that's when something over on the bookcase next to it caught my eye. I closed in and studied the eight-by-ten color photograph with Penny's signature in one corner. It was a stunning picture. Brush in the background.

Trees overhead. At the center of it all was an animal with a gray coat with rusty overtones.

"You like foxes?" I asked Penny.

"Well, they're pretty enough." Penny came to stand at my side, and she looked at the picture, too. "But it's not like I was out looking for that guy or anything. I just happened to see him and thought I'd take a chance catching a picture. I'm pleased with the way it came out."

I took a closer look. "He's not as red as the foxes I've seen around."

As if she'd forgotten, Penny bent closer to take a better look. "Isn't he? I guess maybe the lighting was lousy. It was dusk, I think. I happened to be out in my backyard just as he walked through."

I thanked Penny for her time, and Violet and I walked toward home, side by side. We stopped on the bridge over the canal, watching the water glide by. To be honest, I wasn't thinking about what it must have been like nearly two hundred years ago when raw manpower dug the canal that eventually stretched from southern Ohio all the way to Lake Erie.

Oh, no.

I had murder on my mind.

"Did you take a good look at that picture?" I asked Violet. "Did you notice what I noticed? That's right." I gave her head a rub. "A great big bushy tail on that fox. Just like the phony one the cops found out at the ranch."

Chapter 12

It wasn't often that Charmaine and I had a chance to have lunch at the same time. Most days, the shop was hopping from open to close and for that, I was grateful. She was busy. I was busy. When one of us wasn't, we snuck in some time—and a sandwich—for ourselves. But that Wednesday, the sky was filled with dark threatening clouds, the heat soared, and every breath of outside air was packed with more humidity than a rain forest.

I couldn't blame people for staying home, and besides, a little quiet time gave me the opportunity to do all the things I didn't have the chance to do in the course of a normal day. Instead of having to devote my evening hours to it, I designed and ordered postcards that I'd send out to our loyal customer base publicizing an upcoming author signing. I culled some books (always painful!) from the gothic section and put them in a box that I'd donate to the library. I got to sit down—actually sit without jumping up and down to answer questions or take care of sales—with the chicken salad sandwich I'd brought for lunch.

"Ah, thought this is where you'd be." Charmaine came into the historical room, her lunch bag with her. I was already sitting near the window, so she took the other wing-back chair, stretched out her legs, and took two pieces of double-pepperoni, mushroom, and green olive pizza from her bag.

"Nick's." She leaned over the pizza and breathed in deep. "I don't know what that man puts in his sauce, but ever since he moved to town and opened his place, I've got to have pizza at least once a week."

I totally understood. I was addicted to Nick's Italian sausage and banana pepper combo.

Pizza, however, wasn't what I wanted to talk about.

"I was over at Junk and Disorderly," I told my aunt. "Watching security tapes with Max."

"I heard!" She grinned and wiped pizza sauce from her lips. "Glory told me all about it. Max told her. The two of you. In the back room." Her sigh was monumental. "Honey, it's the stuff romantic dreams are made of."

"Not so much." I bit into my sandwich and chewed. "It was actually pretty ordinary."

"Oh?" She sat up and fluttered. "Does that mean you're finally getting the hang of flirting? Or . . ." Just as quickly, her excitement dissolved, her shoulders drooped. "You don't like him. You don't think he's any big deal. You acted normal because you don't think he's cute."

"He's plenty cute." I shouldn't have had to remind her. "I just . . ." As if it explained everything, I lifted one shoulder. "We weren't talking silly stuff. You know, not like you usually do when you're just getting to know a guy and you're floundering for things to say. Max and I, we were talking murder."

When she shivered, the shimmering crystal beads she wore that day with a red sundress caught the light and winked at me. "It's been a week. Can you even wrap your head around it? A week since Brody was killed."

"Yeah. But the security tapes we watched were from the day before. You know, the day Glory found that fifty-dollar bill at her booth."

Charmaine chewed and considered this.

"And that's why we were watching the tapes," I told her, hoping to coax the truth—or at least some version of it—out of her. "Max wanted to see who came and went and maybe who left the money, and since he doesn't know everyone in town very well yet, he wanted my input."

She nodded and chewed some more.

"You were there."

She swallowed. "Was I? At Junk and Disorderly? The day before the murder?"

"You don't remember?"

"Hard to keep it straight. I'm there all the time."

"Yes, but that day it was raining."

Her eyes lit. "Yes! Of course I remember that. Cats and dogs! But you don't think . . ." The corners of Charmaine's mouth pinched. "You can't think that I . . . Why would I leave money at Glory's booth?"

"That's what Max is trying to figure out."

"Well, I didn't." She jiggled her shoulders. "And just in case you're wondering, I didn't pick up the murder weapon while I was there, either."

Since it was exactly what I was thinking—and exactly what I was hoping not to prove—I denied the statement as soon as I swallowed a bite of sandwich. "You can't possibly think that anyone would suspect you of—"

"Well, actually, I hope that's exactly what they think!" A rumble of thunder shivered in the air between us. "That's how the police have to think. They have to suspect everyone. If they don't, they can't get all the facts and then they never find out the truth."

"The truth." I set down my sandwich, the better to aim a level look at my aunt. "It would be nice to know the truth about—"

"Ooh, what do you suppose he's up to?" Her gaze on the window, Charmaine was out of her chair in a flash, and I turned and saw what she was looking at. Ned Baker was walking down the sidewalk. "He's still wearing those sunglasses. In this weather! Like he thinks that's going to fool anyone."

I'd been meaning to talk to Ned about what we'd seen on the Junk and Disorderly security tapes and I saw this as a golden opportunity. I stood and set aside my chicken salad. "I'll be right back," I told my aunt.

Honestly, I had every intention of returning in a jiffy, but no sooner did I get outside than Ned hopped into his car. He sat for a minute, checking his phone.

It was all the time I needed. Though I usually walk to the shop, I'd driven that morning, thinking it was going to rain. My car was parked right up front, and since I knew Charmaine was bound to be looking outside to see what I was up to, I pointed to it and made crazy back-and-forth movements with both hands, like they were on a steering wheel. Satisfied she'd know what it meant—that I was leaving and she had to take care of the shop—I got into my car and kept my eyes on Ned.

He pulled away from the curb.

I followed right along.

I kept on following him, too, certain he was going to head to that Mediterranean nightmare of a home of his. I planned to pull into the driveway behind him, where I could talk to him and he wouldn't be able to slam the front door in my face.

Except Ned didn't go home.

He cruised right by the turnoff to his house and kept going, all the way to Hudson, a nearby town where there were more far more homes and shops and office buildings than would ever fit in our little Tinker's Creek corner of the world. When he pulled into the parking lot of a medical building, I was right behind him. He parked. I made sure I stayed inconspicuous by driving right past, swinging around to the far aisle, and parking way down at the end of a row where I could see but not be seen.

Then I waited.

It was my first attempt at tailing a suspect, and I thought about all the books I'd read and all the movies I'd seen where smart women—always self-confident and gutsy— tracked bad guys. I wasn't feeling either gutsy or self- confident, just unsure of what I was supposed to do next. Hop out of my car and confront Ned right then and there? Creep along behind him, stealthy-ninja fashion? Leave before I em- barrassed myself?

My mind was made up for me when Ned went into the building.

If I was going to talk to him away from his home, where he would have every right to demand that I leave, this was the moment.

I got out of my car and hurried to catch up with him, but short legs, oppressive heat. I arrived in the lobby sweaty and winded just in time to see the elevator doors close. A few seconds later, the light above the elevator indicated the third floor. When the elevator came back to the lobby, I got in and went up.

As it turned out, there was only one tenant on the third floor.

PROWSKY AND MARTINGALE, COSMETIC SURGERY

When it came to knowing what kind of facial work caused which type of bruising, it looked like Charmaine knew her stuff.

There was a bench outside the tasteful smoked-glass double doors that led into the practice, and I parked myself and waited.

It was more than an hour before Ned stepped through the door and out into the hallway.

And about two seconds after that when he caught sight of me and stopped cold.

"What are you doing here?" he demanded.

I stood and stretched and considered cobbling together some story or another that might actually sound plausible, then decided to go for broke. And for the truth. "I thought we could talk."

"Here? Now? Have you been following me?"

"Absolutely not," I assured him. "Not until this afternoon, anyway. I saw you in town and wanted to talk to you, but you drove away."

"And you had the nerve to—" He swallowed his outrage at the same time he pulled his sunglasses out of his shirt pocket and put them on. It was a little late to hide his bruises from me, so my only guess was he was trying to spare the citizens of Hudson the sight of the ugly splotches, still purple in the center but a sickening shade of green around the edges.

"Really, Ned, you don't need to hide," I told him. "I get it. You had some work done. Probably a nose job."

"Shhh!" As if we weren't standing outside the office of cosmetic surgeons, as if it were some deep, dark secret, he closed in on me and lowered his voice. "I don't want the world to know."

"There's nobody here but us."

"Yeah, and if that aunt of yours catches wind of this . . ."

I didn't let on that she already had. "Your secret is safe with me," I assured him. "But why are you keeping it a secret, anyway? No one cares if—"

"Oh yes, they sure do. At least in my line of business. I've got a deal in the works. A big business deal. And I haven't met the people I'm hoping to work with yet. Not in person, anyway. I want them to look at me and think energy. I want them to think youth and enthusiasm. I do not want them to think tired and old."

"I've never thought of you as tired and old."

"Maybe not, but I can't take any chances. A little tuck here. A little nip there. And as long as she was at it, I had the doc fix my nose. I've never liked my nose."

Since I couldn't picture it, it must have been an unremarkable nose to begin with, but I didn't point this out. "I don't care that you had surgery," I assured Ned. "And I swear I won't tell anyone. I just wanted to ask you if you were at Junk and Disorderly the day before Brody was killed."

He stepped around me and stabbed one finger against the elevator call button. "Why?"

The elevator arrived, and Ned stepped into it before I did. The doors closed.

I looked straight ahead. "Glory is trying to get her accounting straight and I told her I'd help out. Someone left money at her booth."

"It wasn't me."

The elevator clunked to a stop and the doors swished open. Ned bustled out past me and was all the way to the main door of the building before he turned and looked my way. "You're not worried about Glory's money. You think I had something to do with Brody's murder."

"I didn't say that. I—"

Before I could say another word, he was right up in my face, his finger pointed at my nose.

"I didn't," Ned growled, "and I can prove it. Go ahead. Go back upstairs." He poked that same finger toward the elevator. "Ask the nurses. Ask Dr. Prowsky. She'll tell you. I had my procedure on Wednesday, and that night I stayed in a suite right here at the clinic so they could keep an eye on me. I was nowhere near my house, or Brody's ranch, the night he was killed. What do you think of that, huh?"

He twirled away, then whirled right back around. I couldn't see Ned's eyes. But I saw the way his eyebrows shot up above the black plastic frames of his sunglasses. Like he had an idea. Like he was about to prove to me just how far off base I was.

"In fact . . ." His voice was as sly as I imagined the look in his eyes must be. "If that isn't enough for you, I can prove I wasn't the one there at the ranch. And I can show you who was."

My heart clutched. "What are you talking about? How would you—"

"Security cameras. Haven't even shown the footage to the cops yet because I only thought about looking at it this morning. I left a message for that cousin of yours, but he hasn't called me back. You want to see who was at the ranch on Wednesday night?"

Did I?

I chortled in a way designed to convince Ned (and maybe myself) that it hardly mattered to me and shrugged, too, just to prove it. "It can't be anyone I know."

"You think?"

I swallowed what I can only describe as abject fear. Maybe I didn't want to know. But maybe I couldn't afford to turn away from it, either.

"You'll show me?" I asked him.

"Come on," he said and stalked out the door. "You followed me this far. Now follow me home. I'm about to turn your little world upside down."

I followed, all right, my heart beating double time and my breaths coming in short, quick gasps that made it hard for me to think. Did Ned have proof? About Charmaine following Brody home that night?

My stomach soured. My mouth went dry. My hands trembled against the steering wheel.

All the way to Mediterranean villa à la Tinker's Creek.

I parked outside the four-car garage and hoped the rumble of thunder that punctuated my footsteps wasn't as foreboding as it always was in gothic novels. Before I walked inside, I whispered a prayer. "Please, please don't let him have anything that shows Charmaine at the ranch."

When Ned motioned for me, I walked into his garage and waited along with him for the garage door to close.

I was right behind him and wondering what I may have just gotten myself into when we stepped into a pristine laundry room.

"This way," Ned said, and we crossed a kitchen bigger than my house. It was all shiny and incredibly over-the-top—cabinets painted gold, marble columns, miles of quartz countertops. Ned's banging footsteps echoed against the marble floor. My pink sneakers slap, slap, slapped behind him.

We negotiated a maze of hallways and entered Ned's office, and I took a quick look around.

A desk as big as Ned's ego.

A wall filled with certificates proclaiming who knew what about the man.

A floor-to-ceiling bookshelf.

One look and my nose crinkled. Honestly, I'll never understand people who have bookshelves with plaques and pictures and trophies on them—and not a book in sight. It offends my soul on the deepest level, and I was still trying to wrap my head around it when Ned's voice rang out and I winced.

"Over here!" He motioned to me from where he stood behind his desk, pointing to the screen of his computer monitor. "Security camera runs twenty-four-seven."

This did not surprise me. When your house is too much, your security system has to live up to it.

I bent closer for a better look at the monitor and the picture on it, a wide swath of grass, a few trees, a bit of driveway, a tall fence.

"Bison." I did not need Ned to confirm or deny. "You have a security camera devoted to the fence between your property and Brody's?"

"Well, one of the cameras is. There are others. Too bad I wasn't here in my office monitoring this one the evening that critter came over the fence. Then I might have had at least a little bit of warning about what was about to happen. But oh, no, there I was out at the pool. With the principal partner of Hanover, Harcourt, and Hemmingway, and the

CEO of a tech giant that's about to surprise the world with their initial stock offering, and the visiting president of a charming little bank in the Cayman Islands. It was not the best way to start the evening."

"Which is why you had every right to be angry at Brody."

"But not enough to make me want to kill the man. And as I've already said, I couldn't have done it. I was in Hudson, recovering, relaxing, and being waited on hand and foot."

"And the camera just shows the bison!" Yeah, that was me, sounding way too perky, way too relieved, when in all actuality I was just scared to death of what Ned was about to show me. I backed up a step. "I guess I'll just be on my way then and—"

"Oh, no!" With one hand, Ned latched on to my arm to keep me in place. With the other, he clicked the appropriate keys and I saw a date flash in the right-hand corner of the picture.

When I hiccuped, he mistook the sound for excitement rather than fear.

"Take it easy, Nancy Drew." Ned moved us through the evening, from just before the sun set until after dark, and I was amazed at how good a security system that wasn't Glory's old VCR could be. The picture was clear and perfect, the colors were true.

"You'll see here . . ." He'd been zipping through the night and he stopped the picture now. "The time stamp shows. See. It was just after eleven."

After Brody left Charmaine's and she went racing after him.

Even before I backed away another step—from the security tape and all it might reveal—Ned was waving me closer.

"What are you doing? You're the one who wanted to see this. Look, here's Brody coming back from somewhere."

Brody's fancy pickup truck chugged by the camera, starting, stopping, lurching, just like it had when I saw him leave Charmaine's.

"And just a couple minutes later—"

"Isn't this something you should show . . ." I almost said *the police* and swallowed down the words. If we were about to see what I thought we were about to see, the police were the last people I wanted to see it. "I really don't think you should be showing me this." I backed away a few more steps, already panicking. Would I be forced to turn over my aunt to the authorities? Or would I help her pack and shuffle her off to Mexico before the cops could close in?

"You watch this." Ned's hand tightened around my arm. "And you tell me what you see."

What I saw was another car pull into the driveway, not long after Brody's.

"It's dark and hard to see and . . ." In spite of myself and the terror that ate away at my composure, I couldn't look away. "Can you rewind it?"

Ned rolled his eyes, but he did just that.

"And now slow it down?"

He did that, too.

My knees got weak and I let go of a breath.

"It's not a purple Volkswagen Beetle," I said.

He looked my way. "Is it supposed to be?"

"Well, no. I'm just sort of talking my way through what I'm looking at. I mean, it's not a Jeep or a van. It's not a Volkswagen Beetle."

"It isn't," he agreed.

"What it is . . ." I wanted to be sure, so with a motion of one hand, I asked him to run the clip again.

What I saw was a sedan.

Beige.

Solid and dependable.

A car so plain and sensible, it could only belong to one person.

Chapter 13

By the time I got back to Love Under the Covers, Glory was there for her daily gossip session with Charmaine. Neither one of them blinked an eye when I picked up that box of gothics and told them I was taking it to the library.

I drove. Hot, remember? And just as I got to the library, fat raindrops plopped onto my windshield. When I hopped out of my car, the rain was coming down in buckets. I hurried inside to keep the box and the precious books inside it dry, then stopped cold, upended by all those pictures of Brody that looked out at me from the display case.

I shouldn't have been knocked for a loop. After all, I knew Meghan was preparing the display. I knew she was Brody fan numero uno. Yet now, looking at his rugged face, studying the rock-hard set of his shoulders, the stubborn tilt of his chin, the gleam of courage—not to mention sexiness—in his eyes . . .

I wondered what he'd thought when quiet, orderly, systematic Meghan showed up at the ranch that last night of his life.

It was hard to believe Brody would feel threatened by anything, so I imagined he would have welcomed her. Hesitantly, maybe, not understanding what the town librarian wanted or what she was doing there. He may have been getting the bison in for the night and maybe he invited her into the barn while he worked, all rippling muscles and masculine energy.

Had she snuck up behind him?

No, the wound—that awful gash—was in his chest, so he must have been attacked from the front.

I guess when the woman who's about to stab you is the last person on earth you'd think of as bold enough to commit a murder, your guard is down.

Brody's sure must have been.

The automatic doors swished open and another patron rushed in out of the rain, and the whoosh of humid air that accompanied her pulled me out of my thoughts. My head still swirling with theories and possibilities, my brain still questioning if it was even possible for a woman like Meghan to commit a murder, I hoisted the box of books against my hip and went looking for the librarian.

I found her in the back room where orders are received and processed, busy taking books out of a shipping carton and making neat stacks. Mysteries here. Science fiction there. A third, smaller pile for Westerns.

I had to wonder that she wasn't wearing latex gloves as protection against genre cooties.

When I chuckled, Meghan glanced up.

"What can I do for you?"

"Book donation." As if she couldn't see it, I lifted the box a little higher, then set it down on the table where she worked. "Gothics, and most of them aren't that old. If you don't want to catalogue them into the system—"

"Yes, yes, the semiannual book sale. I'm sure there's someone out there"—the way she caught her breath told me it was hard for her to even imagine—"who likes that sort of thing."

"If selling these books means money to support library programming, I'm sure it's worth it." She might have noticed my upbeat smile if she didn't go right back to unpacking books.

When I still didn't move, Meghan lifted her gaze, but not her chin. "Is there something else I can do for you?"

"As a matter of fact, there is." Just to mess with her and her ever-so-neat piles of books, I grabbed the book on top of the mystery stack. Cute cover. Clever title. An author I enjoyed when I had time to pull myself away from romance and read something with a little blood and guts. I set the book down and apparently it wasn't exactly as I'd found it because Meghan straightened it. "How about you tell me what you were doing at Junk and Disorderly a week ago Tuesday."

Meghan had been about to take another book out of the shipping box and she put it down, stepped back from the table. "Why are you asking?"

"Oh, come on, Meghan. You want to find out what happened to Brody as much as I do. Maybe more than I do. I'm just asking some questions, trying to line up the answers. You can help."

Her head tipped, she considered this for so long I thought she was going to blow me off. At least until she said, "Is that the day it was raining?"

"It is."

"Well, then that explains it, doesn't it? I was on my way

into work and stopped for donuts. Library Clerk Appreciation Day. Before I could get near the bakery, the skies opened up. I had to go somewhere, didn't I? To keep out of the rain."

"You had an umbrella."

"Of course I did. But sometimes even an umbrella isn't enough."

"You didn't buy anything?"

Meghan puckered her lips. "How do you know all this?"

"Word gets around."

"Word about me trying to keep dry and out of the rain? Oh, I get it." She clasped her hands at her waist and raised her chin. "I suppose since I was overcome with emotion at Brody's memorial service I've been the talk of the town."

It wasn't right to mention the thong, and let's face it, that's all anybody was talking about. And not what Meghan was talking about. She was talking about Brody's attachment to her, her devotion to Brody. And as far as I could tell, I was pretty much the only one who cared about that.

"Not really," I told her.

Her stony expression wilted. Yeah, she was that disappointed.

"I'm glad we cleared up the mystery of you at the antiques mall." I backed away a few steps, giving her a little breathing room, hoping to catch her off guard with my next question. "That explains what you were doing at Junk and Disorderly on Tuesday. Of course, it doesn't say where you were the night Brody was killed."

As if I'd slapped her, Meghan reared back. Her face, usually so porridgy, flushed a color that reminded me of the stream of blood (or was it marinara sauce?) on the cover of the cozy mystery I'd just set down. Her fingers fluttered, twined together again, clasped so hard, the bones underneath the skin stood out like sticks.

"If you must know," she said, "I was in Cleveland that fateful night. At a meeting. The Society for Shakespearean Studies. We meet every month to discuss . . ." The only way her smile could have gotten any stiffer was if it were painted on. "I won't even try to explain. Not to someone who doesn't understand real literature."

I ignored the dig. "Come off it, Meghan. You weren't yakety-yakking with your fellow literary types. You were at the ranch."

"How did you—" She knew she'd made a mistake the moment the words tumbled out of her mouth, and as if she could call them back, she clamped her lips shut.

"It's not like I'm accusing you of anything," I was sure to tell her. It was technically true. I was on a fishing expedition. Accusations, arrests, indictments. Those were for Josh and Max to take care of. "I'm just trying to understand what happened. Obviously, someone hated Brody."

A strangled sob escaped her. Her knees gave out, and I was glad there was a chair right behind her. Otherwise, I would have had to pick her up off the floor. "Poor man. So much life! So much vitality! So much potential! And to have it all snatched away." Dispirited, she shook her head. Her words fluttered over tears. "You know, whoever it was"—she gave me a hard look—"I think they'd tried before."

"They? Tried what?"

The way she pursed her lips said more even than the sudden coquettish tilt of her head. "Maybe no one in town paid as much attention to dear Brody as I did. Otherwise, they might have noticed."

"The cut on his forehead." I remembered the last time he'd been in the shop, the day he bought the card he sent to Charmaine. "Are you telling me—"

"That cut on his forehead? He said he slipped in the garage on some oil he hadn't realized he'd spilled. A bruise on his arm a few weeks before that? He tripped over a tree branch near the barn, one he swore wasn't there the last time he passed that way. That little limp last month? He told me he'd parked where he always did over at Ken's Diner, that last spot way in the corner. And when he got out of his car, there was a big rock there. One that had never been there before. Naturally, he wasn't looking for it. He stepped down and twisted his ankle." She poked a finger at her chest and the navy cardigan she wore over a cream-colored blouse. "I know Brody wasn't careless, and let's face it, those stunts he did in his commercials proved he wasn't clumsy. He'd never admit to being concerned or afraid. You know what Brody could be like."

"Not really," I admitted. "I hardly knew the man."

"Well, I did." She fanned her face, sending the silent signal that she wasn't talking about what I was talking about. "He wasn't one to moan or complain or look to have anyone feel sorry for him. Maybe he hadn't even put two and two together yet. But I think those accidents he had weren't accidents at all."

I remembered the shadow in my garden that night Brody visited Charmaine.

The light in the woods on the night of the murder.

The binoculars I was sure were used to keep an eye on the rancher.

"You think someone had been trying to kill him for a while?"

"Absolutely." Convinced, Meghan gave me one quick

nod. "Obviously, that person didn't succeed. Not until last week. No big surprise there. It would be hard to get the jump on a man as manly as that man."

I excused her word choice. When it came to talking about Brody, Meghan was obviously not in possession of all her faculties.

Which brought me right back to the night of the murder.

"Want to explain why you lied about what you were doing? You said you were at a Shakespeare meeting."

"I . . . I was." I wasn't sure if she was trying to convince me or herself with the set of her shoulders. "But the meeting didn't go on all night. Of course it didn't. Besides . . ." She stood, as prim as a Regency miss. "I don't see why it's anyone's business. What Brody and I did together—"

"You and Brody? Did things? Together?"

She ignored the disbelief in my voice. "What Brody and I did together that night or any other night is my business and mine alone."

"But you were there. At the ranch. No matter what you were doing there, it's important for the cops to know."

"Then I'll call that cousin of yours and I'll tell him exactly what I'm going to tell you. I was on my way back from Cleveland when Brody called. He knew I'd been to the meeting, of course, and he knew that after hours of discussing serious literature, I'm always atingle with energy. He invited me to stop over for a drink. When I arrived, he was . . ." There was a packing invoice on the table in front of her, and she slid it to her right, slipped it to her left. "There was no sign of him. Not anywhere."

"You looked in the barn?"

"Of course I did. After all, Brody was a man of his word. If he said I should stop by, I expected him to be there."

"But he wasn't."

She slipped the invoice to her right, slid it to her left. "No sign of him," she said. "And after that . . ." I have a feeling the little shrug she gave was meant to show me that at the time, she was convinced she'd done all she could. Instead, when her bony shoulders rose and fell, she reminded me of a scarecrow battered by the wind.

"I left immediately," Meghan told me. "And nobody can prove any different."

"One more question."

I saw her suck in a breath and hold it, and yes, the wicked side of me wanted to drag things out and see how long it took her to turn the color of her cardigan. I took pity on her, though, when a blast of thunder rattled the room, and I took it as a sign to get a move on.

"Did you see anyone at the ranch that night?" I asked Meghan.

"The bison were there."

"Bison don't count. I mean a person. Maybe one who was wearing a phony fox tail?"

"Fox. Tail." Her laugh wasn't as amused as it was just plain batty. The high-pitched sound pinged against the walls and the tiled floor. "Why on earth would anyone wear a silly fox tail?" A little more laughter, designed, I was sure, to convince me of something. Too bad at that point I didn't know what that something was.

Meghan came around the table and put her hand on my shoulder, the better to escort me to the door.

"Fox tail." Her chuckle was deeper now. "Why would you even ask anything so silly? Did someone find a fox tail out at the ranch?"

At the doorway, I slipped away from her so I could turn and look at her when I said, "As a matter of fact, the police did. And when they figure out who it belongs to, my guess is they're going to have the murderer."

I t was luck that I ran into Max as I was leaving the library. Good luck or bad luck, I couldn't say.

"Hey, I've been wanting to talk to you." He waved me closer to where he was sitting in the front seat of his Jeep, and since it was raining so hard that rivulets ran through the parking lot and my sneakers were soaked in seconds, it's not like I could have come up with an excuse to avoid him even if I wanted to.

I slipped into the passenger seat and shook my head, and I didn't even realize the damage I'd done until Max brushed the drippy fallout from his face.

"Sorry," I mumbled.

He cocked his head to look out the windshield, though since it was sheeted with rain outside and clouded with condensation inside, I wasn't sure what he hoped to see. "The weather today is just like it was on the day of those security tapes we watched."

"Yeah, and by the way, Meghan says she only stopped into Junk and Disorderly to keep dry," I told him. Then, as long as I was at it and we were talking murder, I figured I might as well add, "Penny admits to being there but says she didn't buy anything. She showed you the receipt for what she did buy a few days later. I haven't had a chance to talk to Ernest yet, and by the way, Ned claims to have an alibi for the night of the murder that looks airtight. As for my aunt being at Junk and Disorderly that day, she says she didn't leave the money or pick up a murder weapon, and I believe her."

It must have been the accumulation of humid air inside the Jeep. Max's eyes were a little glazed.

He blinked. "You've been busy poking your nose where it obviously doesn't belong. You're awfully—"

"Nosy. Yes. I confess, I am. It's just that once I get my teeth into something—"

"I was going to say wet. You're awfully wet." He reached into the back seat and tossed me a towel.

I caught it in midair and scrubbed the towel over my sopping hair, then dabbed my shirt.

Max, in the meantime, rubbed a hand over the window for a better look at the library. "I know what she told me. What did she tell you? What's her alibi?" he wanted to know.

I sat up and kept scrubbing. "Then I'm right! You think she's a suspect, just like I do."

"I think I've got a lot of people to think about when it comes to this case. Ms. Watkins is one of them. Let me guess, you marched in there and asked her outright what she was doing the night of the murder."

"She says she was at some Shakespeare meeting. Is that what she told you?"

"It is."

"But you know she wasn't. Or at least she wasn't all night. She was at the ranch."

I could forgive Max the squint-eyed look. "She told you that?"

"She didn't need to. Ned Baker has a security system. And it's better than Glory's, by the way."

He drummed his fingers against the steering wheel. "Josh told me he'd gotten a call from Ned. He's on his way over there now to talk to him. But you've already watched the tape on Ned's security system?"

I nodded, blotted a drip from the tip of my nose. "Don't get too excited. Ned's camera isn't aimed at the barn. But it does show the driveway and the fencing. Ned was keeping an eye on the bison. But the tape clearly shows Meghan's car in the driveway the night of the murder. Just a little while later, you can see her driving away. Ned says he should have told you earlier, but he's been preoccupied. Cosmetic surgery. But no one's supposed to know that."

Max grinned. "Does he think I'm blind? I figured that out the minute I saw him at the memorial service. We'll see what he tells Josh, then maybe I'll have a talk with him, too."

"And you might want to check on Callie Porter and Tasha Grimes, too. They both dated Brody, you know."

"That I did know. No luck there. Alibis. Both of them."

The rain let up a little. Instead of getting saturated going to my car, I'd only get soaked if I jumped out of the Jeep now. I put my hand on the door, all set to leave before the conversation turned from murder to something more ordinary and my insides turned to jelly and I didn't know what to say. Another thought occurred to me, though, and I turned in my seat to give Max a look.

"What are you doing here anyway, just hanging out in the library parking lot? Were you following me?"

"I told you I needed to talk to you."

"I didn't date Brody. You know that."

Even in the dim light, his eyes gleamed. "I know you've got better taste than Brody. And that's not what I wanted to talk to you about anyway. It's that card."

Oh, how I wished I'd taken the opportunity and hopped out of the car when I had the chance.

"What card is that?"

"Come on, you're smarter than that!"

I guess I was supposed to take that as a compliment. It felt more like an accusation.

Max scooted a little closer. "The card Brody bought at

your shop the day before he died. I heard all about it. From Callie. And Tasha."

"Oh, that card. It was nice. Handmade. Brynn makes them, the handmade cards. She does wonderful things with dried flowers and little add-ons like buttons and—"

"And if I ever need a special card I'll know where to buy one. But that's not why I care. What I'm wondering is if Brody told you who the card was for."

I didn't have to lie, so it was easy to look Max in the eye. "He did not."

"Did he happen to mention if it was for a special occasion, a birthday or something?"

"The way I remember it, he said it wasn't."

"And you don't remember anything else?"

"He wanted the card to be blank inside."

"But on the outside it was plenty romantic-looking."

"Was it?" I pretended to have to think about it. "Flowers, so yeah, maybe."

"And a cupid. Ms. Grimes told me. Definitely a cupid." Max pinned me with a look. "I thought your specialty was romance."

"Romance novels," I reminded him.

Right before I opened the door and hopped out of the Jeep.

The good thing about being soaked was that it gave me an excuse to stop home and change clothes.

The good thing about stopping home and changing clothes was that I knew while I was there, Charmaine was still back at the shop.

The good thing about Charmaine being back at the shop

was that I was able to duck into her house, race upstairs into her bedroom, and grab the card from Brody.

What did I plan to do with it?

Good question, and as it turned out, the answer didn't matter.

I searched high and low and everywhere in between. And that love letter Brody wrote to Charmaine right before he died?

It was nowhere to be found.

Chapter 14

I am smart. I am logical. I am pragmatic.

If I wasn't, I couldn't run a successful business.

In the great scheme of things, this isn't just good, it's wonderful. These qualities and a few more (like my hard-headed determination, my deep love of literacy, my honest-to-goodness belief that my mission in life is spreading the word that romance novels empower women) allow me to stretch my entrepreneurial wings. My work lets me express my creativity when it comes to marketing and programming, to support myself and build the life I dreamed of all those years I had my nose pressed in a book and my head in the clouds of imagination.

But there's a downside, too, and lately, I was feeling it more and more, as real as a weight on my shoulders.

Smart means I should be able to see the big picture. Right?

Logical means I should be capable of understanding problems and considering them from all sides.

Correct?

Pragmatic means I should come up with solutions.

Can I get an amen?

Only now, faced with something far more important even than Love Under the Covers, my devotion to the romance genre, and my hope to be self-employed forever and ever, I couldn't manage any of those things.

The missing love letter.

The found fox tail.

The mysterious fifty-dollar bill.

The trail of Brody's love-'em-and-leave-'em lady friends.

The rancher himself, of course.

The dead rancher.

The cold-blooded killer who'd taken his life.

The more I looked for answers, the more confused I got, and the more confused I got . . .

I must have grumbled my frustration. After all, it was the only thing that explained why one of the first customers who came into the shop on Thursday had stopped midstride on her way to the checkout counter and had given me a look that clearly said she wasn't sure if it was safe to approach.

"Just a computer snafu," I told her, and as if it would actually prove it, I set my hand on the keyboard in front of me. "You know how these tech problems can drive you crazy."

She did. Which is why, she confessed, she liked to lose herself in historical romances.

I knew exactly how she felt. Ah, the good old days.

Like before I had a murder to solve.

The customer taken care of, I drummed my fingers on the front counter, thinking more and getting to exactly the nowhere I was before. I wasn't sure how long I stood there like that, but I know that's how Charmaine found me.

"Too bad you had to run out to the bank so early this morning." She was carrying a packing box from a new supplier who rescued vintage glassware by making homemade candles in it, and she took out one candle and breathed deep. "Lemon chiffon." She stuck the candle under my nose. "Nice, yes?"

It was, but I wasn't as concerned about candles as I was with what she'd said. "Why?" I asked my aunt. "Why is it too bad I had to go to the bank this morning?"

"Well, because that nice ranger stopped in, of course." Grinning, she arranged the candles on a shelf we'd cleared off near the front counter, stepping back now and then to make sure the glass vases and tumblers and the handcrafted candles in them caught the light just right.

Charmaine was so busy admiring her own work, she didn't notice the way my hand tightened around the front counter. My blood ran cold, too. "What did Max want?"

Charmaine tipped her head and chewed on her bottom lip. "I'm surprised he didn't ask about you."

"Why would he?"

"Why else would he be here?"

Why, indeed.

Unless he had a line on a murder suspect.

Trying to look casual in spite of the sudden pounding inside my ribs, I rounded the front counter and checked out Charmaine's display. It looked perfect. It smelled divine.

"So . . ." I cast a sidelong look in her direction. "If he didn't ask about me, what did you and Max talk about?"

"I thought so." Now that her hands were free, she could

wag one finger at me. "You like that young man. Otherwise you wouldn't care why he was here. I don't blame you one bit for being attracted to him. He's a cutie, and he's very polite. That tells me he comes from a good family."

"Which doesn't tell me what you talked about."

"Oh, this, that, and the other thing. The weather, and a program the park system is doing at the gazebo on Sunday all about local animals. Oh!" As if she'd just remembered, Charmaine pointed to the rack where a little over a week before, Brody had chosen the card studded with flowers, buttons, and that cute little cupid. "He looked at the cards."

I darted over to stand in front of my aunt. "Why?"

"Well, I suppose because he was thinking of buying one. I showed him a few, asked if the card was for a special occasion or . . ." Her smile was sly when she looked my way. "Or for a special person."

"And he said?"

She puckered. "He said he wasn't looking to buy a card. He asked about that card Brody bought."

"And you told him . . . ?"

"That I was here that morning and I saw Brody talking to you, but I couldn't tell him much else. Not even when he asked if I knew who the card was for."

I let go a breath of relief.

At least until she added, "Not at the time Brody bought the card, anyway."

My mouth went dry. "But . . . does that mean . . . you told him you knew who Brody meant the card for?"

"There didn't seem to be much point in not telling him."

I gulped. "And what did Max do then?"

"Told me he'd stop by if he needed to talk to me again."

A spurt of panic erupted inside me. My hands shook. "If you need someone to help you—"

"Help me talk to Max? See! Didn't I tell you? You're looking for any excuse to get together with him."

"No, I'm not, but—"

"You're searching for things to talk about with him."

"Not really, but—"

"You'll want to make the most of the time you have. Once Max and Josh solve this case, Max will be heading who knows where."

"That may be true, but—"

"Of course"—Charmaine gave me a wink—"now you've really got something to talk to him about."

I thought bail money.

I thought attorneys.

I thought sentencing recommendations, media frenzy, having to visit Charmaine in a place where there was a glass wall between us and we had to talk to each other with phones.

The gleam in my aunt's eyes told me she was worried about none of those things.

She leaned nearer and looked around, but since the only other customers had made a beeline for the erotica room the moment they were in the door, we were alone. "The will."

"Brody's will?"

"Who else's will would we be talking about?" Charmaine hustled around me, chuckling, and headed to the back of the shop to get rid of the packing box.

I followed right along.

"What about Brody's will?" I asked her.

"Well, you didn't hear it from me . . ." Charmaine's standard disclaimer when it comes to gossip. She paused outside our coffee alcove, the better to make sure I was listening to every juicy detail. "But I heard it from Margaret over at the hair salon and she heard it from her husband, Paul, and you know he's friends with Mark Graham. And Mark was Brody's attorney."

"Isn't that breaching client confidentiality or something?"

"Like I said, you didn't hear it from me. Besides, the will's been prorated or probated or whatever they call it. It's all official so it's not really a secret. Or at least it won't be by this afternoon when Mark's letter to Ernest is delivered. Ernest is the next of kin and Brody's only living relative, so of course he has to be informed." Her eyes gleaming, she shuffled nearer until there was only that box between us, pressing Charmaine's midsection and my collar bone.

"Brody left the ranch and the bison and everything else he owned to the national park," Charmaine confided. "With the stipulation that they use the land and the livestock for educational purposes. You know, for college farming students, so they can try out new methods of bison breeding and growing crops. And even for younger kids, so they can get a look at bison and learn about how they live."

"That was remarkably generous," I said, nudging the cardboard box away. "It's not like I didn't think Brody was a nice guy, but that seems pretty altruistic."

Charmaine grinned. "Not totally. There are a couple of conditions. One is that the whole kit and caboodle be called the Brody Pierce Center for Bison Education. And the other . . ." Her grin turned into a laugh. "A statue of Brody. Right there outside the house, because that will be the education and conference center. Imagine Brody standing there!" She struck a pose, feet apart, shoulders back, chin high. She might have looked more forceful if not for that packing box. "Immortalized in bronze, looking like he just stepped out of the barn." Just as quickly, her shoulders sagged and her voice clogged. "He certainly was larger than life. How I miss that man."

I could be excused for not sympathizing. I was stuck on something she'd said a little while back.

"Farming?" I said. "Educational center about bison? Ned Baker is not going to be happy."

"He doesn't have much choice. The way it stands now, Brody's land butts right up to the national park on one side, but you know, when old farmer Tussock owned the place, he owned acres and acres more. When the park moved in, he sold them a ton of land. Made a pretty penny off it, too."

Again, as semi-interesting as this all was, my brain was stuck, my thought processes lagged. "Who else isn't going to be happy?" I asked Charmaine, and when we went into the office and she tossed the box from the candles in our recycling pile, brushed her hands together, and turned to me with a question in her eyes, I encouraged her with a flourish of my hands. "You know the deepest, darkest secrets of everyone in town. You must know this. Is somebody going to be disappointed that Brody's money is going to the bison? Ernest, maybe?"

"Well, it would only be natural for Ernest to expect to inherit, so I imagine he'll get quite a surprise when he receives that letter from the attorney."

"True," I conceded. "Did they get along?"

"Ernest and Brody? They were cousins."

"But did they get along?"

Charmaine considered this while she dug her purse out of the bottom drawer of my desk, fished out a granola bar, and opened it. "They were the same age," she said around the crunch. "Went to school together all their growing-up years. Same elementary school, same high school. I was a few years older, but I remember them, all right. Then again, every girl in town kept her eyes on Brody! I think both Brody and Ernest played on the football team for a while, then something happened. Ernest broke his leg or something and couldn't play anymore. Oh, and I remember. They were in Drama Club. Just like I was a few years before. I'd forgotten all about that. It was always such fun to see the cousins up there on stage together."

The Drama Club was the last thing I was thinking about. "What if," I asked Charmaine, "all this time Ernest thought he was going to inherit, and this afternoon he gets the surprise of his life? I've got to imagine Brody's estate is worth a pretty penny."

When she leaned closer, I smelled oats and honey. "A couple million."

"That sounds like motive to me."

"Ernest?" Charmaine finished off her granola bar and tossed the wrapper in the wastebasket next to my desk. "He's too nice a guy."

I grabbed my phone.

"What are you going to do?" my aunt asked.

"I'm going to make sure I can talk to Ernest."

I had to, didn't I? Max knew about the card. He knew Brody gave the card to Charmaine because Charmaine told him so herself. It was only a matter of time before he started asking all the uncomfortable questions she wouldn't want to answer.

Honestly, Liz, I don't know what I'd do without you. You're a lifesaver!" Brynn zipped by and I grabbed a tray of mini quiches out of her hands and took it over to the table where other trays of finger foods and an assortment of desserts were already set up. "Cindy Phelps was supposed to help me this afternoon and, well . . ." Brynn threw her hands in the air and looked around the Tinker's Creek Community College meeting room, all ready for the reception to honor the school's new president. "No sign of her. Cindy's pulled this kind of stunt on me before, and I'll tell you what, it's the last time I hire her to work one of my catering events. And to think, when you called yesterday and asked if you could help, I almost said no. Glad I didn't. I owe you."

"Consider it a lesson learned. Cindy's a flake." We both knew this to be true so there was no use discussing it. "And if you want to repay me, I've got an author visit in a couple of weeks. Chocolate-cranberry-chunk cookies?"

"And some of the new apricot jam tarts I've been experimenting with." Brynn grinned. "No charge."

"Charge." I pinned her with a look. "I can at least pay for the ingredients."

"Deal." We exchanged a high five and gave the buffet tables one last once-over. We were as ready as we'd ever be, and it was a good thing, too. We heard applause from the auditorium across the hallway. The program was over. A few seconds later, people started streaming in.

It was a pleasant room with windows on one wall that looked out over a gorge, lush and green this time of year. The opposite wall was filled with framed photographs of the college's administrators over the years, men mostly, their expressions as serious as their suits and ties. We'd set up the food in front of the windows, and I slipped behind the tables, ready to help in any way I could. It was the perfect spot for me to keep an eye on the food and the guests and to signal to Brynn when trays needed to be refilled.

Needless to say (but I'll say it anyway), it was also the perfect spot for me to watch for Ernest.

It didn't take long for me to catch sight of him. He walked into the room at the head of a group of young people, students no doubt, and stepped back to allow them to hit the buffet line ahead of him.

Fine and dandy.

I was ready for him by the time he got to the quiche.

"Lizzie." About to reach for a mini pie, he stopped and gave me a look. "What are you doing—"

"Just helping out." He already had a couple of rumaki on his plate, and I knew the soy sauce they were marinated in made them sloppy. I handed him an extra cocktail napkin. "I heard about the will," I said.

"I'm not surprised." He bit into a rumaki. "There's always gossip in our town."

"Yeah, but—" He'd been about to walk away, and that was exactly what I was expecting, so I raised my voice a bit to get his attention and to make him think what I was about to say might be heard by anyone in the room. It worked. He backed up a step to allow the people behind him in line to get at the food, and once they were gone and there was no one else in line, he stepped back up to the table.

"But what? I really can't see why my cousin's will is anyone's business."

"Well, it wouldn't be. Except that his ranch is worth a bundle. And, well, he was murdered."

"Horrible. Obviously. But what does that have to do with—" Ernest's eyes got as round as those mini quiches. "You think, what, that I had something to do with his death? Because I expected an inheritance?" He stiffened, blinked. And then Ernest laughed. "You're way off base. Believe me, my academic life . . ." As if we were standing in the hallowed halls of Harvard and not a meeting room of the local community college, Ernest looked around. He smiled. "I like my life just the way it is. I teach, I study, I read. I explore the park and look for artifacts on the land around it. Besides, the news that I was left out of the will, well, in spite of what you might have heard, it really wasn't news at all. Not to me. I've known for years that Brody had no intention of leaving me anything, and in all those years . . . well, like I said, I've never really cared. Why would I want a bison ranch? What on earth would I do with it?"

It was a valid question. "Sell it, I suppose."

The way he popped down a quiche told me just how preposterous the suggestion was. "I don't care about the money. I've got everything I need. Right here. You know, people used to talk about my cousin. Oh yeah, every time he showed up anywhere, tongues would wag. I'm sure you heard it all the time, and I guarantee you know what people always said. Successful. That was a word you always heard when people talked about Brody. Am I right?" Since he knew he was, Ernest didn't wait for me to answer.

"They always said Brody was successful. Why? Because he lucked into that commercial job of his. Because he stock-piled enough money to build that lavish ranch. You're young, Lizzie, and if you're smart, you'll learn this lesson now. Being content is way more important than always trying to amass more money, more land, more bison. Not to mention more women." His snort told me exactly what he thought of Brody's love life. "Contentment, that's real success."

I couldn't argue with him.

I also couldn't let him walk away before I was done talking to him.

"I'm sure the cops have already asked you, but you know, I've been trying to put together a timeline of everything that happened the night Brody died."

"Are you?" He thought about this while he chewed a stuffed mushroom. "What have you found out?"

"Not much," I admitted. "Not much that makes sense, anyway. But I am trying to get a handle on where people were that night. You know, the night Brody died."

"And you're wondering where I was." Since he'd finished all the food on his plate, he reached for another quiche. "That was a Wednesday night, right? So the answer to your question is simple. I was home. Prepping my class for the next day. Unlike some people around here who just sort of wing it"—he put a hand to one side of his mouth—"a great deal of research and preparation goes into every one of my classes. Now"—he backed up a few steps—"if you'll excuse me, I've got colleagues to talk to. Nice to see you, Lizzie. Good luck with your timeline."

He walked away, and I should have gotten busy refilling food trays. I would have if I wasn't so busy staring at what Ernest did next.

He stopped beneath a ceiling spotlight that threw a clear, bright beam down on him.

And maybe that was the first he noticed that he had something clinging to his blue blazer.

With two fingers, he pulled it away from his sleeve, made a face, dropped it.

And I watched it flutter to the floor.

Soft.

Fuzzy.

White.

Violet fur.

"I said, are there any more of those cookies?"

I flinched and realized there was a woman standing across the table from me looking put out about the missing cookies.

"Sure, sure," I told her. But let's face it, my mind was a million miles away.

Ernest had an errant strand of Violet fur on his clothing, and that could mean only one thing. When he told me he never visited the ranch, when he said he and his cousin never socialized, he'd been lying through his teeth.

I wondered what else he'd lied to me about.

Chapter 15

By the time I'd helped Brynn with the last of the cleanup over at the community college, then gone back to the shop, sent Charmaine home, and closed up so I could head home myself, my head was in a spin. What I needed was peace, quiet, and time to think about all the lies I'd been told.

What I got was—

Just as I was about to step off the sidewalk and into the garden I shared with my aunt, I froze. Or at least I would have if I wasn't so busy waving away the clouds of smoke that poured from the far side of the garden, where in the cool weather we pulled our chairs around the steel fire pit, roasted marshmallows, and drank hot cocoa.

"Charmaine!" Since I couldn't see clearly, I called to her, and when there was no answer I headed for the fire and hoped I didn't find my aunt passed out from smoke inhalation.

As it turned out, I didn't find her at all.

The smoky remnants of the fire huffed and puffed thicker than ever on that end of the garden, and the long pole that Charmaine used to tend the fire was lying on the ground, tossed to the side.

But there was no sign of my aunt.

This did not strike me as especially peculiar. Or at least no more peculiar than Charmaine usually was. She'd gone into the house to get herself something cold to drink, I told myself. She'd gotten wrapped up in a phone call and, as she so often did when she talked on the phone, she walked and wandered. The fire was nearly out; it's not like it posed a threat to public safety.

Well, except for all that smoke.

I coughed and fanned my hand in front of my face, and I knew I had to do something before the Tinker's Creek Fire Department was called, like they had been the time Charmaine hosted her own little mini version of a Burning Man–like festival. The straw effigy in the center of the garden was a nice touch. At least until she set a match to it, things got out of control, and one of Mrs. Castille's rose of Sharon bushes went up in flames.

Yeah, our local firefighters could still be heard grumbling about that.

For their sake and the sake of my house, directly downwind, I grabbed the pole and poked the remnants of the fire, and thanks to the air I introduced, the flames came to life and the smoke settled down. I poked a little more. Old telephone bills, bits and pieces of crumbled paper, an odd candy wrapper or two. It looked as if Charmaine had been cleaning and straightening and decided to dispose of the debris the easiest way she could.

A few more pokes and I'd have everything under control.

The Tinker's Creek Fire Department would thank me for it.

I'd just smiled at the thought when something at the center of the fire pit caught my eye.

An envelope.

Half-burned.

I dared to hunker down for a better look.

The paper was ivory, thick, and awfully familiar-looking.

"What are you doing down there so close to the fire, Lizzie?"

When my aunt appeared out of the haze, I caught my breath and jumped to my feet. As long as I was at it, I pointed.

"That's an envelope from one of Brynn's cards."

I was right about the cold drink. She had a glass of lemonade in one hand, and she carefully set it on the stone wall that surrounded the fire pit. "It's like this," Charmaine said.

"It's like this?" Good thing all that smoke hung in the air; it helped muffle the disbelief in my voice. Well, a little, anyway. "I know what you're doing. How can you stand there and look so innocent?"

"Do I? Look innocent?" Charmaine had the nerve to smile. "I was trying my hardest. I'm glad it worked. Really, Lizzie." She lifted her lemonade and held out the glass to me. "Maybe you'd better take a nice, long drink. You're a little worked up."

"I am," I admitted, and accepted the lemonade. I'd already downed a big ol' gulp before I tasted the vodka. I made a face and handed the drink back to my aunt. "I just can't believe you think it's that easy. That you can simply burn evidence and get away with it."

She hung her head. "I didn't want you to know."

"I'm the last person you need to worry about. What about Max? What about Josh? If they find out—"

"About the envelope? Oh, Lizzie!" She pressed her free hand to her heart. "I never thought you'd be the type who would be so petty. I'm more than willing to buy another envelope from Brynn, if that will make you happy. But if you're going to file charges against me for shoplifting—"

I think it was my raised hand that cut her off. It must have been, because her words ran out even before I had a chance to say, "What are you talking about?"

"The envelope." She looked at the last of it crumbling to ash in the fire. "What are you talking about?"

"The envelope. And the card that was in it."

"But there wasn't a card in it. Why would I want to burn one of Brynn's cards?"

As luck would have it, there were two Adirondack chairs nearby. As a short person, I've never been fond of Adirondacks. The seats are too deep and when I sit back, my feet dangle above the ground.

I wasn't about to be particular. Not when my head was swimming.

I waited until Charmaine sat, too, before I said, "Start from the beginning."

"About the envelope?"

"About the envelope."

"Well, you were gone helping Brynn today, and . . ." Her bottom lip trembled. "I try not to be careless. I really do. I know how important the shop and everything in it is to you. But I was drinking iced tea, and I helped a customer with a few cards, and then she left and I didn't realize I hadn't put everything back, and that envelope was on the front counter and I set down my glass and the next thing I knew, there was a giant water stain on the envelope."

I leaned forward. Also not easy for a short person in an Adirondack. "What?"

"I didn't want you to know. I was going to call Brynn, replace the envelope, and you'd never be the wiser. I didn't want you to think—"

"You're burning the envelope because it has a water stain on it?"

"Well, yes."

"And you were afraid to tell me?"

"I just thought that—"

She was so darned serious and so darned worried, I should have jumped right up and given her a hug. And I would, I told myself, as soon as I was done laughing.

Relief swept over her expression. "You're not mad?"

"Of course not!" I did my best to swallow my laughter. "It's just a silly envelope, and who cares that you got a water stain on it? There are plenty more where that one came from. Please, promise me you'll never worry about things like that again. And here I thought . . ." What I thought washed away my laughter. It was time to level with my aunt. It was time for her to come clean.

I gave her a steady look. "I thought you were getting rid of evidence."

"Well, I was, I—"

"Not evidence of water stains. Evidence of murder!"

All the color washed out of her face. "What are you talking about?"

"The card. The one Brody bought. The one he wrote a love letter in and gave to you."

It was Charmaine's turn to laugh. She laughed until she had to clutch her stomach. Until tears rolled down her cheeks. And when she saw me sitting there, stunned and confused, she laughed some more.

"Here." She handed me the lemonade and vodka. "Take a drink, honey. I've got a story to tell you."

Truth be told, I finished that drink. Every last drop of it. I wasn't prepared for the tale Charmaine spun.

"So you're telling me"—I'd sat up and scooted to the edge of the chair while she explained what was going on, and now that she was done, my spine accordioned and I let go a long breath—"Brody didn't write that card to you?"

"Of course not."

"You two weren't—"

"Oh, Lizzie!" Her shriek of laughter split the evening sky. "Brody was the hottest thing this town has ever seen. Nobody can deny that. And let's face it, I don't always make the best decisions when it comes to relationships. Nobody can deny that, either. But even I knew not to get sucked in by Brody. Not that he was ever particularly interested in me. Which was fine. Really. I've had my share of love 'em and leave 'em, and no amount of macho or good looks or fame or fortune can make up for that. Well"—she grinned—"almost no amount. No, no. Brody and I were never involved."

"But he was here," I said. "The night he died."

Charmaine's lips puckered. "You saw him, huh? I wondered if you did and why you didn't say anything."

"Because I wanted to figure out what was going on. Now you're telling me the reason he was here—"

"Like I said, I was helping him write that card."

Of all she'd revealed, this was the one thing that surprised me the most.

"I should have known," I said. "You! You're the one who

writes the love poems and love letters that people around here get."

"Shhh!" There was no one around, but she held a finger to her lips anyway. "We can't let word of this get out. I can't tell you how many women in town think their men are romantic devils."

"When really all they did was hire you to write something mushy."

Charmaine's groan rumbled through the garden. "If Glory ever finds out . . ."

"That letter? From Ted?" I winced.

"It would break her heart if she knew those weren't his last words to her."

I crossed my heart with one finger. "Your secret is safe with me. How long have you been doing this, anyway?"

She didn't have to think about it. "Since high school. It started out as a kind of joke. Wrote a letter for Wally Simpson to give the girl he liked. I don't remember her name. Some skinny girl with bad skin. But Wally was crazy about her, and he never knew what to say when she was around. So I told him what to say. And he wrote it down. And he gave it to her. I'll tell you what, Lizzie, when I saw what happened when she read that note from Wally, it was like magic."

"She fell for it?"

"And fell for him. Big-time."

"And you've been doing it ever since."

"Never thought of it as a career or anything," Charmaine said. "But after a while people offered to pay, and it was hard to say no. Now I advertise over the Internet and write letters for people all over the world. It's not much in the way of an income, but it helps. And just so you know, I've been socking away most of it. You know, to pay you back for rescuing my house when it was nearly auctioned out from under me."

I'd told her dozens of times that she didn't need to feel indebted, so I didn't bother to say it again. "How did Brody know?"

"That I was the mystery letter writer?" She chuckled. "I actually told him one day. Yes, it was supposed to be a deep, dark secret, but that man, he had a way about him. He could coax a woman into doing pretty much anything, and one day we got to talking and . . ." She lifted her shoulders. "He swore he'd never tell, and he didn't."

"But he did come to you when he needed a love poem written."

"Well, I didn't write most of it," Charmaine admitted. "Since you saw the card . . ." I'd told her how I'd gone look-ing for Penny's horoscope, how I'd accidentally found the card, how I'd been worried sick ever since. She didn't hold my snooping against me. "All that *love isn't love unless the person you love* . . . way too schmaltzy for me. No, that night Brody stopped here, he knew what he wanted to say, he just couldn't put the words together. I just helped him remember that silly old thing we used to say back in high school. It took us a while to get it straight, but hey, we didn't do too bad for a couple middle-agers long out of school. Once we got the words right, he wrote it down. He left the card here because . . . well . . ." She had the brass to actually look embarrassed. "I can be a little over-the-top now and then, a little dramatic. You know?"

"I might have noticed."

"I insisted that Brody use a fountain pen. It's so much classier. Soon after we finished, he had to get back to the ranch. You know, so he could tend to the bison. I told him to leave the card with me and once the ink dried, I'd mail it for him."

"Then you know who he wanted to send it to! This is important. Josh and Max are going to want to know."

She made a face. "But that's just it. Brody was supposed to call me the next day and give me the address. But he died before he could do that."

"So the mystery lover—"

"Is still a mystery."

"And that's what you told Max, when you said you told him all about the card Brody bought."

"Absolutely. All Brody told me was that the card was for an old friend. So that's what I told Max. Why would I tell him anything else?"

It all made perfect sense, and there was no reason not to believe my aunt. But that didn't explain . . .

"Why did you go running after him? That night Brody was here. You left the house and went after him like your shoes were on fire."

"I did, didn't I? And you must have seen me and assumed—"

"Well, let's face it, it looked desperate. Like you'd had a lovers' quarrel or like you were begging him to listen to you or to stay with you."

She grinned. "I was trying to get him to listen to me, all right. See, when I was cleaning up and I looked out the dining room window, I saw brake fluid on my driveway. Remember how my brake lines broke recently? Well, one look at him driving down Main Street and lurching along, and I knew that's exactly what had happened to his truck."

"You were trying to warn him."

"Sure. Before anything bad happened. That road out to the ranch twists and turns. I caught up to him right over at

Ken's Diner and told him, but of course Brody knew all about trucks. He'd suspected what was happening and promised me he'd drive slow and safe."

"I've been so stupid! I'm sorry I ever thought—"

"That it was actually possible for me to be having an affair with the one man in town every woman was after?" She shook with laughter. "Thanks for the compliment."

I wished I could laugh, too. "I'm sorry I was so suspicious."

"You were curious, that's all. You followed the facts."

"All the wrong facts."

"So what are you going to do now?"

My sigh pretty much said it all. "I'd love to know who that card was meant for. Brody didn't say anything about Meghan, did he?"

"In her dreams."

"Then what about Penny?"

"Never mentioned her name."

"Which means that old friend is another woman, one we don't know about yet."

Charmaine liked the sound of this. Her eyes glowed. "Oooh, just like in a novel."

"Except in a novel, at least the author has some idea what's going on. Me? I'm totally clueless. And, Charmaine, I feel responsible. I'm the one who found Brody, after all, and . . ." My gaze traveled to my house, and I thought about Violet in her red bandanna. "She misses him so much! If nothing else, I owe it to Violet to find out the truth."

Chapter 16

I was relieved to learn that Charmaine wasn't a killer.

Not that I ever believed she could have actually done it, but there was that niggling worry inside me, that *what if* that wasn't so much about whether she'd actually killed Brody as it was about whether the evidence would lead to her and she'd be charged with the crime anyway.

That would have wounded her to the core. It would have destroyed her place as head gossiper and most lovable kook in the Tinker's Creek community. And it wouldn't have done much good for my shop, either.

By the time Saturday night rolled around, I slept better than I had since the night I saw Brody and my aunt at her house. Oh, I still had plenty to worry about, not the least of which was who really did do our rancher in. But for a few blessed hours, I refused to think about it.

I woke up the next morning feeling refreshed, and since it was Sunday and the shop wasn't open and I hadn't forgotten my vow to try to help Violet overcome her grief, I invited her on a long walk.

It goes without saying that she accepted with enthusiasm.

We stopped at Ken's Diner first, where Mick told me they did not usually allow dogs but that he'd make an exception for Violet, since she was so pretty and she'd once belonged to Brody. While she waited patiently (and shed a lot), Mick cooked up a bacon-and-egg sandwich on an English muffin for me. I got it to go, and while Violet and I wandered the streets of Tinker's Creek, I munched. (And yes, I admit it, Violet munched, too, but I only gave her a little. After all, I didn't want to spoil her.)

We waved to bikers who zipped by on their way to the park. Watched a couple of kids splash through the puddles left from the rainstorm earlier in the week. We ran into Glory and didn't say one word about what we knew in regard to that love letter from Ted that she treasured, though we did promise we'd come see it one day soon.

It was already nearing noon when we headed home, both of us tired and happy. It was a warm day and the clouds that gathered above us promised more rain, but when we walked through the square at the center of town, I saw there was a group gathering in the gazebo.

"Nature program," I reminded Violet, and because I was curious about the program, and she was enticed by the smells of all the people gathered there, we took a closer look.

The last person I expected to see was Max.

Smokey Bear hat and all.

Violet and I closed in on him. "It's a nature program." It seemed a more appropriate greeting than a simple hello, and Max understood. He must have. Otherwise, he wouldn't have nodded and grabbed my hand to drag me closer to the gazebo.

"You've got to help me," he said.

"I am helping you." I would like to say that at this point, I untangled my hand from his, but truth be told, I didn't even try. There was something about holding hands with a good-looking guy on a summer Sunday afternoon that appealed to my romanticist heart. "I found out Charmaine didn't kill Brody."

He wrinkled his nose. "Of course Charmaine didn't kill Brody. Did you think she did?"

"I thought . . ." It didn't seem like the best place to try to explain, what with all the people gathered nearby. The program was aimed at kids, and there were two dozen or so of them milling around, their parents urging them up to the gazebo where they could better see the display set up there. From where I stood, I caught sight of a couple of animals (the dead and stuffed kind) on a table. I suspected they were real—or at least they once had been—their bodies found in the park and preserved for educational purposes. A poster of animal footprints hung next to a map of the park. "It doesn't matter what I thought," I told Max. "What matters is that I am helping. Or at least I'm trying to help you figure out who killed Brody."

"You're not supposed to be. You're a civilian. And that's not what I'm talking about." Was that a sheen of sweat on his top lip? It didn't seem possible. Max was calm and self-assured. Like all athletes, he was comfortable in his own skin, and had enough of an ego to carry off pretty much anything. "It's . . ." His eyes were wide when he looked at the kids clambering around the display at the gazebo. His face was a little green. "This."

I looked around, too, and realized something I hadn't before. "You're the only ranger here."

"Stacy Gilstrap, our nature educator, was supposed to do the program. She came down with shingles yesterday."

I winced for the obvious reason. And again when the not-so-obvious reason hit. "But you said you don't know anything about nature!"

"I was the only one available to step in. Which is why I'm asking for help."

"But I don't know—"

He didn't give me time for more of an objection. Hanging on tight to my hand, Max marched over to the gazebo, and I had no choice but to go right along with him. Brynn and Micah were sitting right up front and before I got tugged up the steps, I handed Micah Violet's leash and the bottle of water and collapsible silicone bowl I'd brought along for her, asked him to please take care of her, and totally ignored the look on his mother's face, which clearly said something in the way of *OMG, he's holding your hand!!!*

Together, Max and I climbed the stairs, and while he stood there scraping his palms against the legs of his pants, I had a chance to check out the display.

A racoon. A beaver. A heron. A hawk. Not just one fox but two.

Something told me his job today was to introduce the kids to wildlife in the park.

Not such a daunting task as far as I was concerned, since I was used to introducing guest speakers when we had programs at the shop. Ten people, twenty, fifty, it didn't really matter to me. Talking in front of a crowd gave me a chance to spread the word about romance novels. And there was nothing I liked more.

Something told me Max did not share in my enthusiasm. Oh no, not for romance novels but for speaking in front of a crowd. There was panic in his eyes. There was a tremor in his hand. No wonder Max Alverez, Major League catcher who'd had a Hall of Fame career ahead of him, had never tried to be a baseball commentator after he was forced to quit the game. Max was terrified of speaking in public.

I couldn't stand to watch him suffer, so I decided to hurry things along. I gave him a poke in the ribs with my elbow.

Max flinched. "Hey." He may be an also-ran when it comes to nature studies, but Max is a commanding presence. He's big. He's good-looking. And let's face it, the whole Smokey Bear–hat thing has a certain panache. The minute he opened his mouth, the kids in the audience shut up. Their mothers, not so much. I heard more than a couple of appreciative sighs from around the gazebo.

"We're . . . uh . . . gonna . . ." Max looked at the crowd of small, eager faces around him. "Today we're gonna . . ."

"Bottom of the ninth." I turned my back to the crowd and spoke quietly so only he could hear me. "Two outs and the pitcher on the mound is the best closer in the league. He's smoking them past your teammates, batter after batter. You've already swung at one curve and missed by a mile. Now, what are you going to do?"

"I can't whack one of these taxidermied foxes with a bat."

He had a point.

I pasted on a smile and spun to face the crowd. "Good afternoon," I called out, and automatically, a dozen little voices echoed my greeting. "I'm here today to find out more about the animals in the park. How about you?" I pointed to a little girl in the front row who nodded enthusiastically. "And you?" This time, I poked my finger toward a little boy. "I don't know very much about the park," I told them all. "That's why I wanted to come here today and see what Ranger Max has to tell us. So, Ranger Max . . ." I settled a hand on the stuffed beaver. "Who's this furry guy?"

Fortunately, someone was smart enough to provide Max with a cheat sheet for each animal. He glanced at the one taped on the table near the beaver and opened his mouth. Nothing came out of it.

The stuffed critter was perched on a wooden platform and I raised it into the air. "Who knows what this is?" I called out.

"A raccoon," one little boy said.

"A possum," a girl replied.

"I know, I know." Micah waved like mad. "It's a beaver."

"It is a beaver. And when Ranger Max finishes his talk today, I want you to come up here and take a close look at this beaver. Look at his webbed feet." I pointed them out and yes, I checked out the cheat sheet, too. Just to be sure I wasn't giving out wrong information. "Beavers are really good swimmers. And their fur?" I ran my hand along the animal's body. "It's waterproof. Did you know that?"

I got a whole lot of head shakes in response.

"And look at his tail!" This, too, I showed off as much as I was able. "See how flat it is? That's because a beaver uses his tail to help him swim. Do you know where you can see beavers?"

The children were small, but they were smart. "At the park!" a bunch of them called out, and I gave them the thumbs-up before I turned to Max.

"What can you tell us about these two foxes?" I asked him.

He looked down at the cheat sheet. "Foxes . . . um, foxes live all over the park. In grasslands and woodlands."

One of the stuffed foxes was vibrant red, like the kind I'd seen around town a time or two. I held him up for the kids to see.

"They . . . uh . . ." Max cleared his throat. "Foxes eat . . . uh . . . they eat insects, vegetables, fruit, and small mammals."

We got the expected chorus of "eeews" in response.

"And they have very bushy tails."

To show them, I ran my hand along the red fox's luxurious tail.

"And that's . . . um . . . that's it about foxes," Max told the crowd.

"Except for this guy." I grabbed the second fox. This one looked exactly like the one in the picture I'd seen at Penny's office, and I held it up for all to see. "Tell us about this one, Ranger Max."

"That one . . . uh . . ." Max peered down at the info sheet on the table. "That's a kit fox, and it says here . . ." He looked up at his audience and had the nerve to blush. Yeah, as if even the kids couldn't tell he was working from crib notes. "This fox is here to show you that there are different kinds of foxes in different parts of the country. This one has large ears."

"See?" I pointed.

"And a gray coat with rusty undertones and a black tip on its tail."

I lifted the fox's tail and waggled it.

"And it's called a kit fox," Max told us. "This one . . . um . . . this animal doesn't live in the park. It doesn't live anywhere east of Colorado."

"No, that can't be right." I put down the stuffed fox so I could look over the notes Max was reading.

"Large ears, gray coat, rusty undertones . . ." Quickly, I read through the list, mumbling under my breath. "Not found east of Colorado." My head came up and I looked at Max. "Not found east of Colorado?"

"That's what it says."

"But Penny—" I remembered we were in public, and that we were surrounded by the good citizens of Tinker's Creek, and I clamped my mouth shut.

"What about Penny?" Max wanted to know.

"Later," I told him out of the corner of my mouth. "Not here. Not now."

I'm actually not sure how we managed to finish the program, and in record time, too. I suppose I kept up my end of the bargain and helped out Max as much as I could, jabbering away and asking questions and trying to keep the kids interested, but honestly, my head was spinning with ideas, my brain packed with questions. Why had Penny lied? She'd clearly told me she took that photograph of the kit fox in her backyard.

"What do you suppose it means?" The program was over, and since Brynn and Micah volunteered to take Violet home for me, I was helping Max clean up. We'd already loaded the stuffed beaver and the heron and the hawk into the back of his Jeep, and when we got back to the gazebo, I picked up the kit fox and gave it a careful look. "Why would Penny tell me she took the picture of the kit fox in her backyard when there's no way she could have?"

"I saw a kit fox at the Grand Canyon. At least that's what the ranger I was with told me the critter was. But maybe that picture Penny has, maybe it's not a picture of a kit fox."

Max hoisted the red fox under one arm and grabbed the kit and tucked it under his other arm. "All these animals look alike."

I laughed. "Beavers don't look like hawks, and kit foxes . . . I mean, look at this one." When we walked over to the Jeep and he set it down, I rubbed my hand over the stuffed animal's ears. "Large ears. And that black spot on its tail. I know this is the same kind of fox in that picture Penny has."

We went back to the gazebo and rolled up the posters he'd brought along. "It could mean a million things," Max said. "Penny likes foxes." One of his eyebrows slanted up. "Maybe enough to wear a phony fox tail. Or someone gave her the picture you saw in her office and she likes to show off so she pretended she took it. Or—" He stopped what he was doing. His dark brows formed a *V* over his eyes. "Penny was out west at some point."

"Yeah, just like Brody was."

"She told me she never met him until he moved here."

"She claims she saw that fox in her backyard, too."

I grabbed the park map, and Max took the poster of the animal footprints and perched it on his shoulder. Yeah, like a baseball bat.

"I'll do some digging," he promised. "Maybe there's more to Penny than we think there is. And now . . ." He swept an arm toward the front seat of the Jeep. "Ride?" When I hesitated, he laughed. "Hey, it's the least I can do for you. You saved my hide back there."

"I helped."

His grin was friendly enough, but there was a sizzle that went along with it that made my temperature soar and my arm tingle. "You did. And I'm grateful. Come on, hop in."

As much as I tried to come up with an excuse to do anything but, I fell flat. It wasn't until after I got in the Jeep that
he said, "I need to stop at the library. We borrowed that
animal footprint poster from them. Then"—he backed out
of his parking space and drove in the direction of the
library—"I'd like to take you to lunch. To thank you."

It had all been going so well. Park animals. Murder. I'd
been able to hold my own. I hated the thought of spoiling
things when it came to making small talk over meals.

"I don't really do lunch," I told him.

"You don't eat?"

"I don't . . . uh . . ." I sounded so much like Max had
when faced with that sea of small faces, we both laughed. I
slid him a look. "I guess you get it, don't you? You understand about being nervous."

"Oh yeah." He cruised into the library parking lot and
stopped right in front of the main door instead of in a parking space, then turned in his seat to face me. "But here's the
thing: You never have to be nervous around me."

"I don't?"

"Well, no." He leaned a little nearer. "See, a lot of guys
who ask you out, I'm betting they're pretty shallow."

"Ha! I'm sure that's what they say about me when they
find out I can't string two sentences together."

"Don't you get it? All they care about is how pretty you
are, how successful you are. They don't bother to try and
find out how smart you are. So they totally blow it when it
comes to interesting conversation. Me, I've got to tell you,
I'm way ahead of the pack. Because sure, I've noticed the
pretty. And yes, I've seen that you're successful. But I know
how smart you are, too. That means you don't have to prove
anything to me."

He'd taken off the Smokey Bear hat when we got in the Jeep, so I couldn't blame the pitter-pat inside my ribs on the dashing chapeau. It was his eyes, I decided right then and there. Rich, deep brown, like chocolate.

And oh, how I loved chocolate!

"What do you say?" he wanted to know. "Lunch?"

I rubbed my arm. "As soon as you're done with Meghan?"

"As soon as I'm done with Meghan."

"Then let's get going." I hopped out of the car. "Except..." I pulled up short. "I thought the library was closed on Sundays this time of year."

He slid out from behind the steering wheel and rounded the Jeep. "It is. But Meghan said she'd be here working in her office all afternoon."

We walked up to the front door.

"I think she did it," I told him.

He brushed a hand through his hair at the same time he slid me a look. "And I think what I've thought all along—that you shouldn't worry about it. But I've got to admit"—his sigh spoke volumes—"I've been thinking the same thing. All we need is some evidence that points to her."

His comment brought me up short. "There really isn't a lot of evidence, anyway, is there? I mean, evidence that points to anyone specifically. If we could find the murder weapon . . ."

"Or trap one of our suspects in a lie . . ."

"Or get one of them to confess." Convinced by the brilliance of my idea, I sidled up to him when he rapped on the glass of the main door of the library. "Maybe we can trap Meghan into admitting she killed Brody."

"Yeah." He tapped on the glass, louder and longer. "But first we have to be able to talk to her. She told me . . ." He pulled out his phone and dialed a number. "When I picked up the poster this morning, she told me she'd for sure be here this afternoon."

"You don't suppose she ran off, do you? Because she knew you were closing in?"

"I don't know. But she's not answering. I'd better check it out. You stay here," he told me before he headed around to the side of the building. Naturally, I followed along.

He didn't turn around. "I told you to stay put."

"That's Meghan's car," I told him with a look at the sturdy beige sedan in the Lilliputian employee parking area. "And I want to know what's going on."

"I'm just going to look . . ." He put his hands to both sides of his face and pressed his nose to the nearest window, but since I'm not as tall as he is, I couldn't see what he saw. "There's a book cart turned over. Books everywhere."

A funny spurt soured my stomach. "No way Meghan would put up with that sort of messiness. Not in her library."

Together, we looked toward the employee entrance, and Max held out one arm to stop me from going any farther.

"The door's open," he said.

Yes, I could see that. The door with the sign on it that said **EMPLOYEES ONLY** stood ajar, the AC pouring out of it into the sultry afternoon air.

Max closed in on it. "Now will you listen to me when I tell you to stay put?" he asked.

"Probably not." I followed right along. "You might need help."

"I need you to call the police." He looked at me over his shoulder. "You tell them what's going on while I go inside."

I did and it didn't take very long. That meant I stepped into the building right behind Max.

That room where I'd seen Meghan sorting books just a couple of days before was over on our right. Her office was on the left. It would have been easier to walk into it if there wasn't debris scattered everywhere. Books, papers, her monitor and computer.

And Meghan in the center of it all, facedown on the floor, the back of her head covered with blood.

Chapter 17

S he's pretty woozy." Josh, Max, and I stood near the library door, watching Meghan get loaded into an ambulance, and since Josh had just talked to the EMS techs, he gave us an update. "She wasn't making a whole lot of sense. But from what I could make out, she didn't see anything. Someone came at her from behind."

I remembered what Max had said about the overturned book cart. "Yeah, out in the library. She must have run and—"

"They caught up to her in her office." Max shook his head with disgust. "If she didn't see anything, did she say she heard anything that might help us identify her assailant? A voice, maybe?"

"Like I said . . ." The EMS crew gave Josh the signal that they were taking off, heading to the hospital with Meghan, and he stepped toward his patrol car. Max zipped over to his Jeep, fished his wallet out from under the front seat, and joined my cousin.

"I didn't get a whole lot out of her," Josh said. "Not anything that wasn't jumbled, anyway. She's hurt and she's scared. We'll wait for her to come around. Then maybe she can tell us something more helpful."

I knew they had to go, but there was so much I didn't understand! I followed Josh and Max to the patrol car.

"This means she didn't do it, doesn't it?" I asked them.

Max had his fists on his hips, and he scanned the area where another one of our local cops was searching for evidence. "If you're talking about Brody's murder, it doesn't look like it," he said. "Unless there's some reason other than the murder that someone might have attacked Meghan."

"She could be annoying," I told him. "That's no big surprise, but annoying isn't enough to attack someone. Unless . . ." I sucked in a breath. "She admitted she was at the ranch on the night Brody was killed. What if—"

"She saw something and someone doesn't want her to talk." Max was quick on the uptake.

So was I. "Or someone thinks she saw something and doesn't want her to talk."

"Another thing we need to go over with her." Josh was already behind the wheel, so Max got into the front passenger seat of the patrol car. When he rolled down the window, I leaned inside.

"What do you want me to do?" I asked him.

Josh and Max exchanged looks, and my cousin was the one who answered. "Well, we should notify someone about what happened, but I can't think of one person. How about you, Lizzie? You know anyone we should call?"

"You mean, like, for Meghan? To let them know what

happened to her?" It was a perfectly normal request, so I don't know why it struck me as odd. Except . . .

"She really doesn't have anyone, does she?" I asked them, and myself. "I suppose the people here at work would want to know what's going on. And maybe the members of that Shakespeare group she told me she was with early on the night of the murder. But as for nearest and dearest . . ." I raised my hands and gave an exaggerated shrug. "If there is someone, no one knows about it, because if they did—"

"My mom would know." Josh chuckled. "And then everyone in town would know."

When he started the car, I backed away.

"Think about it," Max called out. "Call me if you come up with anything."

I did think about it. I sat on the bench in front of the main door of the library and watched the crime scene techs bustle in and out of the building where they were dusting for prints, and I thought about Meghan and realized I knew pretty much nothing about her at all.

She worshiped literature.

She hated genre fiction.

She was crazy about Brody.

Okay, sure, I knew all that. But what I mean is that I knew nothing about her as a person. Sure, she was neat. She was tidy. She was a stickler when it came to everything from arranging books on the library shelves to keeping that umbrella of hers handy at all times. But what was going on underneath all that? In Meghan's head? In her personal life?

Wondering if her office might reveal anything—vacation pictures, a phone number tacked to a bulletin board—I went around to the back of the building and ducked inside.

I didn't touch anything that had been tossed onto the

floor. Honest! I knew better than that. Instead, I looked around at what hadn't been disturbed and was left feeling chilled.

There were no personal mementos, silly things like stuffed animals or shells picked up on a beach.

No personal photographs. Not a one.

Maybe regimented, uptight, sweater-wearing Meghan kept her personal life out of sight.

Or maybe she just didn't have one.

The thought in mind, I bent my head to listen for a moment, and sure the crime scene techs were still busy out front, I opened Meghan's top desk drawer.

Personal life out of sight?

I'll say.

My eyes popped, my lips puckered. I knew better than to touch anything so I closed the drawer, grabbed my phone, and scrambled out of Meghan's office and into the room where I'd found her processing books only a few days earlier.

Max picked up on the first ring. "What's up?"

"I found something else you need to talk to Meghan about," I told him. "There's a plastic hair band in the top drawer of her desk. And I know that doesn't sound very interesting at all except, Max, there are two red fox ears attached to it."

I hadn't been invited.

Heck, I was pretty sure I wouldn't even have been allowed into Meghan's hospital room if I hadn't brought coffee and sandwiches.

Waiting for the heave-ho, I toed the line between the corridor and the room, glancing from Josh to Max where

they sat, one on either side of her bed, and waited for her to
open her eyes and recover her strength.

One look at the bag in my hands, one sniff of the delicious aroma of coffee, and Josh's eyes lit. He waved me in
and took a ham and Swiss cheese out of my hands before
he stood and stretched. "You two will be all right in here
for a couple of minutes?" he asked, and when Max assured
him we would be, he went out into the hallway.

Max unwrapped a roast beef with horseradish sauce on
a pretzel bun but he didn't take a bite, not until he pinned
me with a look. "You put it right back where you found it,
didn't you?"

Automatically, my right hand shot up, Boy Scout–style.
"I never touched it. All I did was look."

"And it matches—"

"That tail that you found at the ranch? It sure looks like
it does."

He looked at Meghan, her head swathed in bandages,
her face as pale as the sheets. There were dark smudges
under her eyes, her left cheek was swollen, a bandage
dabbed with blood covering a wound there. When she went
down, she must have hit hard and landed on something
sharp.

"Is she going to be okay?" I asked Max.

"That's what the doc says. Head wounds bleed a lot, so
her injuries looked worse than they really are. They shaved
the back of her head, cleaned everything up, did some
stitching. She's on a whole bunch of meds, naturally, but
I'm hoping when she comes around—"

On cue, Meghan moaned.

Max rolled his sandwich in the paper it had come in and
handed it back to me before he nudged his chair closer to
the bed. "Ms. Watkins?" His voice was gentle enough to

soothe, but there was a ring of authority in it. "Ms. Watkins, it's me, Ranger Alverez."

Her eyes fluttered open. "What happened?"

"Do you remember?" he asked her. "Anything?"

She winced. "I heard a noise. Left my office. There was someone behind me."

"Did you see who?"

She shook her head, winced.

"Did they say anything?" Max wanted to know.

Another shake of her head before she asked, "Water?"

We raised the head of her bed and helped her sit up, and as long as I was there feeling like the third wheel I was, I held a glass of water to her lips.

Meghan closed her eyes and sighed, and when she opened her eyes again she looked more awake, more aware. "Why would someone want to hurt me?"

Since she'd directed the question at me, I felt justified in answering. "We think it might be because you were at the ranch the night Brody was killed."

"The ranch!" She moaned, the sound like a banshee wail. "I was at the ranch, and—"

"Why?" Max wanted to know. "You told Lizzie that Brody invited you there. Now you tell me the truth. What were you doing there, Ms. Watkins? And why were you wearing a fox tail and ears?"

As pale as she'd been only minutes before, Meghan flushed as red as a lobster now. She turned her head away from Max only to find herself looking at me. A tear slipped down her cheek. "You wouldn't understand," she said.

"Try us." I slipped into the chair Josh had vacated. "I'm finding it a little hard to believe you wear a tail and ears when you're talking Shakespeare."

The tears came faster now. "I can't tell . . . You won't

understand . . ." She carefully turned her head to look at Max. "You can't let anyone know."

"If it's not pertinent to the investigation," he told her, "it stays right here in this room with us."

She looked my way. "Even you? If that aunt of yours—"

"Meghan." I put a hand on hers where it lay on top of the sheet. "All we want to do is find out what happened to Brody. That's what you want, too, right? The details are none of Charmaine's business."

She nodded, but she didn't talk. Not right away, anyway. Not until she'd thought about all of this long and hard. It wasn't until she asked for and got another sip of water that she cleared her throat and mumbled something neither of us could hear clearly.

"What's that?" I bent closer. "Something about fur?"

"Not . . . not fur." She looked up at the ceiling and kept her gaze there, not daring to meet our eyes. "Furries."

I opened my mouth to say something. I'm not exactly sure what. I snapped my mouth shut again. It wasn't until I saw Max looking totally confused that I tried again.

"I'm no expert." I felt it was important to make that clear right up front. "But there are some romance books, urban fantasy mostly, about werewolves and shapeshifters and such, and some of the people who read those . . ."

Max cocked his head, ready to hear more.

I scrambled to make sense of it all, and since Meghan's lips were clamped shut, it looked like I was the only one who could.

"Some of the people who read those books have talked about the furry community. They dress up. In animal costumes. It's like cosplay, you know? Animals who act like humans. They have names and identities."

"Fursonalities," Meghan mumbled.

"Fursonalities," I echoed. "And they get together and have conventions, fur cons they call them. And—" A thought hit, and I sat up and gave Meghan a penetrating look. "You weren't talking about Shakespeare that night, were you? You were at a furmeet!"

"Yes." Tears gushed over her cheeks. "I never go to Shakespeare discussions. It's the furries. I'm always with the furries. Now you know. My guiltiest secret."

If I hadn't been looking directly across the bed at Max, I wouldn't have seen the way he struggled to control a smile. "So, Ms. Watkins, what is your fursonality?" he asked her.

"I'm Faithlynn the Frippety Fox. Only I've never been comfortable in a full costume, not like some of the fursuiters."

"Which explains the tail and ears." I swear, now that he had Meghan talking, the last thing Max was thinking about was lunch, but he waved for his sandwich anyway. I tossed it to him and he took a great big bite. At least when he was busy chewing, he couldn't burst into laughter.

Me, not so much. I was trying to work my way through what must have happened. "You left the furmeet still wearing your ears and tail. Is that when Brody called you to come over?"

She closed her eyes. She gulped. "Brody . . ." When she opened her eyes they were sad, vacant. "He never called me. Not that night. Not any other night. Brody Pierce didn't even know I was alive."

"I'm sorry." It was the only thing I could think to say to a woman who was so clearly heartbroken. "That means when you went over to Brody's—"

"I was watching him, yes. Spying on him." Her gaze shot to Max. "Are you . . . are you going to arrest me?"

Since he was chewing a bite of sandwich, he shook his head before he swallowed and said, "That depends on what else you're going to tell me."

"I sometimes watched him." Meghan's hands shook. So did her voice. "When he came into town and people started talking. You know, the way they always did when Brody was around. They'd come into the library and they'd say, 'Brody Pierce is over at Ken's getting lunch.' Or 'Brody's here again. Looks like he's stocking up on groceries.' And I'd . . ." She ran her tongue over her lips. "I'm not especially proud of it. But when I heard people talking like that, I'd find an excuse to leave the library. I'd go to where they said Brody was. Just to see him. Just so I could say hello and we could exchange some small talk." When she looked my way, her eyes were pleading. "You know?"

I didn't have the heart to tell her I didn't, and what difference would it have made anyway? Instead, I said, "So you were the one in my garden the night Brody came to see Charmaine!"

Meghan's face clouded with confusion. Her brows dropped low over her eyes. "At your place? No. When?"

"The night he was killed." Max didn't know this, either, so I looked at him across the bed. "About ten o'clock. I was out, and when I came home, there was someone in the garden. I couldn't see well," I added because I knew he was about to ask why I'd never mentioned it. "I didn't think it mattered. Are you sure"—I turned Meghan's way—"it wasn't you?"

"At ten o'clock I was just leaving the furmeet in Cleveland. There was an accident on the freeway. Traffic was slow. It took more than an hour for me to get back to town. That's when . . ." Her words were smothered by a strangled sob. "I stopped at the ranch to try and see him. Just to . . ." She picked at the sheets with nervous fingers. "Just to watch him for a while. It was late, so I thought he'd be at the house. I parked by the barn and planned to walk up to the house. Just to, you know—"

"Look in his windows?" Yes, my voice was a little tight. Then again, the whole concept of Meghan as a voyeur made my stomach swoop.

"I just thought . . ." If nothing else, she must have known there was no use even trying to explain. Meghan cleared the tears from her voice with a cough. "The barn door was open and I thought that was odd. It was late. The bison are usually in by that hour."

"You'd been there before." It went without saying, but I knew Max had to get all the details straight.

"Yes," Meghan admitted. "Not to do anything," she was quick to add. "I just wanted to . . . just wanted to see him. To watch him. To go to bed that night feeling like I knew something about his day. That I was somehow a part of it. Only that night—" She thrashed under the blankets. "I parked and I looked in the barn and—"

I could imagine what she was going to say, but before I could open my mouth, Max stopped me by putting up one hand. He had to hear it from Meghan.

"There he was." Her voice was flat. "He was on his back and his eyes were open. And there was blood." Meghan burst into tears. "So much blood!"

"You ran."

She looked at me when I said it. "I didn't know what else to do. I was so upset. So terrified. I went home and I crawled under a blanket and I stayed there until—"

"You called into work sick the next day." I remembered what Ernest had told me, how Meghan wasn't at the library to make sure he got all the books he'd ordered. "You were too upset to go to the library."

"And I've wanted to help ever since. I have, Ranger. Only I didn't think there was anything I could do. And then when I heard you found my fox tail, I thought for sure you'd think I did it. But I didn't. I swear, I didn't kill Brody. I could never harm a hair on that man's head. I loved him."

"We would have had a better idea of the time he died if you'd have let us know what really happened before now," Max said. "It might have narrowed down our field of suspects."

"Field of suspects?" The last thing I expected out of her was a laugh. "I can't believe you haven't figured it out yet."

"Have you?" he wanted to know. "Did you see someone that night at the ranch?"

"I didn't have to see anyone. Just like I didn't have to see anyone today to know who came after me to try and keep me quiet." She looked from Max to me, then back to Max. "It was Penny. It had to be."

Chapter 18

We were back at the library, me and Max. He, because he wanted to take a careful look around Meghan's office and, while he was at it, check out those fox ears that backed up that crazy story from Meghan. Furries. Fox tails. Furmeets.

Me, because he claimed if he didn't keep an eye on me, I was going to get into some kind of trouble. Just for the record, I did not agree with this, but since he said it had been a long day and he really wasn't in the mood for an argument, I didn't want to give him a hard time.

I'd had a long day, too, and I regretted not getting myself a sandwich when I got them for Josh and Max. My stomach rumbled. My head pounded. Since Max was bound to tell me to stay out of the way anyway, I left him in Meghan's office doing whatever it is cops do when they're investigating and went into the room across the hallway.

I plunked down in a chair near a table piled with books

and file folders and fought to put my thoughts in some kind of order.

It was no use. As far as I could tell, all we'd proved that day was that it looked like Meghan didn't kill Brody, and yeah, that was good to know, but it still didn't tell us who the murderer was.

"Do you really think it was Penny?" Since Max was across the hall, I called out my question nice and loud.

"Do you?" he called back. "Meghan didn't have any proof to back up her accusation."

She didn't. "It's like Elizabeth Bennet and Caroline Bingley," I grumbled, and the next thing I knew, Max stuck his head into the room.

"What? Don't tell me there are two other women in town who dated Brody and I didn't even know about them."

He was so serious, I couldn't help but laugh. "*Pride and Prejudice.*"

Blank look from Max.

"It's a novel."

More of the same from Max.

"By Jane Austen."

No glimmer of realization in his eyes.

It was sad, and I sighed. "In the book, Elizabeth and Caroline are rivals for Mr. Darcy."

"And he's . . ."

Honestly, was it even possible I could be having a conversation with a man who had no idea who Mr. Darcy was?

I suppose he had an excuse. Max had spent his growing-up years on the baseball diamond and had missed out on all the truly important things in life.

"Fitzwilliam Darcy," I explained, "is the epitome of the classic romance hero. He's handsome. He's aloof. He's wealthy."

"So all the girls are after him."

"Not all. The first time he proposes, Elizabeth turns him down, and that makes him realize he can rub people the wrong way. Like I said, aloof. And I think a little shy, too, but bring that up in a discussion of the book and you'll get a million different opinions. Anyway, Darcy swears he's going to change the way he acts and—" I had to stop myself. Like all right-thinking people everywhere, I could talk about *Pride and Prejudice* for hours. "What I'm saying is that I was just thinking about Elizabeth and Caroline, and wondering if that's what could be going on with Meghan and Penny. Meghan must have known Penny dated Brody. Penny never made any secret of it."

"And that's why Meghan accused Penny. Meghan is jealous."

"Well, of course she's jealous. She was stalking the guy!"

"And you never told me about the person in your garden."

Oh, he was a tricky one. He changed the subject so fast, I didn't have time to come up with any of the excuses I might have concocted otherwise. With no other choice, I opted for the truth.

"I didn't think it mattered. Except, I guess it really might. I mean, if someone was following Brody—someone who wasn't Meghan—that could have been the person I saw, the person who threw down that rake on the path so that I—"

He took a couple steps into the room. "You got hurt?"

"Sore knee. No big deal." To prove it, I flexed my leg. Which he couldn't see since I was sitting, but it did serve to remind me I'd fully recovered from the mishap. "What does matter is that whoever that was, it couldn't have been Meghan. She was busy playing Faithlynn the Fox." Even after having had time to think about her involvement in the furry community, I wasn't sure if I wanted to laugh or shiver. "And after her meetup, Meghan went right to Brody's and found him dead. No, not Meghan. She wasn't the person in my garden."

"But someone was there."

"Maybe the same someone who had that flashlight I saw in the woods, or the binoculars I saw that Josh told me he couldn't find when he went back to look for them. But if it wasn't Meghan . . . It seems weird, doesn't it? That means there must have been two people spying on Brody. Does that even seem possible?"

Thinking about this, he came farther into the room and perched on the table near where I sat. "From what I've heard, Brody was that kind of guy. He attracted attention everywhere he went."

"And he enjoyed every minute of it."

"Some of that might have been good attention. But some of it could have been bad."

"And Meghan did say she believed those accidents Brody was having weren't accidents at all. She believed someone was trying to kill him."

Meghan had repeated the story for Max before we left the hospital, so he knew the details. He thought them over, nodded. "Penny?"

"Or Meghan pointing at Penny because she's jealous of Penny's relationship with Brody."

"Rivals, like Elizabeth and Caroline."

I liked a man who caught on quickly when it came to life, jealousy, and *Pride and Prejudice*. I gave Max the thumbs-up.

"Well, we might know more by tomorrow," he told me. "I've requested a background check on Penny. Maybe there's more to her than we realize."

"Like if she really did take the picture of that kit fox, she might have spent time out west."

"If so, I'd like to know why she kept it a secret."

"And I'd like to know . . ." I slapped a hand onto the book on top of the pile in front of me. "I'd like to know everything." My spirits flagged along with my shoulders, and when they did, my hand fell to my side and that book on top of the pile slid and fell onto my lap.

Brody's high school yearbook.

It was the first time I gave the stuff stacked on the table a close look. "These are the things Meghan looked through when she was making up that display about Brody," I told Max. "What are the chances there might be something in here that would help us figure out what's going on?"

"Slim to none."

"You a gambler?"

"Absolutely not."

"You want to try anyway?"

He came around the table and sat down next to me. "Give me one of those folders."

In the romantic suspense novels I read and love, even the canny heroines often take hundreds of pages to glom on to a clue of any real significance.

That, I was sure, was why I was flabbergasted when just a few minutes after I started to page through Brody's high school yearbook I found myself looking at the picture of the Drama Club. This in and of itself was not especially significant, and I would have zipped right by if not for the words printed under the group shot.

"'Love isn't Love 'less the person you Love Loves Love

like you Love Love.'" I grabbed hold of the sleeve of Max's shirt. "Did you hear me?"

He glanced at the yearbook. "It's Brody's Drama Club, and that's got you spouting off about love?"

"It's not me talking about love." I rolled my eyes because, yes, he deserved it. "It's what's written here. It's the same thing Brody wrote on that card that I thought was meant for Charmaine."

"Really?" He reached for the book and I handed it over, and Max read the caption under the club picture. "'Love isn't Love 'less the person you Love Loves Love like you Love Love and Loves you like you Love, like the person you Love Loves Love.'"

He slanted me a look. "That's what you thought was a love letter from Brody to Charmaine?" He rubbed a finger behind his ear. "It's pretty lame when it comes to the love letter department."

That card and the message in it had been the cornerstone of the suspicions about Charmaine that had rocked my world and threatened to destroy my trust in my aunt. Yes, I was thrilled it had all been a colossal mistake, but that didn't mean I appreciated having my investigative thought processes questioned.

I yanked the yearbook out of Max's hands. "Oh, and what, you're an expert at love letters?"

His eyes glinted. Deep chocolate. Flecked with fire. We were talking motives and murder, but he was smiling. "Maybe."

My mouth went dry. Which totally explained why my tongue stuck to the roof of my mouth.

"Maybe I'm like one of those poets, you know?" His smile inched up a notch. "Maybe I'm the guy who wrote,

'It's *corny* but I'd sure like to *ear* you say you'll be my Valentine.'"

He was kidding.

And I was so relieved when he laughed, I let go a breath I hadn't realized I'd been holding.

"All right then, Mr. Poet," I said, "tell me this. If you're right, if it's lousy poetry and worse when it comes to love letters, why would Brody try so hard to get it right that he needed Charmaine's help to remember the words? Why would he want to write it in a card to somebody?"

He thought about this. "I guess it depends on who that somebody is," he said, and again, he took the book out of my hands.

"There's Brody." He pointed to the handsome young man standing in the front row of the group shot. Even then, Brody had a presence. He was tall, with wide shoulders and a grin I bet knocked girls off their feet. Max skimmed his finger from face to face. "There's Ernest in the back row. This one"—he tapped a finger against the face of one of the girls in the group—"looks too old for high school. Oh." He read the caption beneath the picture. "'Miss Helen Podgorny, English teacher and club moderator.'"

Miss Podgorny sat front and center, a chunky woman with wire-rimmed glasses and graying hair stiff with hair spray. She had one of those faces it was hard to put an age to, wrinkle-free but with crow's feet around her eyes that said she'd seen a thing or two. Fifty, maybe? She probably seemed as ancient to the kids then as she would be now if she was still alive.

"So why . . ." I wrinkled my nose and studied the black-and-white photo and those words written beneath it. "Why would Brody write that crazy thing about love in a card?"

He thought this over. "Maybe because that saying, or poem, or whatever it is, maybe because it would mean something to the person he sent it to."

"Exactly." I don't know why I felt stabbing my finger to the picture of the Drama Club would help, but I did it anyway. "I'd bet anything that card was meant for one of these people."

He scanned the group of kids. "Which one?"

I'd been sold on the idea, so having him bring me back down to earth with logic and reasoning didn't sit well with me. "How do I know which one? Maybe . . ." I looked at the caption beneath the photo, noted the names, then flipped the pages of the yearbook to find each student's personal picture and the information underneath each one. "Maybe one of them will say something, something that will give us some sort of clue."

No dice.

At least not until I got through each and every club member and was left only with Brody. I turned to his picture and read the information beneath it. "'Football team, four years. Homecoming king. After graduation, Juilliard in the fall, then on to Broadway!'"

Max interrupted me. "I've read over the background materials on Brody. He never went to Juilliard."

"Maybe not, but maybe that's not what's important. Listen to the rest of this. I kept reading, "'Thank you, Miss P, Love isn't Love 'less the person you Love . . .'"

I snapped the book closed but kept my finger in it to mark the page. "Helen Podgorny? That middle-aged Drama Club moderator? You think Brody was carrying on with her?"

"Think any of those other people in the picture might know?"

I hopped up and went to the copy machine to make two copies of the Drama Club picture, one for me, one for Max.

We had phone calls to make.

Fortunately, though, Max is reasonable when it comes to meal times. It was late afternoon and he was ready to eat. I hadn't had a thing since that bacon-and-egg sandwich from Ken's long before noon.

Before we got down to business, we went to Nick's, picked up a pizza, and went back to my place.

Violet was thrilled to see Max, and when he offered to walk her before we ate, I took him up on it. My place is a former carriage house and not large, but it is big enough to acquire a little dust and a lot of clutter when I'm busy with the bookstore. I am not fussy. And I'm sure not meticulous. But I can be self-conscious when it comes to my house. By the time Max and Violet returned, I had the table in the dining room set, my downstairs TBR pile (there was another one next to my bed up in the loft) arranged, and the dust—at least most of it—dealt with.

We dished up slices of Italian sausage and banana pepper and talked strategy.

"For starters"—Max took a bite of pizza and chewed—"take a look at these names and tell me if there's anyone you know who's still around town."

The guys were easy. "Ernest, of course," I told him. "And that's Al Little from the hardware store. Been in his family for years. Him, him, him . . ." My finger drifted over the young faces. "All dead now, unfortunately. I remember Charmaine talking about it. How tragic it was that three guys from the same class died so young."

"And the girls?"

They, of course, were a little tougher. Last names change, and the faces . . . I picked up the copied photograph and peered at it so intently, I got pizza sauce on it. "That's Callie Porter, but you've already talked to her."

"Yeah, but I didn't talk to her about Helen Podgorny and Love, Love, Love."

Too bad I was taking a sip of iced tea when he made me laugh. I choked, pounded my chest, held up a hand to let Max know I was all right when he looked concerned. "We're going to need to talk to everyone we can get a hold of. If you want to stay in here when we're done, I can make calls from out in the garden. The house isn't very big. Hard for two people to hear when they're both talking at the same time."

He let his gaze wander the room. When I bought the property, the carriage house wasn't just in disrepair, it was falling down. The good news was because of that, I wasn't constrained by what was here and what had to be kept. The basic bones of the building stayed, and I kept one entire wall of exposed brick. The rest of the inside was brand spanking new, from the whitewashed wood walls to the double-height ceiling and the fireplace that had never existed before.

"It's nice," Max said. "Cozy."

"Cozies are mysteries." He totally didn't get it, and I didn't try to explain. "It's just right for one person." Though she'd been lounging in the living room, Violet picked that exact moment to pick up her head and woof. "One person and one dog!" I corrected myself.

We finished the pizza, and Max helped me take the dishes into my tiny kitchen, with its cream-colored cabinets and sage-green walls. He rinsed and I set the dishes in the dishwasher, and when we were done, he sat down in the living room to start making calls, and I went to the garden to do the same.

"Fifteen girls in the Drama Club," I told him nearly two hours later when we were all done and we reconvened in the living room, this time with a bottle of wine open on the table in front of the couch, "and nine of them live out of town. I talked to most of them, told them I was doing a retrospective piece for the local newspaper about the high school. Asked about the Drama Club and heard nothing but what a great experience it was. I even asked if there were any scandals, any gossip that would add color to my article, but they're either good at keeping secrets or they didn't know a thing. Four of the girls"—my finger floated over the picture, poking one, two, three, four faces—"they haven't been heard from since they graduated, and no one has any idea what happened to them. I did talk to Jennifer Manz." I pointed out the tall, thin girl with straw-colored hair in the second row. "She says she has no memory of ever being in the Drama Club, and from what I've heard about her and what a party girl she was, my guess is she's telling the truth. The last one was Callie, and when I told her we were just trying to get some facts straight, just wondering if there was any chance there might have ever been anything between Brody and Helen Podgorny . . ." Remembering how Callie had gone up like a rocket, I whistled low under my breath. "I won't repeat what she said. Let's just settle for the fact that 'how dare you besmirch Brody's stellar reputation and how could you ever even think of something so incredibly stupid and maybe you should be locked up because you're obviously out of your mind.'"

Grinning, Max poured and handed me a glass of pinot gris. "I had a little more luck. Nine guys in the club. Brody was one, of course, and obviously I couldn't call him. Tried Ernest, no answer, but I can get to him another time. That left seven. Three dead like you mentioned, two more moved away and were never heard from again, and I had no luck locating them. The other two, to a man, swear there was never anything between Helen and Brody. They say Brody was too busy chasing after all the girls his own age to bother with anyone as old as the club moderator."

"Where does that leave us?"

He sipped his wine, nodded his approval, settled back. "We could be really off base about this whole Love, Love, Love thing."

It was a given.

Violet trotted over and sat next to Max, and he ruffled a hand over her red bandanna. "Maybe," he said, "we could—"

"Lizzie!" Charmaine called to me from right outside my door. "Lizzie, are you home?" She opened the door that led from my stone patio, took a look at me on one end of the couch and Max on the other, and stopped cold.

She was a plenty good actress. As if she actually hadn't seen Max's Jeep parked nearby, she let out a surprised "Oh!"

"Oh, what?" I waved her closer at the same time that Violet hurried over to escort her. "Come on in. Have a glass of wine."

She came as far as the couch and stopped, scraping her hands on the legs of her red shorts. "I don't want to intrude."

I bit back the "Yeah, right" so I could say, "Not intruding," as I popped up and got a wineglass for her, then Max poured. "We've just been taking a little walk down memory lane. Calling everyone Brody was in Drama Club with."

She saw the photograph on the table and picked it up to take a better look. "Those were the days! Look at how young everyone looks. Jennifer and Callie and, oh my gosh, look at Helen."

"Helen?" Yeah, Max and I spoke the name at the same time, but I was the first one to ask, "Is she still alive?"

Charmaine's laugh was silvery. "Of course she's still alive, silly. Age is not something she ever talks about, but my guess is she's in her eighties. Or maybe she's ninety by now."

"And she lives near here?" I wanted to know.

"Used to live right in town. Down the street from the church. She'd invite me for tea sometimes, and that was always nice. She had a collection of china cups and teapots and she made the best shortbread cookies. Now"—she set her wineglass on the table—"she's over at Autumn's End. Assisted living," she added for Max's benefit. "Though last time I saw her, poor thing, I thought maybe she wouldn't even be able to stay there much longer, that they'd have to move her over to the side of the building where she can get a little more care."

As my aunt spoke, I felt a tingle like excitement building, and by the time she was done, I was out of my seat and heading for the door. "And she's still there, right? We could stop in? We could talk to her?"

"Not at this time of the evening, honey." Charmaine laughed. "It's happy hour at Autumn's End, and that's followed by the Sunday night classic movie. You want to talk to Helen, you can't do it now. She misses Cary Grant, and she'll never forgive you."

Chapter 19

We couldn't go to Autumn's End first thing the next morning, either.

Monday. Cinnamon rolls for breakfast, served warm and gooey fresh from the on-site bakery.

Apparently, Helen took her cinnamon rolls very seriously.

Then there was lunch, of course. But that was only after a morning of manicures, bingo, and crafts.

It wasn't until three that Charmaine gave us the all clear, and since she said she hadn't seen Helen in a while and it wouldn't hurt for us to have a formal introduction, she came along with us.

The facility was on the very edge of town, a pleasant building with a brick facade and three stories and a balcony or porch outside every room. There was a sparkling fountain out front, and inside, the wide entryway led directly to a dining area where even though they'd already served the meatloaf sandwich, potato chips, and chocolate pudding lunch that was on the day's menu, there were still a few residents milling around, reading, some visiting, some talking to staff.

We signed in and followed Charmaine down a long hallway decorated with reproductions of soothing famous paintings. Monet's *The Artist's Garden at Giverny* was a big favorite.

Even without Charmaine to escort us, I would have easily found Helen's room. Her door was decorated with golden masks, comedy and tragedy. When Charmaine knocked, the volume on the TV got turned down (*Key Largo* if I wasn't mistaken) and a lively voice beckoned us inside.

Helen sat in a recliner, hanging on to her TV remote and peering at us through round wire-rimmed glass. She was still as chunky as she had been in that long-ago yearbook picture, and her face had hardly changed. Her skin was smooth. Her eyes were bright, inquisitive. Her hair was still done up in a beehive, so stiff with hair spray, I wondered if it had moved since the day that yearbook picture was taken. She turned off the movie and hauled herself out of her chair, looking from my aunt to where Max and I waited just inside the door.

Charmaine, not usually known for her patience, kept her place and apparently she knew the drill. She gave Helen a big smile along with, "Hello, Helen. It's me, Charmaine."

The reminder was all Helen needed. She stepped forward and folded Charmaine into a hug, and while the two of them dropped phrases like, "It's been too long," and

"You look so well," and "How are they treating you?" I had a chance to look around.

Helen's room was actually an efficiency apartment. There was a sink, a mini fridge, and a microwave to our right, a bathroom on the left. With clever decorating and furniture arrangement, the rest of the big square room had been divided into two completely different areas—bedroom with a dresser and a chair next to the four-poster, and the living room where Helen and Charmaine chatted. There was a bookcase on a nearby wall, and I couldn't help but scan it. *The Complete Works of Shakespeare. Broadway: The American Musical.* Pretty much the kinds of books I'd expected from a former Drama Club moderator. But there were also books by LaVyrle Spencer, Diana Gabaldon, Georgette Heyer.

I decided I was going to like Helen.

I had to wait to find out for sure until the two longtime buddies caught up, then Charmaine waved us closer and took care of the introductions.

"Sit down." Helen led the way to a table with four chairs near the windows that looked out over the back of the wooded property. "Char, you make coffee. And there are some cinnamon rolls in the cupboard." She gave us a broad wink. "I've got an in with the chef."

We made small talk. After all, it was rude of us to show up and start asking questions. Especially when those questions had to do with Helen and the boy who would become the man who was the icon for tough guys everywhere.

When we were done with the rolls and had settled into sipping our coffee, Max sat back and patted his (plenty flat) belly.

"Dang, those are the best cinnamon rolls I've ever had."

"Told you." Helen gave him a wide smile. "It's so nice to have company to share them with. Only now . . ." Her gaze skimmed Charmaine. It took in Max. It stopped on me. "Tell me what you're doing here. Because something tells me it has nothing to do with my baking skills."

Did she think she'd made the cinnamon rolls?

Rather than ask, rather than point out that she might be the slightest bit confused, I sipped my coffee, set my cup on the table, and folded my hands in my lap.

"We're trying to figure out who did something," I said. "Something very bad."

"I'm old, honey. I am no Banbury cheese." She leaned closer to Charmaine and pointed out, *Merry Wives of Windsor*, act one, scene one."

"Of course you're not." I reminded myself not to forget it even though I wasn't sure what a Banbury cheese was. "I'm sorry. I didn't mean to sound patronizing. We're here to talk about Brody Pierce."

"What a shame!" She shook her head. "Such a nice boy."

"Was he?" How's that for subtle on my part? Way better than me coming right out and asking if they had some sort of illicit relationship. "What do you remember about him?"

"Him. Yes." Helen's gaze wandered the room. "Loved digging in the dirt, that one did. Always said he was going to be an archaeologist."

I glanced at Charmaine for help, but no worries, she had things well in hand.

"That was Ernest, dear." She patted Helen's hand, and that seemed to snap her out of the piece of the past she'd been lost in. "Ernest was Brody's cousin. Ernest teaches. At the community college."

"Always digging around the park." Helen smiled. "Always

in search of that one thing that would make him famous. He knows all about the canal, you know," she told Max.

"I've heard." Max finished his coffee, and since mine was gone, too, Charmaine got up to get more. She poured. "It's Ernest's cousin we're here to talk to you about, Helen. Brody Pierce was murdered."

A single tear slipped down Helen's cheek.

"And we're trying to figure out who killed him," I told her. "We have some questions. About a poem. We think he might have wanted to send it to you and we wondered—"

As if she wasn't closing in on ninety, Helen popped out of her chair, glided to the middle of the room, and held out her arms. She threw back her head and her voice, as clear as crystal, rang through the room. "Love isn't Love 'less the person you Love Loves Love like you Love Love and Loves you like you Love, like the person you Love Loves Love."

Because we weren't sure what else to do, we all applauded. Helen took a bow and, smiling, sat back down.

"That's the poem," I said. "Brody wrote it in a card and—"

"Did he? How lovely."

"We just wondered . . ." Even a seasoned law enforcement officer like Max wasn't sure of the best way to broach the subject. He motioned to Charmaine for the card she'd admitted to us earlier that she'd been carrying around in her purse since Brody's death because she wasn't sure what else to do with it, and when she handed it to Max, he put it on the table in front of Helen.

She touched a gentle hand to the flowers and the cupid on the front of the card, then flipped it open and read over the words quietly.

"Do you think Brody wrote that to you?" I asked her.

"Oh, I should think so. He sent me cards now and then,

you see. Sometimes for my birthday or Christmas. Sometimes for no reason at all. How sweet of him to keep remembering after all these years."

"Remembering"—Max scooted his chair closer to the table—"what?"

"Well, 'Love isn't Love,' of course. It was what we all said. Before every performance. You remember that, don't you, Char?"

"I remember we went through drills, but no," my aunt admitted, "I didn't remember all the words. That's why Brody and I got together to try and figure it out. Now Lizzie tells me it was in the yearbook all this time. All I ever had to do was look."

Helen nodded. "Actors always do it. To loosen their tongues. To get rid of the jitters. Tongue twisters. You know, things like 'jiggle jungle jangle joker.' Or 'rubber baby buggy bumpers'! That's a famous one." Her eyes clouded with memory. "The kids enjoyed that one, 'Love isn't Love.' Oh, how we'd practice it, over and over, and the students who really concentrated, the ones who really tried, they always got it down pat."

I don't know why I thought looking at Brody's card would make anything clearer, but I pulled it closer. "Which means when Brody wrote this to you—"

"He was remembering the good times, of course. What fun we had in Drama Club. It was a great experience for the kids. Taught them poise. Taught them the value of hard work. They don't put on real plays anymore," she grumbled as an aside. "Not plays like *Much Ado* or *Marty*. These days, it's all *Mamma Mia!* and *The Addams Family*, and that's all well and good, but the good plays, the meaty plays . . ." Her memory was lost in a sigh.

Max brought her back to the present with his pointed

question. "And that's all it was? Just a tongue twister? Mr. Pierce, he wasn't talking about a relationship you two might have had?"

I never knew an old lady could squeal with that much laughter. "Oh, honey!" She plopped a hand on top of Max's. "You couldn't be more wrong. Not only would that have been unethical, not to mention illegal, but believe me, Brody wasn't about to waste his life and take his chances with a woman older than his mother. And I wouldn't have risked my career or my pension. Not for him or any other boy in school. No, no. Brody only went after the girls in his class, maybe the ones a couple years younger. Or older. That's the way it should be. After all, he had big plans."

"He said he was going to Juilliard," I commented.

She smiled. "He was going to be a serious actor. He had the talent. And certainly the looks to get noticed. I have to admit to being as proud as a mother hen about the whole thing. Juilliard! I'd never had a student who'd even dared to dream it, much less apply and get accepted."

I leaned forward to catch her eye. "But he didn't go."

Helen sat back and thought about it. "It's all he ever talked about. The big city. The bright lights of Broadway. I remember the day he got his acceptance letter. That boy's face glowed. I bet you could see his smile up on the moon."

"But, Miss Podgorny," Max took over, "he may have been accepted, but we know Brody never attended Juilliard. He left Tinker's Creek. He went out west."

"And made those lovely commercials." She grinned. "You say he never went to Juilliard?"

"That's right," I told her. "Can you remember why?"

Her silvery brows dropped closer to her eyes. She bit her bottom lip. "Was that Brody? Or was it Ernest?" she asked no one in particular.

"What did one of them do?" I inquired.

"Well, it was about the scholarship essay. The one he had to write to get accepted at Juilliard. Yes, yes. It was Brody. He was the one who was accepted into Juilliard. No one would have known the truth if not for Brody coming forward and telling."

"Brody told the truth?" I asked. "About something terrible?"

"No, no. Not Brody." She gave me the same sort of understanding smile I was sure she got a dozen times a day from staff when her brain got mixed up with details and memories. "Ernest. Ernest was the one who told. He didn't want to. I remember how painful it was for him. But he knew he had to do the right thing." She plucked at the nothing in front of her on the table. "He was such a nice boy."

"Ernest?" Max asked.

"No, not Ernest. Though Ernest was a nice boy, too. No, no. I'm talking about Brody. Aren't you paying attention, young man?"

He assured her he was and Helen went on.

"Brody was so brokenhearted. So ashamed, I suppose. And you know, his parents, they were nice hardworking people. But they couldn't afford to pay for Juilliard. Once we knew the truth, we all agreed to keep it quiet. Why pile misery on top of misery? Ah, 'Some rise by sin, and some by virtue fall.' *Measure for Measure*," she added for our sake. "Act two, scene one. Brody fell because of Ernest's virtue. Once they took the scholarship away."

"Who?" Max asked her.

She nodded, confirming something to herself. "Well, the school, of course. Juilliard. They not only withdrew his scholarship, they told him they would never accept him as a student. Not once they found out he'd plagiarized his essay."

* * *

That's why Brody left town," I said when I slid into Max's Jeep. "That's why he stayed away all those years. He blew it with his scholarship, and he couldn't stand to let anyone in Tinker's Creek know he cheated and lost his chance at Juilliard."

"Yeah, and he stayed away until he'd made a name for himself and showed the world he didn't need a prestigious education to become a household name." He started up the Jeep after he reminded Charmaine to buckle up. "I wonder why Ernest never mentioned it."

"Maybe to save Brody's reputation?" I suggested. "Like Helen said, everyone involved swore they wouldn't talk about it. And what difference does it make after all these years anyway?"

"Sounds to me like Ernest should have been the one who got killed," Charmaine grumbled from the back seat.

I turned to give her a look.

"Well, just think about it. Brody cheated and yes, of course that was wrong. It was terrible. But Ernest blew the whistle on him. That must have made Brody very angry. So you see, if anyone should have been murdered, it should have been Ernest."

"Good thing Brody had more sense than that," I said. "Besides, it's like Max says, once Brody came back to town, he didn't need to be angry anymore. Years had passed. Brody had made a name for himself and a fortune from his commercials." I remembered what Ernest had once said. "Ernest told me they never socialized, and if it's true, it's no wonder. But if they never did . . ." I thought back to that tuft of Violet hair I'd seen on Ernest's clothing.

"I saw a strand of Violet's fur on Ernest, and if he never saw Brody, how would he have been around Violet?"

Charmaine chuckled. "In case you haven't noticed, you don't need to actually be around Violet to drag bits and pieces of Violet everywhere with you," she reminded me.

"Your bedroom." I hung my head. "That explains the Violet fur on your bed."

"Was there?" This got another laugh out of my aunt. "Well, I can guarantee you, the dog was never up there. As for the man—"

Thinking she had another revelation in store, I spun in my seat to find her grinning.

"Just kidding!" Charmaine's cheeks were pink. "I'm sure the fur traveled from Brody's clothes to the upholstery on the dining room chairs and from there, it ended up on my clothes."

Max cleared his throat. "That must be the same way Ernest got Violet's fur on him. He was somewhere where Brody had been. The fur just happened to hitch a ride. I believe that more than I believe they hung out together. It must have been hard for Ernest to face the man whose life he essentially ruined. At least at the time. Sure, Brody ended up with his own special kind of happily ever after, but—"

"He wanted to be a serious actor." I thought about what Helen had said. "Commercials must have felt like the bottom of the barrel."

"Yeah"—Max grinned—"until the money started rolling in."

He pulled into Charmaine's driveway and she got out, but when I made to leave, he stopped me. "I'll drive you around to your place."

"It's only on the other side of the garden."

"Hey"—he wheeled out of the drive—"I like living life on the edge. Besides, I didn't want your aunt to know." He pointed at his phone where it lay on the dashboard. "I got a text from Josh. They got back that report on Penny's background. I thought the fewer people who knew we were looking at her . . ."

"I get it." When he stopped near my carriage house, I hopped out, but I didn't walk away. "Where do you think this leaves us?" I asked him.

"Wish I knew."

"And when you find out?"

"We'll see what the background check says about her and then, well, technically I shouldn't share. But I guess I owe you. For everything you've done and everything you've told me. I promise, Lizzie, you'll be the first to know."

Chapter 20

I wasn't expecting *first to know* to happen just an hour or so later.

That's when Max showed up at my place, a bag with takeaway dinner salads from Ken's in one hand, a file folder in the other.

Violet welcomed him and for the second time in as many days, I set the table for two.

We settled down and munched awhile, but let's face it, that file folder was mighty intriguing, and he had promised to let me know what he found out about Penny. Nobody could blame me if I squirmed. And shot looks at that folder. And started to ask questions he always stopped by pointing to his mouth, a way to tell me he was busy eating and I should be, too.

Halfway through dinner, he finally took pity on me and flipped open that folder. "Penny's background check."

Finally he decided to talk, just when I'd popped a slice

of mandarin orange into my mouth. It was my turn to point to my mouth, chew, and swallow before I blurted out, "And? What does it say? What did you find out?"

"Well, for one thing, this proves once and for all that I know my kit foxes."

"You don't know your kit foxes," I reminded him. "You admitted you didn't know your kit foxes. You said the photograph Penny has might not be a picture of a kit fox at all."

"But now I'm thinking it is."

I caught the subtle inference of the statement and sat up like a shot. "She's been out west."

"Oh, it gets better than that." His salad was Mick's famous Black and Blue. Plenty of blue cheese crumbled over greens and topped with steak that Max had ordered rare. He picked a strand of Violet fur from his steak.

It made me remember what I'd told him. About Ernest. And the fur.

"Have you checked out his alibi?" I asked, and I'm not exactly sure how Max knew who and what I was talking about, but he sliced a piece of steak, popped it into his mouth, and shrugged.

"Home alone isn't much of an alibi, and it's not what I wanted to talk to you about anyway. Let me tell you a story," he said.

Now that we'd started talking murder suspects, I could barely sit still. "I don't want to hear a story. I want to hear—"

"A story. Exactly." He pointed at my salad with the tip of his steak knife, a way to tell me to cool my jets and keep eating so he could tell me everything he'd found out.

"Once upon a time," he said, "a girl named Penny was born in a place called Ten Sleep, Wyoming. And before you criticize small-town America, Ms. Chicago, let me remind you that I myself"—he poured on the Texas accent, as thick as the extra blue cheese dressing he added to his salad—"am from Wickett, Texas, and those of us from small towns do not take kindly to criticism from city folk."

"I don't care how small Ten Sleep is," I'd already said before another thought occurred. "And where on earth is Wickett, anyway?"

"Conversation for another dinner," he said. "Back to my story."

The sooner the better.

The longer he dragged it out, the antsier I got. Eager to get rid of the anxiety, I stabbed a shrimp and realized Max's interrogation techniques must have extended to Mick at the diner. Otherwise, how would he have known to order my favorite beet, mandarin orange, and grilled shrimp salad?

I twirled my fork and watched that shrimp spin. Just like my brain. "So the story is . . ." I did my best to put together the pieces of the little he'd already told me. "Penny grew up in this tiny little town and—"

"I didn't say she grew up there. I said she was born there. Fact of the matter is, our Penny didn't let any grass grow under her feet. Even at a very young age, she did a lot of traveling. With her father."

I might have made some smart-alecky remark about Dad being with the circus. Or running from the law, but Max's expression was so serious, the look in his eyes so grave, I couldn't say anything at all. I crunched a crouton.

"Her father, you see, had an interesting career, and for years, he took his wife and his daughter with him on his assignments. Penny did not necessarily take that photograph of the kit fox right there in Ten Sleep, Wyoming. As a family, they traveled all over the West. And beyond. When you think about it, it's actually pretty cool giving a kid that kind of experience."

"It is. But—"

"But what did Dad do for a living? Hold on there, I'm getting to that. First, though"—he waved his fork, a magician doing a trick—"we're going to test that encyclopedic brain of yours."

"Max!" I groaned my frustration. "We're talking murder. Motives. Suspects. I don't want to talk about baseball."

He slapped a hand to his heart. "I thought you loved baseball."

He may have noticed I had my fork clenched in one fist. Maybe that's why he gave in with a laugh.

"All right. No baseball. Not this time. Let's focus on something a little closer to home. What if I told you Penny's dad was Dean O'Brien?"

The name sparked a memory, distant at first. I scrambled to put it together with everything I knew about Penny, everything I'd heard from everyone we'd talked to about Brody's murder.

Max knew exactly when the truth struck.

I think the fact that I dropped my fork was a dead giveaway. "Penny's dad? The cameraman who was injured in that accident? When Brody hang glided onto the open bed of a truck and—"

"One and the same."

"Wow." This was not a good *wow*. Not an I'm-impressed *wow*. It wasn't even a what-an-incredible-detective-you-must-be-to-find-these-things-out sort of *wow*.

This *wow* had *oh no* written all over it, and it was no wonder why.

In spite of my favorite salad, my stomach soured. "Penny's been leading a secret life. She's been hiding her identity."

"She didn't have to," Max told me. "Mom and Dad got divorced years ago, and Penny took her stepfather's last name, Markham."

I picked up on that much. And Max may have said more. At this point my brain was spinning and I couldn't be sure. Theories overlapped with questions, and those questions piled up and multiplied, each and every one of them screaming in my ear, demanding answers.

I wanted to jump out of my chair and do the happy dance. We had our perp! I wanted to ask if Max and Josh had put the cuffs on Penny yet. If she confessed. Was she remorseful? Or only sorry she got caught? Did she admit to a long-simmering hatred of the man who'd ruined her father's career? Or did she act like she had no idea what the cops were talking about?

Somehow, logic forced its way past all that, and the words that came out of my mouth were, "Why would she still be angry? The lawsuit against Brody and the commercial production company was dropped."

"It was."

"O'Brien got a big settlement."

"He did."

"But—"

"He could never work again, and the sheriff over in Ten Sleep tells me O'Brien is a broken man. Not just physically. Ever since that accident he's changed, and these days he's pretty much a hermit. And as much as he loved filming and teaching his daughter photography, he hasn't touched a camera in years. He sits at home, drinks, feels sorry for himself. Penny used to visit regularly, but the last couple times she was there, she told the sheriff her dad wouldn't even let her in the house. Told her to go away and never come back."

"That's awful."

"It's also motive. And a darned good one, too."

"Wow." Yes, repetitious and hardly original. I let everything he'd told me swirl through my brain. "Penny must have hated Brody. But . . ." Chomping on a grilled shrimp helped me think. "She dated the man. I mean, he destroyed her father's life. How could she possibly tolerate sitting across a dinner table from him?"

"Ah, the mysterious ways of women!" Max finished off a piece of steak in two efficient bites. "You tell me."

"Tell you why a woman would date a man she hates?" It took me a while (and a couple more shrimp) to wrap my head around the question enough to try to form some kind of answer. "What if she wanted to get close to Brody so she could find out more about what he was up to? But . . . no." I discarded the theory as quickly as I'd come up with it. "Everyone in town knew what Brody did and where Brody went. There was nothing secret about his life, that's for sure, and Penny wouldn't have to have gone undercover."

"Okay, then. What else would make her do what she did?"

I thought some more. "To keep an eye on him? Maybe since she was planning on killing him, she wanted to know his every move and she figured if she was close—" My eyes flew open. My breath caught. "Could she have been the one following him? The person in my garden?"

"You tell me."

I thought about that night. It felt like a lifetime ago. I did my best to picture the shape of the person. The size. To try to remember any sound or scent.

It was no use.

"I don't know." I hated to admit it. "But you think she killed Brody, don't you?"

"I think it's a distinct possibility."

"Are you going to arrest her?"

He was finished with his salad and he pushed his plate away. "Not my job. I'll leave that to your cousin. Though I would like to be there when it goes down."

"Are they after her now?"

"No hurry. Penny's not going to go anywhere. Josh is waiting for search warrants on her home and her office. We'll serve those, see what we come up with, and take it from there. A little tangible evidence would go a long way toward supporting her motive, that's for sure. I'll tell you what . . ." He scraped his chair back from the table. "I hate to eat and run, but I want to be there when the warrants arrive so I can help with the search. I don't want to miss a minute of this."

I stood. "Neither do I. I can come along, can't I?"

He spared me having to hear him say *no way.* Then again, the look he gave me pretty much took care of that.

I hate to whine. I mean, usually. But if any situation ever called for a little whimpering, this was it. "I've been in on this investigation from the start. I've done a lot of legwork. I'm the one who told you about the photograph of the kit fox!"

"You did. Even though I told you from day one to mind your own business." He patted Violet on the head and went to the door, and I got the distinct impression he would have given me a pat, too, if he thought he could get away with it. "That's why I'll let you know what happens as soon as it happens."

"But—"

"I'll call you later."

"But—"

"I gotta go."

"Great." He'd already closed the door behind him so he didn't hear me grumble to Violet. "I've worked just as hard as everyone else on this case, and not only do I get left in the dust, I get treated like I was just playing some sort of game."

Violet's whimper told me she understood.

"It's not fair and it's not right, and you know what?" I grabbed her leash and hooked it to her collar. "There's only one thing that can soothe a bruised ego. Frosty Cones. You up for ice cream?"

She was, even when I told her she had to get vanilla.

It was muggy, and I didn't have the heart to make Violet walk through town in her fur coat, so we hopped in my car, turned up the AC and the music, and cruised toward the park. Frosty Cones was just outside its border—wise marketing for the ice cream stand owner, who could always count on the park tourist trade.

On our way to the promised land that was Frosty Cones, we sang along with Adele on "Rolling in the Deep" as we drove down Main Street, looped around the square, and turned onto a side street that would take us around the far side of town so we could avoid any traffic coming out of the park. That was when I saw Penny pull her car into the library parking lot.

"What do you suppose she's doing here?" I asked Violet, and since she didn't have an answer, we pulled in, too, and I parked far enough away from Penny so she wouldn't see me.

I watched her walk inside, stop at the reference desk.

Then she disappeared.

It was too hot to leave Violet in the car, so I got out and took her along, and together we went around to the back of the building. There were windows there and plenty of shrubberies, too.

Negotiating a maze of long-ago planted arborvitae that desperately needed trimming was not Violet's idea of a good time.

"It's okay," I told her, keeping my voice down, hoping to convince her this was just another of our adventures. "Don't worry about your fur. I promise to brush you when we get home." I gave her leash a little tug, and together we wound our way through the greenery. Branches plucked at my clothes. Briars and bits of foliage tangled in Violet's fur. We didn't let that stop us. At least not until we closed in on the bank of windows that ran along the back of the building.

As luck would have it, that's where the public computers were located.

And Penny was sitting at one just a few feet away.

"Shhh!" I put a finger to my lips and pressed my back against the wall, all too aware that I'd be in full view if Penny looked up. "I want to see what she's up to."

This I couldn't do until Violet and I inched even closer. From where I stood, I could see Penny log on to the Internet with her library card number.

"What's she looking for?" I asked Violet and myself.

I found out in just another minute.

"'Incendiary fire basics.'" How I managed to say the words when there was a lump in my throat, I don't know. "She couldn't be . . ." I looked down at Violet. She looked up at me. Neither of us had the answer.

I watched Penny carefully read the information on the

screen in front of her, then very slowly and deliberately back out of the page and close the Internet.

"Covering her tracks," I told Violet, and this she fully understood.

Still, I couldn't wrap my head around what Penny was up to, and talking it out made the most sense.

"She must have acquired a new property to sell," I told the dog. "Or the house someone wants to buy has fire damage and Penny's trying to figure out how much and what kind of renovations will be needed. It's the only thing that makes any sense, don't you think?"

She did, and she barked to prove it.

At the sound, Penny's head came up. Good thing I'm quick on my feet. I fell to my knees next to the dog and held my breath. If Penny looked out the window . . .

She didn't. At least not for the count of one hundred. That's when I felt safe enough to slowly get to my feet and peek into the library.

Penny was nowhere in sight.

"Come on, sweetie." Violet and I took off through the shrubbery. "Let's see if she's still around."

She was, walking out of the library and toward her car, parked near the front entrance.

Back to the building, peeping around the corner, I had a bird's-eye view.

Penny went to her car. She opened her trunk.

And my breath caught in my throat.

"Gas cans!" I clapped my hand over my mouth. Yeah, like that was going to somehow call the words back.

Luckily, Penny didn't hear me. Her check of the gas cans finished, she got into her car and drove out of the parking lot.

Violet and I were close behind.

* * *

I called Max three times, and when he didn't pick up, I tried Josh. He didn't answer, either, and for a minute, I wasn't just annoyed, I was in a panic.

That is, before I told myself to settle down. Maybe Penny had just bought gas for her lawn mower. Maybe there wasn't any gas in those cans at all and she was on her way to the recycling center with them.

"Maybe she's planning to burn something down."

Violet may not have understood the words, but she understood the groan that came out of me along with them. "We'll wait," I told her, remembering the thanks-for-playing-along way Max had treated me when he left my house. "I don't want to call in reinforcements yet. Let's see what she's up to."

It didn't take long.

We headed out of the town and no, I am no psychic. I didn't need to be. I knew exactly where Penny was going.

Except for a few bison I could see from the road, the ranch looked peaceful, empty. I slowed and stayed far behind Penny, watching the flash of color wink in and out as her teal blue SUV made its way into and out of the shadows that shaded the drive.

"There's only one thing she could be planning to do," I told Violet, and I stopped outside the gates of the ranch and grabbed my phone.

I got Max's voice mail.

I got Josh's voice mail.

I left him a message, told him where I was, told him what was up.

And then I took off toward the ranch.

By the time I got there, Penny's car was parked outside the house, trunk open, two gas cans missing.

And there was Penny herself, pacing the front porch, hoisting one of those open red cans, and leaving a trail of gasoline everywhere she went.

Chapter 21

I parked far from the porch and even from there, I could smell gas in the air. I couldn't stand the thought of Violet trapped with the horrible odor, so I opened the door and let her out of the car. She knew the ranch. She'd find a safe place.

I raced to the house, calling Penny's name.

She didn't hear me.

Her shoulders were set in a rigid line. Her gaze was fixed. Her mouth moved over words I couldn't hear and didn't want to imagine while she marched back and forth, splashing gasoline all around her as she went.

I finally stopped in front of the house and waved my arms to get her attention. "Penny, stop. You don't want to do this."

The first gas can was empty and she tossed it aside, reached for the second one, and flashed me a look that told me she wasn't surprised to see me. Or sorry she'd been caught red-handed. She was a woman on a mission, and her mission, it was all that counted. "Yes," she said, "I do."

"But what good will it do? Brody's already dead."

"Dead. Yeah. And I never got my revenge. He loved this ranch. Destroying it and everything he worked for, it's going to be perfect."

I dared a step closer. "I totally get it," I told her, praying I could get through to her. "You're angry and nobody can blame you. Not after what Brody did to your dad."

It was that one word that did it. *Dad*. It somehow penetrated the madness that fueled her.

Penny froze, gas still pouring from the can, puddling on the porch around her, soaking her shoes, and I knew the situation had just gone from bad to worse.

"Penny!" I motioned her closer and at the same time waved away the noxious gas fumes. "Get down from there. It's dangerous. Come on over here." Gas splashed onto her legs. It dotted her denim shorts. "I don't want you to get hurt. Come on." Another wave, my voice pleading. "Let's sit over there by the pond and talk about your dad."

Maybe it was the promise of reminiscing about the dad who'd taken her on adventures and taught her a love for photography that finally knocked some sense into her. Maybe it was because the gas fumes made her gasp. At that point, I didn't care about anything except for the fact that she staggered off the porch.

I actually might have breathed a sigh of relief if (a) I could breathe with all the fumes in the air and (b) she didn't reach for the candle lighter she'd left on the steps.

"No! Don't!" Fumes or no fumes, I darted toward the porch and yanked the lighter out of her hands. While I was at it, I grabbed her arm and didn't let go. "You've got gas

all over you, Penny. If you set the house on fire, you're going to go up with it."

She looked down at her clothes, looked over at me.

Penny's eyes, usually so vibrant, were vacant. Her breaths
came in short, sharp bursts. Before she could do anything
else both of us would regret, I dragged her across the driveway and over to the pond. There was a big, flat rock at the
edge of it, and I sat her down, tugged off her shoes, and
tossed them in the water.

When I filled my hands with water and poured it over
her legs, Penny squirmed. "What are you—"

"You've got gas all over you. It's dangerous, Penny.
What the heck did you think you were going to accomplish
here?"

She shot a look of pure hatred toward the house. "Burn
it down. All of it. Wipe out his memory."

I poured more water over her legs, doused her shorts,
scrubbed her hands, and when I was all done, I washed off
my hands, too, then sat down next to her.

"Nothing you do here is going to change what happened
to your dad," I said.

Penny sniffled. "He was a great dad."

"I heard. About the adventures you had. About how he
took you on his assignments. What was your favorite?"

"Alaska."

"I've never been and I've always wanted to go. I bet it's
beautiful."

"It's . . ." A single tear slipped down her cheek. "It
doesn't matter now. The adventures are over. My dad—"

"I heard about that, too. And I heard you've tried to con-
tact him. You're a really good daughter."

As if she'd never thought of it that way, her gaze shot to

mine. "I thought because he didn't want to see me, I was just a loser."

"Only if you stop trying."

It was plenty warm, but Penny shivered and wrapped her arms around herself. Her shoulders shook. Her bottom lip quivered. "It's all Brody's fault."

"Yeah. I know about the accident while they were filming. I also heard there was a nice settlement."

Her laugh was sharp. It echoed across the ranch. "You think the money makes any difference? My dad—" She choked on a sob. "My dad's life was ruined. Because of that scumbag, Brody Pierce."

"That's why you wanted to kill him."

"I hated him."

"You dated him."

She hung her head. "It seemed like a good idea at the time. See . . ." When she looked up again, there was high color in Penny's cheeks, a gleam in her eyes that made me think that must have been how she looked when the plan first occurred to her. "I thought I could get him to fall in love with me. But Brody . . ." Her shoulders drooped.

"So it wasn't like you told me. You didn't just get tired of his stories and his ego?"

"I was going to dump him." She nodded and kept on nodding, like one of those bobblehead dolls. "I was waiting for that magical moment. For him to finally declare his undying love. Then I was going to pull the carpet out from under him. I wanted to break his heart and watch him try and crawl back to me. I wanted him to suffer."

"But it didn't work. Because he dumped you first."

She scrubbed a finger under her nose, and the sound that erupted from her was almost a laugh. "You got that right, girlfriend. And you know, that's the day I decided there was

only one punishment fit for Brody Pierce. He had to die."
The corners of her mouth turned down. "I'm really good at
what I do. You know that, Lizzie, don't you?"

I patted her shoulder. "Best real estate agent in town."

"I always make the Million Dollar Club. I am the tough-
est negotiator. I never fail my clients. Never!" She shot to
her feet and, yes, I was afraid she was going to grab that
lighter out of my hand and march back over to the house.

I tossed the lighter in the pond and took her hand so I
could tug her down beside me.

Penny groaned. "I'm lousy at murdering people."

"I know you tried for a while. Those accidents Brody
was having—"

"Lame, lame, lame." She pounded her knee with her fist.
"Like pouring oil on the garage floor and waiting for him
to slip and crack his skull open was ever actually going to
work?"

"He cut his forehead."

"Yeah"—she narrowed her eyes and growled—"but his
brains didn't ooze out."

"And that night you were in my garden . . ." If she was
surprised I'd figured this out, she didn't show it. "You were
lurking outside Charmaine's because you cut the brake
lines on Brody's truck. You wanted him to have an accident
on the way home."

"Even that didn't stop the creep." Penny's hands curled
into fists. "The man was made of iron."

"Until that Wednesday night a couple of weeks ago." I
let the words settle between us. "That's when you finally
got your revenge."

Her head came up. "Huh?"

Chapter 22

I shouldn't have had to explain. I mean, it seems clear that a murderer would know all this stuff, right?

I guess in the great scheme of things it was just as well I never had a chance to rehash it. That's because I heard a sound, the deep booming growl of an engine.

Not close.

But hey, what did I know about incendiary fires and the volatility of gasoline? I did know that gas vapors are dangerous. Otherwise, there wouldn't be signs posted at gas stations about turning off engines and not using cell phones.

Fumes we had. Plenty of them.

And I didn't want to find out how close a running engine had to be before it lit up the place like the Fourth of July.

"Hear that?" I asked Penny, and apparently she did, because she tilted her head and listened for a while.

I stood and looked around and though I couldn't see anything, I could still hear the noise. Grinding. Groaning.

"Come on." With hurried motions, I urged her to stand. "Let's get away from the house. We can go to . . ." Starting either car probably wasn't a good idea, so I zipped in the direction of the barn. Shoeless, Penny hobbled along behind me.

"Come on, come on!" I urged her on. "We've got to find whoever that is and tell them to turn off that machine." Away from the house, the sound rumbled louder, and by the time we got to the barn, I could tell it was coming from the stand of trees on the far side of the property, the place where I'd found the binoculars the last time I was at the ranch.

Far away.

But far enough?

"Let's go," I told Penny, and started across the meadow.

"But my feet hurt." She could whine with the best of them, and she leaned back against a fence post and massaged one foot. "I can't walk anywhere."

I propped my fists on my hips. "And I can't trust you with a couple more cans of gas."

"But I won't—"

"Oh, no. Not going to take that chance. You're coming with me. Now."

Yes, I might have raised my voice. But really, could anyone blame me? It's hard to get a woman with mayhem in her heart to listen, and I couldn't take the chance of leaving her there and seeing the whole ranch go up in flames.

The downside?

My raised voice attracted the attention of a certain massive male bison grazing nearby.

His head came up, and when he pawed the ground, I swear I felt a tremor beneath my feet.

He snorted.

Penny stood up like a shot.

"All right. Okay. I'll come with you. Just don't leave me here with . . ." When the bison lowered his head and took a couple steps closer to the fence, she swallowed hard. "Just don't walk too fast."

Tell that to a woman who was afraid some errant electrical spark was going to somehow ignite everything around us.

By the time we got to the trees, both Penny and I were breathing hard.

The sound of the machinery groaned on.

We followed it. Down a path. Around a bend that looped us back toward the ranch.

Too close to the fumes? I wondered. I didn't want to find out.

The sound rattled my collarbone and pounded through my head. A dragon in its lair. A monster in the forest.

We pushed through a dense outcropping of bushes and found ourselves face-to-treads with a compact excavator with a mechanical auger on the front of it.

Ernest Hoyt was at the controls.

I guess me jumping in front of the machine was enough to get his attention. He sat back, turned off the excavator, and jumped down.

"Lizzie . . ." He looked to his right and at the woman who was rubbing her bare feet. "Penny, what on earth are you two doing—"

"It's kind of a long story," I told him. "And it really doesn't matter. What does matter is that there's been a gasoline spill at the ranch. I wanted to warn you. I don't know how fumes can ignite and with you digging and—"

My own words knocked me over the head.

"Ernest, you're digging."

"Technically, I'm augering."

"But . . ." I glanced around at the worktable he had set up nearby. At the tools laid out on it. At the maps and copies of what looked like old diary pages, the handwriting on them cramped and scribbled.

"Brody left this land to the park," I reminded Ernest.

"He did." A smile came and went. "Of course he did, but I didn't think anyone would mind if I just—"

"Why would you want to start an excavation here? We're miles from the canal."

Another smile from him was fleeting. "Two point one miles, to be exact."

"And all you care about is the canal."

"I do. But you never know, Lizzie"—he put a hand on my shoulder to turn me back the way I'd come—"where history may lead you."

"Like the history in these old letters?" They were right there, within easy reach, so I picked up a pile. I would have read them over, too, if Ernest hadn't snatched them out of my hand.

"It's really none of your business," he said.

"And digging here is none of yours."

"Lizzie . . ." When he took a step toward me, I automatically took one back and banged into the table. "I'm just taking some soil samples. Looking around. Checking things out."

"You're looking for something."

He took another step forward, and maybe he would have come even closer if Penny hadn't moaned. "My feet are killing me!" She leaned so hard on one end of the table it tipped, and everything Ernest had arranged on it went flying.

Diary pages flew in the air.

Old maps fluttered and landed on soggy ground.

Shovels, trowels, spades, brushes. All went flying.

Ernest grumbled and got to work picking it all up. I offered Penny a hand, since when the table tumbled she did, too. Just as she got back on her feet, I saw that something else had slid off the table.

It was a piece of metal, maybe twelve inches long, that had been slipped into a wooden holder along the length of one side. Along the other side, the metal was bare. It was old, the surface was pitted. Short ends of metal stuck out a few inches from either end of the holder. They were crusted with rust.

I picked it up and looked from the instrument in my hand to Ernest.

And that's when he knew that I knew.

"Run, Penny," I shouted, only she was so busy brushing mud off her shorts, she didn't pay any attention. I bumped her shoulder. "Run. Back to the ranch. Now!"

I had every intention of taking off after her, and I would have, too, if Ernest's arm hadn't hooked around my neck.

When I let out an *ooph*, Penny turned to see what was wrong. I would have told her to leave, that the only way we were going to get help was if she found someone and told them what was happening, but with the way Ernest's forearm pressed against my windpipe, I couldn't say a word.

"You didn't have a clue, did you?" When he yanked me back, my feet lifted off the ground. I fought for a toehold, trying to settle myself, struggling to get my feet on solid ground and keep the pressure off my neck. "You still don't know what's really going on, do you?" Ernest rumbled in my ear.

I squirmed enough to loosen his grip just a little and gasped for breath. "I know you took this old farm implement from Glory's stand and used it to stab Brody."

"Old farm implement!" I still had it in my hand, and Ernest

snatched it away so quickly, the metal cut into my skin and my hand was instantly wet and slick with blood. "That's what Tussock's family thought it was. Even Brody, when I showed it to him that night and told him how important I thought it was. That night . . ." He growled. "That's when he told me there was no way I'd ever inherit the ranch."

"But you told me—"

"That I'd known it all along. What did you expect me to say? What did you expect me to do? Brody thought this was nothing but a piece of junk. But this . . ." He flourished the tool in front of my face. Too close to my neck.

I squirmed a little more.

"You see?" Ernest asked. "It was found right here by someone in the Tussock family years ago." He stomped a foot, and because the earth was torn by his excavator, he lost his footing. I slipped out of his grasp and turned to face him, waving a hand wildly behind me.

"Go, Penny," I said again, but she was frozen with fear.

Ernest recovered in a heartbeat and swished the instrument through the air. "Old farmer Tussock had no idea what it was. He had no idea how valuable it was." He held the instrument up and gazed at it the way Violet looked at Max. "The Tussocks used it as a weaving shuttle. That's why they encased one side in wood, so they could use the metal edge to level off the threads in the weaving. But this . . ." He whipped the instrument toward me and I automatically jumped back. "This is a piece of a Viking sword."

"Those books you got from the library." Yeah, all right, not exactly the best moment to be talking literature, but once a book person, always a book person, and at the moment it seemed to matter. "You were researching Vikings because—"

"Because I saw this at Glory's booth and I had my suspicions. I didn't steal it." I have a feeling that was supposed to make me feel better. It didn't work.

"They were here!" Ernest threw his arms out at his sides. "There have been stories, theories. We all know the Vikings arrived in North America long before Columbus did. But don't you see? This proves they explored. They had an encampment here. Maybe a settlement. And Brody didn't care, not even when I showed him proof. Brody wouldn't give me permission to dig on his land."

"So it wasn't . . ." I swung my head around and found Penny clutching a sapling as if it could offer her some kind of protection. I turned back to Ernest. "You killed Brody."

"A moment of anger." He shrugged it off. "After a lifetime of putting up with his arrogance and his ego. And now . . ." He swung the sword blade from me to Penny then back to me. "With this auger, it won't take long to make this hole a little bigger." He glanced down at where he'd been working. "A little deeper and it will be plenty big enough to accommodate two."

"Think again, buster." I ducked down, grabbed one of the hammers that had landed on the ground when the table collapsed, and wrapped my fingers tight around it. "Penny's just about to start running back to the house to get help!" This time I yelled because, honestly, was the woman that dense? "And I'm not going down without a fight."

He came at me.

I set my feet apart and braced myself.

A second later, something that sounded like thunder echoed through the little patch of woods, and the next thing I knew, that gigantic bull bison came through like a freight train.

Ernest jumped back and tripped in that hole he'd been

digging and got knocked out cold. Penny screamed. I leaped out of the way.

That bison kept on running, mowing down every bush and small tree in his path.

He wasn't gone but a heartbeat when another creature appeared out of the underbrush.

"Hey, Violet!" When she sat down at my side, I looked from her to the path of destruction left by the bison. "You didn't have anything to do with . . . You didn't go into the bison pasture and . . . ?"

Violet never owned up to it. But the tail wag and the way her tongue flopped out of the right side of her mouth, well, that told me everything I needed to know.

Chapter 23

The next day, Violet got the full spa treatment over at Deb's Dogs. After all, she was a hero, and she deserved it, from the nail buff to the bath to the brushing to the aromatherapy finishing spray that finally got rid of the nasty scent of gasoline and bison that clung to her fur. She now smelled like lavender, and that's never a bad thing.

The pink ribbons on her ears were my idea, but Violet was not a fan. She pawed them off as soon as we walked into Love Under the Covers and insisted that I tie on her newly washed red bandanna.

"Oh, look at her. What a sweetie." Charmaine had been weepy ever since I showed up back in town the night before, after a trip to the ER for a tetanus shot and to get my hand bandaged. She sniffled and kissed Violet's snout and when she was done, she folded me into a hug. "Don't ever do anything like that again," she said.

"Yeah, well, I've heard that before. From Josh. And from

Max." Just remembering the lectures I'd gotten once the fire department had doused Brody's house with water and Penny and Ernest were loaded into squad cars made me shiver. "Believe me, I prefer all my excitement in the pages of the books."

"But not all your romance, I hope." Suddenly smiling, Charmaine glided away. Just as Max walked into the shop.

He gifted Violet with a smile and a treat and, smiling right back, she disappeared into my office.

"I've got news," he told me.

"Penny confessed."

"Well, it was kind of hard for her to deny anything. I mean, there was the gasoline. And extra containers in her car. And your account of the incident."

"You'll throw the book at her?"

"We'll work something out. Might have been a whole lot different if you didn't get there in time and stop her from setting the place on fire."

My stomach bunched. "She wasn't thinking straight. She would have gone up, too."

"Then she has you to thank for saving her life."

The store was extra busy that morning. Word had gotten out about everything that happened at the ranch, and customers were eager to hear the details. I wasn't so eager to talk, and it was just as well. As both Josh and Max had reminded me the night before after they'd taken my statement, heard all the details, and had me walk them through every minute of my visit to the ranch, it was better to keep quiet until all the legal ducks were in a row.

Besides, it was way more fun to talk romance, and I took the opportunity when a customer came up to the front counter with a classic Kathleen E. Woodiwiss.

Callie Porter was next in line. Even though she had

nothing in her hands to purchase. "We heard all about it," she crooned. "It's like you were in a book yourself. Tasha . . ." She looked over her shoulder at Tasha Grimes, who took the look as an invitation to step up to the counter next to Callie. "She thinks—"

"You need to write this." Tasha danced from foot to foot with excitement. "Come to our next meeting of Writers of Romance. We can talk marketing and agents and—"

"I don't think so." The person in line behind Tasha had four books in her arms, and I motioned her forward. "I'll stick to reading the books."

Callie wasn't convinced. "But don't you want to talk about—"

"Actually"—Max stepped closer—"I'm the one who needs to talk to Lizzie. If you ladies will excuse us . . ."

I finished the sale, thanked the customer for coming, and watched all three ladies walk away.

"It's about Ernest," I said, because I saw the serious look in Max's dark eyes, and I knew this wasn't just a social call. "He's denying everything, isn't he?"

"Forensics has identified that tool you found as the murder weapon."

"Glory thought it was a weaving shuttle."

"Well, according to Ernest, the Tussocks did use it as a weaving shuttle at some point."

I turned the thought over in my head. "And do you think it actually might be a Viking sword?"

Max held up a hand. "Way out of my league to decide."

"But Vikings? In Ohio?"

One corner of his mouth pulled tight. "I've been talking to the historian over at the park. She says Ernest is right. There are theories that the Vikings explored North America, and Ernest found notes in the Tussock diaries that told him where they'd found artifacts over the years, including that sword, if that's what it really is. If Ernest actually had proof—"

"He'd be an archaeology superstar." I wrinkled my nose. "I guess wanting to be noticed runs in the family. Brody was always front and center, and maybe if he hadn't cheated on that scholarship essay, he really would have gone on to Hollywood stardom."

"That's one of the things I wanted to talk to you about. I brought it up. With Ernest. Down at the station. Brody never cheated on that essay."

My mouth fell open. "Ernest lied about it and Brody lost his scholarship because of that? Wow, Ernest must have always been jealous of his cousin. And then when he asked Brody's permission to dig on his land and Brody refused—"

"And Ernest found out he'd never inherit the land—"

"It sent him over the edge. Families are funny things."

As if to prove it, we heard a burst of Charmaine's laughter from the contemporary room, and both Max and I smiled.

My smile didn't last. There was something about the way Max stood there, chin high, fists clenched, that made me think this particular visit might very well have been social, too, but it wasn't going to have a happy ending.

At least until the truth hit. "Your temporary assignment is over."

He nodded.

"You're going on to something different."

He nodded again.

And in the great scheme of Lizzie Hale, lover of romance novels and zero when it came to real-life romance, I should have rejoiced. The murder was solved. Which meant the only thing Max and I could possibly discuss was baseball.

And there's only so much baseball you can talk about.

At least with Max gone, I didn't have to worry about him finally discovering what a total dork I am when it comes to romance.

Tell that to the sudden cold that flashed through my bloodstream.

I pasted on a smile. "How soon do you leave?"

He propped his elbows on the front counter, leaned closer. His eyes were dark pools. His lips were a hair-breadth from mine. He brushed a strand of hair from my face. "Who says I'm leaving?"

Panic flooded through me and I stammered. "But you said . . . your assignment . . . and leaving, and, and . . ."

"And until they come up with a permanent replacement . . ." He stood tall and poked his thumb at his chest. "I've been put in charge of the Brody Pierce Center for Bison Education. Yup." I wasn't surprised by the swagger. The wink, though, immediately melted that ice inside my veins. "There's a new rancher in town, ma'am. What do you think? I may have to trade my Smokey Bear hat for a ten-gallon Stetson."

Grinning, Max strutted out of the store.

And me?

I stood there for a few moments, torn between feeling relief and giving in to the utter panic.

There was a new red-hot rancher in town.

It was enough to make my arm itch.

ACKNOWLEDGMENTS

It's never easy to write acknowledgments for a book, not because there is nothing to say and no one to thank but because there are so many things to remember to mention and so many people who help with ideas and support, input and enthusiasm. Each one of them becomes a part of the heart and soul of every book.

The Love Is Murder series started thanks to a conversation I had with my agent, Gail Fortune. We were tossing around ideas, and as soon as we landed on one that involved a romance bookstore, we knew we'd hit a winner. Haven't we all dreamed about owning the perfect bookstore? Felt the siren song of a story calling? Sighed with satisfaction when characters and a compelling plot wormed into our souls and warmed us through and through? Thank you, Gail, for always being there to listen.

I would also like to thank Sareer Khader at Penguin Random House for her careful editing of the book and her encouraging comments. Writing a book is a solitary activity, and getting enthusiastic feedback brightened my writing days!

My brainstorming group is never far from my mind as I work through plot points, character studies, clues, and red herrings. Thank you, Stephanie Cole, Serena Miller, and Emilie Richards for all your input and ideas. Here's to the day we can meet in person again.

When writing about a romance bookstore, it's impossible to ignore all the wonderful people I met early on in my career when I was writing solely romance. Maureen Child, you are one of them! Thanks for always listening.

And, of course, I have to add my usual thanks to my family. David (mostly) leaves me alone as I write. Eliot the Airedale takes advantage of every break I take to make sure we get a little playtime in. And Lucy . . . Lucy came to us four years ago straight out of a prison where she lived with and was trained by one of the inmates. It was a great program, and he did a wonderful job with her. She's sweet, she's quiet, and I'm convinced she has the ability to read my mind. Yes, she is the inspiration for Violet in *Death of a Red-Hot Rancher*, and if you can imagine how much Violet sheds, double that and you'll know what I deal with as far as fur here, there, and everywhere. It's a pain to have to vacuum constantly, but having the joy of Lucy in our lives makes it all worthwhile.

Don't miss the next thrilling
Love Is Murder Mystery by Mimi Granger.
Coming in Summer 2022!

Ready to find
your next great read?

Let us help.

Visit prh.com/nextread